No Oath Sworn
Book 1 of the
No Glory Sought Series

By

Phil Geusz

No Oath Sworn, Phil Geusz

Published by
Melange Books, LLC
White Bear Lake, MN 55110
www.melange-books.com

ISBN: 978-1-61235-180-3

Cover Artist: A. Bratt

No Oath Sworn
By
Phil Geusz

Is War What Makes Us Human?

Tommy Longo was just fifteen when his brain was removed so he could become a superfighter pilot. Any older and it would've been too late. The separation was only meant to last a year or two, and he was supposed to remain a civilian. Instead he gets caught up in a surprise attack and is asked to help cover a major retreat, a thankless and difficult job for even the most seasoned veteran. Can a civilian boy find the inner strength to stand up to such a grueling task? After it's done, will he have what it takes to fight an even dirtier war alongside the guerillas long after his high-tech fighter is gone?

What does war mean? What sense can be made of it, and what purpose does it serve? For that matter, what can war mean to the no-longer-quite-human?

Perhaps most important of all, can young Thomas survive it?

* * * *

Dedicated to SGT Jeffrey Ice, US Army

* * * *

Author Website
www.resistingarrest.net

Chapter One

Everything was blue. A blue sky rose above me, a blue sea floated below, and the haze-blue painted skin of my 'hopper obscured part of the view through some of my cameras. Blue, blue, blue.

The mission was only an hour old, and already I was sick of blue.

"Attack sequence commences in thirty seconds," Otto whispered into my aural nerve endings. "All systems normal."

"Yeah, yeah, yeah," I answered back in equal silence, letting my interface translate the thoughts into electrical impulses my aircraft could read. "Whatever." Who would have thought doing something as cool as demonstrating an attack 'hopper' for a living could ever become boring?

"Fifteen seconds," Otto continued. "Ten. Five. Three, two, one."

The sky and sea spun and tumbled around me as if alive. Virtual gauges flashed and whirled. Even the blue skin of my Skybolt rippled and fluttered under the twenty to forty G stresses of the preprogrammed maneuvers. It would've been terrifying had I not ridden through it all a thousand times before to demonstrate my father's product.

In fact, it might still have been terrifying if I'd still had a full set of the appropriate glands.

"Launch. Launch. Launch!" Otto shouted. Three stylized missiles projected onto my consciousness. I blinked in surprise, though the gesture was only figurative since I wasn't equipped with actual eyes. The Del Rio complex had a bearing on me long seconds earlier than anticipated. Reflexively I turned right and sped away from the simulated incoming weapons to gain time to think.

"Preprogrammed attack sequence terminated," Otto interjected.

From here on out I was improvising, having been forced to abandon my original plan. Otto, a basic sort of computer, wasn't much more than an autopilot. No computer of any real sophistication could function anywhere near a full-power antigrav, whick made a pilot necessary.

Del Rio was equipped with old-fashioned Rapiers I remembered as I sped along at many times the speed of sound in the wrong direction.

While plenty fast, they hadn't been designed with the Skybolt in mind. I pulled up and then throttled back a little.

Our 'war zone' had only been cleared of civilian traffic to the top of the atmosphere, and I didn't want to give the missile crews even the flimsiest of pretexts for claiming a rules violation. Still, the sky's blue deepened noticeably before the Rapiers began to close.

It was the easiest thing in the world for me to pull the Skybolt up and around and over in a much smaller arc than the computer-equipped missiles could manage. Their antigravs were small, shielded, and inefficient in response to their electronics-dependant design philosophy. Before they managed to reverse direction, I'd completed a fifty-G turn and dived right through the center of the trio.

"Structural overload," Otto mumbled, "Structural overload."

"Yeah," I acknowledged automatically. I'd pulled a lot more than fifty G's before and probably would do so again before this particular demonstration ended. The main structure was stressed for a hundred G's. The weapons pods were the only things I had a slight chance of losing. That wasn't much of a worry on this run though. I was loaded pretty light. Nukes didn't weigh much. Now I had a few seconds to develop a new plan.

"Emphasize the human element," my older brother always advised me. He was a military academy graduate, though his alma-mater wasn't particularly popular hereabouts. "Try and help the customers understand the importance of initiative and creativity in the cockpit. Show them not only is your aircraft more capable than any computer-controlled weapon can ever be, but also that you're smarter than a computer."

Well, if I were truly smart, I'd be back home in New Orleans racing skimmers on Lake Pontchartrain and studying math instead of inhabiting a little titanium brain box and creating high-order sonic booms over swampy, inhospitable colonial worlds. Yeah, I wasn't the family genius and my job was just to push the iron. So I throttled back a little, giving the missiles time to lock on again and then dove full-bore on Del Rio.

Rapiers, as it happened, were equipped with tactical nuclear warheads. Perhaps I could make good use of that fact.

It wasn't hard to imagine the confusion down below as I zoomed towards the missile base. I flamed like a meteor towards the end. At fifty G's of acceleration, you come down in one heck of a hurry. I'll bet the missile controller was frantically stabbing at the self-destruct button on his console, but that wouldn't do him any good at all given the degree of space-distortion that my drive created directly between him and his simulated charges.

I stole a glance at my rear radars. Sure enough, the Rapiers were still hot on my tail and closing fast. Perfect. I activated my own weapons pods and fired off an anti-radar missile to ensure the people at the radar base were in no danger of growing bored. At just the right moment, I pulled up, hard.

"Structural overload," Otto cautioned me again. "Struc—"

All of my gauges spun and wavered once again as the three interceptor missiles detonated over the ocean fairly near to Del Rio. The result was an impressively realistic simulation of a nuclear strike, so realistic, in fact, that I felt it necessary to check my backup cameras and verify that the defense base and the sleepy little village that'd grown up around it were still there.

Having compromised the air defenses, I focused on my main assault. Dole Field was located near the center of Churilla Island, the largest semi-dry land mass on this swamp of a planet. All of the high-value targets clustered right in one compact area— railroad hubs, highway nodes, chemical plants, even what little manufacturing existed on such a backwater world. The whole planet put together wasn't worth a single nuke. I swung around towards Churilla City. New Orleans alone was worth three Churillas. The place wouldn't even have been worth settling, if it hadn't been for its proximity to the Orion Nexus. Therefore Longo Industries had one heck of a good chance to make sales here, if I did my part.

I would've shifted in my seat, if the fighter plane had been equipped with anything resembling a seat and if I still had anything resembling a body. A standing patrol of Polecats over Dole Field, backed by all the 'alert' units they could scramble in the next few seconds came next. Polecats were easy meat for a Skybolt. The pilots wore human bodies so their performance was strictly limited.

However, the Top Bananas were one of the finest fighter units anywhere. I'd watched them do a formation flyover back on Earth when I was still just a kid, and the holo I'd snapped hung on my wall for years. They were the cream of the crop, all of them—tall, confident, even swaggering a little with their well-earned pride. My Skybolt was more than a match for Polecats and their pride, I knew. Unless I screwed up something terrible, I should win hands-down. Still, I had to admit to myself that deep down I was a little nervous. The Top Bananas had once been my heroes, and I was still pretty young.

"Tallyho," Otto whispered into my brain. "One…three…eight bogeys…" Seamlessly, the data flowed into my pipper. The little red blips represented Polecats, at one-hundred-seventeen. It was a quarter of the squadron, the standard combat air patrol permitted by the rules of the engagement, up and waiting for me. Even as the facts flowed into me, the red icons first grew fuzzy and then sprouted red vector arrows.

Now they raced at me, balls to the wall.

Otto wasn't much of a computer, but unlike most 'hopper-borne comps', he could at least perform time-and-distance equations. "Negative," he answered my half-formulated question, and once more I wished that I had a fist to clench.

In most of my previous demonstrations, the defending pilots had underestimated the Skybolt. They had followed routine procedures and orbited several miles away from their airfields so that the base personnel and nearby civilians wouldn't be disturbed by the unavoidably noisy growl of the patrol's antigravs. That several-miles lead had often been all I'd needed to scoot in, lay my egg, and vanish. It wouldn't be so simple this time. Either word about my capabilities had finally gotten out, or the Bananas simply didn't do things the easy way.

Somehow, I suspected the latter.

Eight fully-alerted and well-positioned Polecats was a lot to ask even of a Skybolt. Then, as I peered through my high-magnification forward-looking camera I saw several more shark-like shapes taxiing down the strip at well over regulation speed. More rule-breaking. They'd be off in seconds.

Hit the base first. That way I would catch as many on the ground as possible. Then the dogfight.

"Structural overload," Otto warned me as I swung my nose hard to the right. "Struc—"

"Shut up," I commanded, concentrating on doing five things at once.

It would've been impossible for a fully human pilot, who had only two hands. Yet due to my very *lack* of appendages, I fired my remaining two simulated anti-radar weapons, throttled up my antigravs, and armed my nuke at the same time. I also locked a targeting laser onto my aiming point, fired with my simulated attack laser, and watched as the Top Bananas nosed over to intercept me at a point far short of where I could release my simulated bomb.

I bet they're laughing now, I thought to myself. *They think they've got me.* I waited, waited, waited as the seconds crawled past.

The Bananas flew farther and farther away from the airfield with every tick of the clock. Just short of intercept, I rolled hard, swung ninety degrees away from the Polecats, went to full emergency thrust, and showed my attackers what a Skybolt could do.

Boooooom.

My oversized antigrav roared out, shattering windows for miles around. My father had deep pockets. I was accelerating at almost sixty-five G's, where a Polecat's frail human pilot would begin to fall apart at fifteen or so. Being just a disembodied brain floating in fluid had advantages. The ability to withstand massive acceleration stood high among them.

"Sayonara, suckers," I whispered to myself as I watched my antagonists fading away to nothing.

I reached the other side of the base and attacked. A single defensive missile launched, but failed to lock on to the Skybolt. My bearing had changed too fast for its onboard computer. As my anti-hyper-radar missiles struck home, I sighted the targeting laser dead on the parade ground in front of the CO's office. The nose lifted just a tad, I lofted my simulated bomb.

Suddenly all hell broke loose. Everything went red and flashed, wall to wall. I'd been hit. Somehow I'd been hit. That had never happened before. What on Earth? Then my radio crackled to life, the sounds heavily distorted by my antigrav.

"Splash one Skybolt," someone cried out in triumph on the common channel, the frequency everything in the sky shared regardless of which side we represented. "This is Top Banana One. I say again, splash one Skybolt."

"Roger," another voice answered. "The bomb is already airborne. We're tracking it, Banana One. It's gonna be a direct hit. Our air defense is out. We can't do a thing about it. He's nuked us."

"Damn," the Polecat pilot complained. He wasn't accustomed to losing his base, I gathered. "God damn it to hell." There was a long silence, then another burst of static. "Call it a tie, Skybolt?"

Technically I'd won, and I knew it. My single aircraft, under the worst possible conditions and bereft of the element of surprise, had in simulation taken out not only the primary air defense center of an entire planet, but also much of its government and economy. Such an achievement was well worth the loss of a single 'hopper, even a Skybolt. My father had drilled that fact into me over and over again. Delivering the bomb was the important thing, not surviving. That was what impressed the politicians. Yet I'd never been shot down at all before, had I?

"A tie," I agreed, feeling inexplicably warm and tingly inside. "We'll call it even, Banana One. That's a big roger on that one. I'm looking forward to talking it over with you."

"Good," the Polecat pilot replied. "The beer's on me, Skybolt-buddy."

"Hey," I answered. "You're getting off cheap then, Banana One. I don't drink."

"Oh" There was a long pause. "Because of the no-body thing?"

"No," I answered, wishing I could grin. He had to know, but somehow everyone kept forgetting. "Because of the under-age thing. I'll gladly drink a soda-pop with you."

Chapter Two

"A railroad tunnel?" I asked, cocking the head of my mannequin body a little to one side. It helped when I added a little body language to enhance my difficult-to-read facial expressions. Otherwise, people often didn't understand me. "You hid half a squadron by hovering in a railroad tunnel?"

Commander Knight nodded and smiled. "We busted the Adam and Eve squadron that way too, three years back. When they visited for cross-training exercises."

"Damn good thing you didn't wait another half hour to attack," Lieutenant Pollocks added. "There was a heavy freight scheduled to come through."

"The birds on the ground were lame," Knight continued. "Unserviceable. Didn't you notice that it took them too long to get into the air? They never did make it, you know. Because they couldn't. They were just taxiing around to rush you a little. To make you want to complete your strike before they could lift off."

Well, I certainly fell for it hook, line, and sinker, I admitted to myself as I took another tiny sip of soda. My mannequin body could deal with only a limited intake in a bag mounted in my torso where socially-consumed food was stored for disposal later.

"But a railroad tunnel? I mean, come on. If the Dracans ever attack you guys, what makes you think that they'll be so accommodating as to fly right over your favorite ambush site?"

"You did," Knight pointed out. "Everyone does. The missile defenses are weakest from the ocean side, right?"

"Yes," I agreed, taking another tiny sip. "That's obvious."

"We could fix that easy enough, but we never will. We want folks to come in that way." Knight took a long pull from his mug of beer.

"So you're approaching over the water, from the west," Commander Porter continued for his boss.

He was just a Lieutenant-Commander. However officers of that rank were called Commander too, as a courtesy. I'd had to learn a whole bunch of military-courtesy stuff like that before leaving home.

"You take out Del Rio, that's a gimme. Poor bastards are gonna be the first to go, no matter what. It gets you going, though. Gets your heart pumping and the old adrenaline flowing. Then, the next thing on your pipper is gonna be our Polecats on standing patrol."

I nodded my head. "Uh-huh. That's just how it was." Except that I didn't have a heart anymore.

Knight swallowed his beer, belched, and then took the lead once more. "Our patrol-Polecats might move a lot slower than your ride, kiddo, but they were enough to make you break off from that line of attack. That leaves you with a decision to make. You can either break north or break south. You broke south. Everyone does."

The lights began to come on in the room and in my brain. These men hadn't outperformed me. They had out-thought me.

"Because the other missile base on Duncan's Rock my course was predictable."

"Exactly." The Polecat commander smiled.

He was really old, almost forty or so. He even had a few streaks of gray in his crew cut. He didn't carry an ounce of fat on him. Even a Polecat pulled a good fifteen G's, and, at that kind of acceleration, no pilot could afford even a trace of excess body-mass. The Top Banana aircrew all looked like spokesmen for the diet from hell.

"We expected you to break south from the beginning, and deployed accordingly."

"The burst that got you was fired at point-blank range. High-deflection, too," Lieutenant Pollocks interjected, "We were close. You didn't have time to notice us, much less react."

I sighed and looked down. "You're right. I never saw it coming, not even a hint. You guys killed yourselves a Skybolt, and you did it fair and square."

Knight smiled and tousled my 'hair'. The psych people had insisted that the mannequin-head on my social body be designed to look as human as possible, complete with camera lenses for eyes. Otherwise, they feared, I might suffer extensive personality trauma. They'd even replicated my long blonde Esteppan hairstyle, though in my opinion it looked rather silly framing my mannequin-like face. At least it never needed to be cut, and only seldom washed.

"It wasn't easy, kiddo. Not by half. Your father's come up with a superior weapon system, that's a fact. You were tons faster than us, could turn inside us..."

"...and tossed that bomb a lot further than we expected, too," Porter interjected.

"Yeah," Knight agreed. "It wasn't just the plane. We figured you'd have to come in real close to lay your egg, because we counted on at least part of the air defenses still being operational. But after that trick at Del Rio, using their own missiles on them…" He smiled and shook his head. "You surprised us on that one, and as a result had enough hardware left to suppress Dole Field's air defenses."

Lieutenant Pollocks nodded. "We lost our base—the base we were supposed to defend. That's the bottom line."

A long silence followed, and, for no good reason at all, I felt a little guilty. "Well," I said after a time. "You did better than anyone else has so far. You're still the Top Bananas."

"For now, maybe," Porter said, frowning and looking down into his beer mug as if his drink had suddenly turned sour. "Soon it'll all be over."

"Skybolts," Knight agreed. "Skybolts are the future, sure enough." He took a long sip of beer.

"Even I'm too old," Pollocks added, looking up at me for a moment and then staring out the window. "At twenty-six, I'm already too old."

"Much too old." I looked down at my feet.

The right one was planted in the middle of a small puddle of spilled beer. It was just as well I'd checked because the sensors there weren't nearly sensitive enough to allow me to detect the slippery dampness. A little awkwardly, I clunked half a step to one side.

"That part sucks," I agreed. "Really, really sucks."

Knight grinned, then crossed his arms and looked at me appraisingly. "You know," he said after a time. "I've been flying for almost twenty years now."

I didn't have a real digestive tract any more, but my subconscious still hadn't figured that out. So I wasn't too surprised when the stomach I no longer possessed suddenly developed a big lump of cold lead.

"Really?" I asked.

"Really," he agreed. "I've seen combat, too."

I sighed and looked down. There was only one place where Commander Knight might've participated in a shooting war, and I knew it. At the time my father had already been an aircraft designer of considerable notoriety.

For the other side, unfortunately. The losing side.

"Sir," I explained, "we were obeying the law. My father and his company have cooperated with the United Systems government in every possible way. Our production facilities have even been relocated to Earth. We…"

Knight shook his head and held out his hands to stop me. "Wait a minute. You didn't let me finish." He smiled, then stepped over and tousled my hair again. "It's all right, son. I've met your dad, back on Esteppe during the Occupation. He's a hell of a smart guy, and, in his way, a gentleman." Then the commander's face fell, and he gestured at my clearly-artificial self. "Still, it gives me the heebie-jeebies to see human beings all wired up like you. That's what we fought to prevent—the alteration of the human genome. To keep the essence of humanity sacred."

I looked away. "My genes are one-hundred-percent natural. I'm a pure human."

"Are you?" Knight asked, his eyes narrowing. "Are you really and truly still human, Thomas?" He sighed. "It just doesn't seem right, somehow. No, we're not slicing genes anymore, mixing and matching and whipping up creatures that God himself wouldn't recognize. Instead it's perfectly okay to core the brains out of fifteen-year-old kids and turn them into electronic Frankensteins. It's perfectly fine to do this to children?" He sighed.

"It's not your father so much that I have a problem with, Thomas. He's obeyed every law and regulation. The powers-that-be granted him special permission to do this to you because there may be no better way. Then what did I fight so hard for, if not to prevent this kind of thing? Why did so many of my friends die?"

I shook my head. "A normal human body can't tolerate the accelerations of a truly modern aircraft. Fighters have been detuned for years, simply to accommodate the frailties of their human pilots. You have to brain-core a mammal while it's still growing, or the nerves won't connect up right." I paused and looked up. "It's not like this is permanent. I'll get my body back."

"So long as the surgery is performed before your body is too mature," Lieutenant Pollock observed.

"I have a good five years before then," I countered. "Maybe even six. There've been an awful lot of fighter pilots whose entire careers lasted four years or less. Most wars aren't even as long as that." I paused.

"The Skybolt system depends on the use of disembodied brains, and we need the Skybolt. You know that, deep down. You must."

Knight shook his head again. "I don't know," he said. "I think it's damned strange that at the moment it seems likely that Esteppe's supposedly inhuman and immoral technology might help us beat the Dracans. All of a sudden your father is back in the arms business and being encouraged to do the very same thing that we once forced your people at gunpoint to stop doing. Does reshuffling a few genes matter more than a kid losing his whole body?

"I just don't get it. What the hell is 'human' supposed to mean anymore, anyway? My own son..." He sighed and looked away. "I'm just an over-aged, broken-down, fighter pilot. It's my job to go zoom-zoom and blow shit up, not sit around and think about why I'm doing it." He smiled and extended a hand. "Truly, Thomas, I mean no offense."

I reached out to meet him halfway, and we shook. He didn't hesitate, even though my hand was a chromed five-digit claw. Not the slightest effort had been made to simulate a human appearance, because all attempts to do so had failed miserably in the practicality department.

"None taken," I agreed, as my surrogate face "smiled" for me. It didn't do a very good job of it. "I can't even remember the war. I was too young."

The commander of the Top Bananas pressed his lips together. Then suddenly he smiled. "Say," he declared. "I have an idea. Tomorrow night's the big Army-Navy game, you know."

I hadn't known actually. Nor did I care much about football, to be perfectly honest. However, I was a company representative, after a fashion. Therefore, I had a duty to socialize. Besides, I rather liked Commander Knight. He was cool, just like I'd always thought that the leader of the Top Bananas would have to be.

"Really?" I asked.

"Really," Knight agreed. "It's the biggest social event of the year around these parts. Everyone who's anyone meets down at the stadium to listen and drink beer and place bets. Unfortunately, we're not quite on the same schedule as Earth. Kickoff will be just after three in the morning, local time. So, I'm holding a big late-night dinner at my place first. Would you like to come and eat, then sit with the Top Bananas at the game as our honored guest?"

"YES," a chorus of male voiced declared as the other pilots suddenly clustered around us. "Please come."

My surrogate face smiled again. "It'll be my very great pleasure," I replied. "Thank you for inviting me."

Chapter Three

Even though the main demonstration was over, I still flew the next morning. I injected myself into high planetary orbit no less than five times in two hours to impress the local brass. Earth could recommend, but each world controlled its local defense budget. The ability to fight in orbit and, in many cases beyond, gave the Skybolt a major plus.

A 'hopper's antigravs operate under an inverse cube law in proximity to large masses. The huge engines of the 'Bolt were strong enough to make her a useful exo-atmospheric fighter as long as one didn't wander out too far. True spacecraft required more expensive and delicate thruster-based power plants, and those engines didn't scale down enough to serve the needs of fast, nimble fighting vessels. The Skybolt remained a viable fighting machine out to where the stars stopped twinkling and well beyond. I'd now demonstrated this fact to the satisfaction of all involved.

Touchdown always came as a bit of an anticlimax after hitting vacuum. There was something about maneuvering in zero-gee that was cooler than simulated combat. Like all modern combat 'hoppers, the Skybolt was VTOL. It was the work of but a moment to bring my ship into a hover over the Navy hardstand my aircrew had borrowed, then lower myself until I felt the pressure on my "feet" that indicated a safe landing. We had been able to stay on-base instead of having to rent a commercial hanger.

Here military types guarded the Skybolt. This close to Dracan territory, even civilian governments seemed to understand that they shared my father's interests in protecting his secrets. I was still rocking back and forth on my landing gear when the special little ground cart rolled up underneath the geographic center of the 'hopper.

"You ready, Tommy?" a voice asked over the radio link. I recognized it as Johnny Repp, the tech in charge of my biosystems.

"Ready," I agreed, after scanning my virtual instruments one last time to ensure that everything still showed green.

"Confirmed," Johnny answered. After a moment's delay, he got everything lined up just right. “Here we go.”

I sighed and closed my nonexistent eyes, shutting off all sensory input even before Johnny disconnected me from the Skybolt. Changing bodies was disorienting as hell and sometimes even nauseous. It was the only part of being brain-cored I truly despised. Somehow though, shutting off my own inputs was better than letting Johnny do it. An endless time passed, during which I floated free from all reality, seeing, feeling, experiencing nothing.

Then, I was lying on my back in my mannequin-body, choking, wheezing, and thrashing about like a wounded beast.

“Easy, Tommy,” Johnny whispered into my brain from his chin-mike wired to my audio nerves. “Easy, son. You’re just fine.”

Pulling back my fake rubbery lips, I reached out with my manipulators and tried to grab something—anything—solid. I experienced a brief out-of-control period when I switched interfaces. It came from switching out one set of neural responses for another. My gyros always gave me trouble at first, which was why everything spun. When I got my own natural body back after such a long separation, it would be far worse. I’d be helpless as a baby for weeks.

“How’d it go?” demanded Dr. Layton as my involuntary spasms first ebbed, then faded away. He was my personal shrink, and I didn’t like him. His job was to make sure I didn’t go nuts from not having my proper body. It wasn’t nearly as bad as most people seemed to think. The government had sort of forced him on Father and me. Otherwise, I’d have fussed until they got someone else.

“Just fine,” I replied. “At least I didn’t get shot down today.”

“That’s always a good thing,” he answered with artificial cheer. Then his eyes narrowed. “Did you have nightmares last night?”

I sighed, then met the psychiatrist’s eyes with my own paired lenses. “Look,” I explained for about the thousandth time. “Being shot down in simulation didn’t hurt, like you seem to think it should. It didn’t upset me, except that I feel like if I’d done a better job, it wouldn’t have happened.”

The shrink smiled, displaying pointy teeth. “When you’re a machine, do you often feel like you’re not doing as good as job as you should?”

I closed my eyes and looked away. If the United Systems government had to burden me with a shrink, I wondered, why in the name of everything holy did they have to settle on such an obtuse one?

“I should be perfect in every activity,” I recited in the mechanical singsong that, in the early days after my surgery, had been all I could manage. “My design specifications call for perfection in all things at all timestimestimestimestimes…”

"Umm," Doctor Layton chuckled, reaching out to tousle my long hair but somehow not quite getting the gesture right. "You're fine."

I sat up and shrugged. Movement grew easier now as my nerves found the right connections. "The Top Bananas invited me to have dinner with them this evening, if you don't mind?"

Along with Father Murton, Doctor Layton was my legal guardian for the duration of the demonstration tour. Thankfully, this was our last planet before heading back home to New Orleans. I actually liked Father Murton. He'd been tutoring me since I was little. The more time I spent around Dr. Layton, the phonier he seemed.

"Then, they want me to go to the big Army-Navy game party with them. It's an all-nighter."

"Of course," Layton replied, straightening his spine. "It's clearly a business obligation." He frowned. "Are your lessons caught up?"

If my shrink had really cared about me, he would already have known that I was done with my entire syllabus. A month early. As usual.

"Yes, sir."

"Good," he answered with another oily smile, reaching out to help me stand up on the hot tarmac. I was still a bit unsteady on my feet. "Then I'll figure on you sleeping in tomorrow. We'll do your regular morning session in the afternoon."

I nodded my head. The gesture was slow and unnatural, reflecting the limitations of the electric motors that created it.

"Tomorrow afternoon," I confirmed, hoping that perhaps the universe might end before then, thus sparing me the hour of excruciating boredom.

I walked over to the little electric runabout that was part of the equipment package I was supposed to be demonstrating and mated my mind to the special fitting on the dashboard. Cars were simple things to control in comparison to arms and legs and faces. In a moment, with no more effort than a thought, I was on my way to prepare for dinner at Commander Knight's place.

Chapter Four

Churilla City proved to be a busier place than I'd ever have expected on such a remote planet. Masses of humanity, half of them mounted on cyclescoots and seemingly bound and determined to find kamikaze's deaths before sundown, packed the streets. The electronic maps hadn't offered me any warnings about the traffic. If I hadn't been brain-cored, my lips would have been white with concentration, and I'd have been forced to inch along through the throngs. I hadn't driven much yet. By Earth standards I was still too young for a powered ground-vehicle license. As things were, however, I just let a little more of my "self" merge with the car than was my usual practice, and, in a few minutes, I was flowing effortlessly along, avoiding collision after collision by mere millimeters just like the natives.

I'd read that Churilla was an impoverished world, but reading was not at all the same thing as seeing. Every time I stopped at an intersection, mobs of kids not that much younger than me came rushing up with extended hands, begging. Apparently, there were no schools for them. This was a problem on many of the frontier worlds.

Interstellar trade was expensive and difficult during the best of times, and there'd been a long gap when things had fallen apart because of wars and piracy. Populations had soared out on the edges of things, while technology and development hadn't evolved much at all. Hardly anyone traded for almost a century, and some parts of the United Systems had even broken away entirely, like my native Esteppe and the Dracans. My father had coached me on how to handle myself under such circumstances, and his instructions paid off. I'd stashed several rolls of United Systems pennies in the glove box and showered a few of them out the window at each intersection to the accompaniment of joyful shrieking.

At one stop, the begging took on a particularly memorable form. Churilla was the wettest world ever colonized. Even here on the biggest island, rivers and streams of considerable size meandered everywhere.

Near First Landing Park, where the city traffic was at its worst, I had to stop on a large, high bridge. Almost instantly a boy my own age was rapping at my window.

"A gold piece," he demanded, smiling and not letting my bizarre appearance distract him in the slightest from his business. "I'll dive for a gold piece, sir."

"I...Uh..."

"Look," he said, pointing at a yellow shiny-something flashing through the air from the window of the truck in front of me. Almost at once a dozen or more young men leaped over the rail after it and went falling, falling, falling fifty feet or more down to the water below.

"The one who catches it gets to keep it," he explained, still smiling. "Come on, you're a rich man. The best divers all went after the last one. Except me, of course. I'm Louis, the finest diver of all. Give me a chance, sir?"

I had not one but several gold coins in my pocket. Father was very scrupulous about paying my brother and me properly for our work, even though we were family and I was still a minor. Suddenly I pitied Louis, who couldn't have any idea he was older than I. He didn't have a personal tutor and teacher-machine filled to the brim with the most expensive sort of tapes waiting at home for him. He didn't have an assured future.

"I...Ah..." I stuttered, trying to buy time as I dug, and dug deep. My fingers weren't the most sensitive, but eventually I succeeded in fishing out a twenty-credit coin.

Louis's eyes bulged. Apparently, he was more accustomed to seeing singles. "Sir," he cried out, head bobbling up and down in excitement. "Honored sir."

I couldn't throw in the normal human fashion. My electrical arm couldn't generate enough velocity. I was able to sort of 'flick' the coin over the rail with my thumb.

"Honored, sir." Louis stuttered again. Then he was off, chasing after the glittering speck and making his dive into the muddy brown water so far below.

It looked like it might have been fun, I decided before traffic lurched forward again. A special kind of devil-may-care dangerous fun that I might never know. At least I got to see Louis rise back up to the surface well downstream of where he'd entered, waving the coin excitedly back and forth above his head and then placing it safely in his mouth for the long, hard swim to shore.

Commander Knight lived in one of the better parts of Churilla City. I knew I was getting close when traffic eased, the buildings gradually grew further apart, and isolated patches of lovingly-cultivated green began to pop up here and there among the eternal dreary rocks. His house might've been described as a mansion anywhere else. As an officer of the United Systems Space Navy, his wages were paid in gold System credits. Those went a long way on an impoverished world like Churilla.

A lot of folks were already there when I arrived. I had to park almost three blocks away. One of the good things about my not having my own body anymore was that I didn't get tired or sweat no matter how much I exerted myself. So I was still fresh when I raised the ornate family-crested knocker on the front door.

"I'll get it." I heard an excited young voice ring out. Next came the sound of running feet. "Hi," a fifteen-year-old gushed before the door was even halfway open. "Welcome to..." Then the voice stopped cold as the boy recognized me. "Oh," he said, his eyes widening as they took in my unusual form. "W-w-w-welcome to the Knight residence, Mr. Longo" he said formally, bowing a little at the neck. "Come in, please. I'm Jimmy."

It had been a long day, and I had a grueling dinner party ahead of me that I wasn't at all looking forward to facing. "I'm Tommy," I explained, smiling as best I could and extending my hand. "I won't be 'Mr. Longo' for a long time yet, except when I have to work."

I smiled a little wider, hoping against hope. It'd been so long since I'd been able to play with anyone that I'd almost forgotten how. "I like *Rocket Sledder*. Do you?"

"*Rocket Sledder*? Way cool!" Suddenly, my host was feeling far more at home, and so was I. He turned and raced halfway up a flight of steps. "I'll get the consoles out." he turned to explain. "Dad said that you'd probably want to play a game with me."

Chapter Five

Several hours probably passed while Jimmy and I lay on our backs and fiddled with our controllers. *Rocket Sledder* was a cooperative game, one that required more in the way of strategy than dexterity. This was just as well since my fingers weren't what they'd once been.

"Yes," Jimmy declared at one point when I caromed my sled just so off of his, nudging it over the last little hump that we needed to surmount in order to move onto the next world. He pounded his fist on the floor in triumph. "Level eight. I've never made it this high before. You're great!"

"You're pretty good yourself," I agreed, watching the victory-fireworks flash in full holographic splendor across my new friend's ceiling.

Camera-eyes weren't quite as good as human ones at color and stuff, or the ones in my mannequin-body weren't. Those in the Skybolt, however, were another story. There, money was no object. It was unfortunate that I spent a good hundred or so hours in my mannequin for every one in my 'hopper. I felt a lot more alive there sometimes, and the improved vision was probably part of why. This was something that I was careful to never even hint at to Dr. Layton.

"You are so cool," Jimmy said, freezing the fireworks at their climax so that we could savor our victory for a moment.

I shrugged. "Not really."

"Humph," Jimmy snorted. "Come on. Even Dad thinks you're a great fighter pilot. He said so last night, and you're, like, almost a kid."

I shrugged again. This time the gesture was accompanied by a slight mechanical sound. Apparently, one of my joints needed lubrication. "It's not as much fun as you probably think. I mean, at first it was, sure. Being a mannequin gets old in a hurry. There are all kinds of stuff I can't do, like eating real meals. I'm sort of half-numb to everything, except when I'm flying." I sighed.

"Flying is fun, sure. But…" I pointed to the frozen fireworks hovering in mid-air. "Getting to level eight was *much* cooler than nuking your

Dad's airbase. Even though they were both games, really." I sighed.

"Once stuff gets too close to people getting hurt, it's not so cool at all anymore. Trust me on that."

"Really?" Jimmy stared at me. There was a long pause. "Dad says that you're the way of the future. If I ever wanna be a fighter pilot like him, I'll have to join the Navy and have the same kind of surgery. Probably in the next year or so, if the government approves it that quickly."

I shook my head, though in the darkness the movement was invisible. "Jimmy," I said slowly. "I know that—"

A loud rapping sounded at the door. "Thomas?" a familiar voice asked. "Are you in there?"

I closed my eyes for a moment, then let the game controller slip out of my fingers. "Yes, Dr. Layton. I didn't know you were coming."

The door opened, admitting the restrained sounds of adult-type dinner music and my shrink's bespectacled head. "They invited me at the last moment," he explained, looking around the room. "We're so far out in the sticks that Earthers rate high on any social list. Any Earther, for once. Not just you." His gaze lingered first on the suspended fireworks, then on Jimmy. "Are you playing games?"

Somehow, the last two words sounded like an accusation. "Yes, sir," I said, letting my head bonk back onto the carpet a little harder than a real teenager might have. After all, I could turn my pain sensors off and they couldn't.

"He's really good," Jimmy explained, his voice eager and bright. "You should have seen it when he—"

"Thomas has business out with the others," Dr. Layton interrupted smoothly. He pasted on his oiliest smile. "With the *adults*. Representing Earth's business interests. He's come an awfully long way to waste time *playing*."

I sighed and blinked twice. "Right." I sat up and climbed to my feet. I'd taken off my dress shoes, so without asking permission I sat down on Jimmy's lower bunk bed to slip them on. It took me forever to do that and usually Father Murton helped me. Dr. Layton just stood and glared. I'd never had a bunk bed, I mused as I struggled to get the left one lined up with my foot so that I could slide it in. Now, I probably never would.

"What's this?" a gruffer voice demanded from beyond the doorway. It took me a moment to place it as that of my host, Commander Knight. "Is something wrong?"

Dr. Layton turned and scowled. "I was just looking for Thomas."

"Oh," the commander replied, sounding more cheerful. "After having met him, I figured that he and Jimmy might get along." Knight stepped forward a little and looked over Layton's shoulder. "Whoa! Are those fireworks for level eight?"

Jimmy nodded proudly, smiling again. "Uh-huh."

Knight's grin widened enough to match that of his son. "Way cool," he said, looking over at me. I felt myself smiling. "I've never made level eight with Jimmy yet. Maybe you can sleep over tonight and show us both how you did it? Tomorrow, after everyone's left?"

My smile faded as I turned towards Layton. "I…Uh…"

"Of *course*," he agreed, bobbing his head companionably and reaching out to slap Knight on the back. I'd never, ever seen him back-slap anyone before. "Boys will be boys, after all." His not-smile faded, and his eyes bored deep into mine.

I looked away and nodded. His intent was obvious. Knight's opinion of the Skybolt was at least as important as anyone else's. If he wanted to play video games with me, Layton was explaining, then I was to play video games until hell froze over.

"I'd very much enjoy a sleepover, Commander," I replied. "I'm grateful to both you and your son James for such wonderful hospitality."

I don't know just how I expected Commander Knight to react. I didn't anticipate that he'd stare at me for a moment, then turn away and shake his head.

"Whatever," he answered, appearing to lose interest in the whole project. When he turned to face Dr. Layton, his lip curled ever so slightly that no one else probably even noticed. "Whatever."

Chapter Six

Dinner at Commander Knight's wasn't much fun for a long time after that. Dr. Layton eagerly introduced me to everyone in sight, so many new people so fast that I promptly forgot almost every single name and title. Soon I had a sort of permanent cluster of fellow guests hovering around me, each of them seeking an eyeful of my obviously-plastic skin and metal claw-hands, but none wanting to be caught staring. The fact was that I'd rather they'd been up-front about it and admitted that they wanted to stare. None of them were honest enough. Not one of them at any of the dozens and dozens of stupid dinner parties I'd been forced to endure on as many planets.

At last the lights dimmed once, then brightened again. At this hint the string quartet changed tunes in mid-number, accomplishing the unlikely feat of selecting an even duller tune. Clearly, dinner was served.

I couldn't eat normal food. In fact, my social body couldn't ingest very much of anything. What nourished me instead was a small tank filled with predigested material that kept me going for ages. I was also equipped with an even smaller tank that dealt with wastes. My biosystems crew dealt with that sort of thing so I never had to worry about it. Except when people were trying to force-feed me.

"No thank you," I replied to the man sitting to my right, once we'd all gathered around the long table and found our names on the cards perched atop the highly-starched napkins. Without my father's careful lessons regarding such matters, I'd have been totally lost.

"I won't actually be eating much, you see. Because I can't." I'd made the same explanation a thousand times before. Of course, I endlessly re-explained and repeated it to people who, could never quite accept how things really were.

This time, I was lucky. "I see," the Minister of Agriculture replied. Then, he simply dug into his salad.

"I hear you play a mean game of *Rocket Sledder*," the man sitting diagonally across from me observed. There were two empty spaces next to him, one directly across from me and the other caddy-corner to my right. No-shows, presumably. My dinner-mate was wearing a Navy uniform and had the ultra-lean look of a combat pilot, but I'd never quite figured out how read the rank insignia on mess-dress blues. Nor had I caught his name. Judging by his age, however, he was probably quite junior.

I smiled. "Word apparently gets around fast."

The young officer smiled back. "I'm Jimmy's older brother Ted. You won't believe how hard I pulled eldest-son rank to get a seat near you. Jimmy's seat, in fact. Plus I had to promise to buy him a model Skybolt to build and get you to sign it." His expression softened a little. "I hear that you can't have the procedure done over age twenty-one?"

I nodded. "Right. In mammals, the brain still has to be growing. Or else the nerve endings won't hook up."

"Both on the way in and on the way out," the elderly woman to my left observed. She was really old. Maybe even fifty.

I nodded. "That's why we have to begin so young," I explained. This was the real reason I attended such functions, to explain things and help important people face up to cold reality. "I was five days short of my fifteenth birthday when they brain-cored me. It took weeks before I adapted enough to operate a mannequin body, and even longer before I could mate up with my 'hopper. All the time, they were teaching me fighter tactics and stuff just as fast as I could learn."

"You must've been an excellent student, by all accounts," the Minister of Agriculture interjected. "Though they might have taught you to fly a little higher. You shattered a quarter of the greenhouse panes on Churilla Island yesterday, you know. It'll cause a noticeable blip in tomato production."

"My father will pay," I responded, shrugging.

"Yes," the woman replied. "Of course he'll pay us. With our own money. Money we're being *forced* to spend to upgrade an already perfectly good fighter fleet."

"Not so perfectly good," Ted countered. He took a bite of salad and chewed thoughtfully for a moment.

"Madame Parliamentarian, with all due respect, this young man and his single, lone Skybolt waxed our asses yesterday. He nuked this very city, for crying out loud. Against the finest fighter squadron in the galaxy forewarned and ready for him." He took another bite, chewed slowly, and swallowed again. "Have you ever considered what he might have accomplished had he taken us by surprise?"

The Parliamentarian, she had introduced herself earlier, but for the life of me I couldn't remember her name, frowned. "That fighter's fundamentally Esteppe-tech," she replied. "Forbidden."

"Forbidden to us, perhaps," Ted countered, "but not to the Esteppans during their war against us. Or, perhaps, the Dracans. Who knows what kind of devilry they're up to, over on their side of the frontier? We haven't a clue, and you know it. "He pointed to me. "Ask my dad what it was like to face down a whole squadron of 'hoppers not all that much less potent than Skybolts. With brain-cored pilots in them every bit as good as him. Even better, ask his brother's widow or his other brother's widow. There's *lots* of 'hopper-jock widows you could ask, when you get right down to it. Hundreds of them. Also thousands of ground-pounder widows. All because of thirty-six fighters not quite as good as the model we want you to buy."

The Parliamentarian frowned again, then delicately pushed her salad bowl away from her. "You're the Top Bananas. You can defend us without forcing us to double our defense budget, without leaving us unable to educate and feed our young, and without making us brain-core little boys into something less than human. We, sir, are above that level of savagery."

Ted pressed his lips into a thin white line. "We're the Top Bananas. We have a proud history. We've been first, or nearly first, into every single war fought by the United Systems in the last century.

"Do you know why that is? Because the people at the Admiralty aren't stupid. As a matter of unofficial policy, they keep us stationed at whatever they consider to be the most likely place for the next war to start. So that we can act as a deterrent, you see. Madame, if you haven't figured it out yet, right at the moment the most likely place is here."

A long pause followed. The Parliamentarian frowned again and pushed her salad bowl the rest of the way to the center of a table. Almost at once, a servant took it and whisked it away.

"The boy's right, Sara," the Minister of Agriculture said after a moment. "We might not like it, but our planet sits right on top of the Orion Nexus. The Dracans want it. Anyone can see that. Half their trade comes through here."

"We don't represent a threat to Dracan trade," the Parliamentarian sputtered. "We make money on it, not much, but some. Every credit is welcome. "

"Their military convoys have to use the Nexus," Ted responded. "In the event of war between the Dracans and the United Systems, they have to take this planet. It's too good a base for them."

"We could declare ourselves neutral," she countered. "Kick you Navy people off of our planet for the duration. Not that we've anything against you," she added hastily. "We *want* to be part of the United

Systems, but...but..."

"But you'd sell out your fellow citizens in a minute in exchange for an empty promise of peace, Parliamentarian Fowler," a new female voice interjected, the tone saccharine. "You'd sell out the one strategic advantage that the United Systems holds in such a war, the key location of this planet, and leave all of your citizens to fight that much harder and suffer many more casualties, just so your personal parade remains unchanged. Meanwhile, you soak up every penny of financial aid the Systems will vote you and continually demand more."

I looked up, and my jaw dropped. Talk about your unexpected sights. The speaker was a female anthro rabbit, of all things, dressed in an old-fashioned yet stunning gown. She was gray, with one black ear. And, standing alongside her, was another anthro-rabbit, this one solid gray. He was dressed in an equally old-fashioned tuxedo. I couldn't help but stare. I knew that such beings existed, of course, but I'd never seen one before.

"This isn't our fight," the Parliamentarian spluttered. "War is obsolete. Why should we suffer for—"

The Minister of Agriculture cut her off by rising smoothly to his feet. Everyone else up and down the table did the same. Clumsily, not really understanding what was going on, I rose as well.

"Governor Wiston," he exclaimed, smiling from ear to ear. "Mrs. Wiston, What a wonderful surprise. We heard you weren't going to make it."

"We were just caught in traffic," the male rabbit-man explained, extending his hand and shaking first the Minister's and then Ted's before reaching out to introduce himself to me. "I'm Spencer Wiston. Former governor of this island, a long, long time ago. This is my wife Alicia."

For a stunned moment, I looked from one bewhiskered face to the other, totally unable to react. Then Alicia rescued me.

"It's a long story," she said. "Once gengineering was legal. Our parents were transhumanists and believed the human genome could be improved."

Mr. Wiston nodded. "When the laws against gene-cutting were passed, what were they going to do? Round up all the transhumanists and shoot them? I was a young child at the time. Who was going to shoot a harmless little bunny-kid? So instead they made it illegal for there ever to be any more of us. Most of us obvious-types headed for the stars, where the villages were smaller and the neighbors more accepting."

The Minister of Agriculture turned to me. "The Governor and Mrs.

Wiston are the last of Churilla's surviving Founders. As such, they're among our most beloved and well-known citizens."

My mouth opened again, then closed. Churilla's First Landing was over a hundred and fifty years ago and they didn't even look old, except for their clothes. Perhaps the Transhumanists had been onto something after all?

We all sat down again amid a renewed buzz of conversation and two huge bowls of salad arrived, one placed in front of each rabbit. I tried hard not to stare, but couldn't help myself. I'd seen pictures of anthros in my history books. Who hadn't? It had been in my native planet's interest in similar practices that had led directly to my becoming what I was. Governor Wiston's movements were so unstudied and natural, and the way his wife's nose wriggled as she sniffed at her tomato was uncanny and not like anything I'd ever seen.

Then, Governor Wiston caught me staring. "We're in an awkward position, both of us," he said. "Let's make a deal, son. You stare just as much as you'd like at the missus and me, only you've got to allow us the same privilege. There's no sense in trying to hide it. We're both condemned to live out our lives in the center of fishbowls. So for once, let's just be honest about it and keep things out in the open. You stare as much as you'd like, and so will we. So let's put all the nonsense aside, shall we?" He smiled and so did his wife.

"Spencer hates it when people say things they don't really mean," she explained for her husband. "Or at least he hates it when they say them and he's sure that it's only because they're trying to be polite."

The male anthro-rabbit reached around behind his wife and gave her a little squeeze in the midsection. "I'm getting old. There's so much to do in life, and so little time to get it all done. Why should we waste so much of it on polite nonsense? Besides, how many modern cultural taboos are we already breaking through our very existence? What's one more, eh?"

I thought about the little bubble of not-starers I'd been dragging around with me all night, then I smiled too. "All right." I extended my hand-claw again to seal the bargain. "Stare away, then. Perhaps we *do* have a few things in common after all."

Chapter Seven

Everyone's dinner except for the Wiston's and my own was served in seven courses. By the time my Parliamentarian neighbor was chewing on her roast lamb, the discussion had worked its way back around to Skybolts.

"...don't have the faintest idea where you think the money is going to come from, Chester," she said to the Minister of Agriculture. "It doesn't matter how good the damned things are. We can't afford them."

"We can't afford invasion, either," the minister countered. "Now can we?"

"War is always more expensive than peace," Governor Wiston added, breaking a long silence. "We experienced a few little intramural frays of our own here during the Breakdown, you might recall. Rebellions."

"You think that broken greenhouse-panes are expensive?" Mrs. Wiston said. "You ought to see the bill for putting down an insurgency. The cost isn't tallied just in terms of cash, either. The killed and maimed. War rips the very heart out of a culture, Sara. It twists and corrupts whole peoples, children not exempted. It's far cheaper to deter an aggressor than to fight him."

The lady Parliamentarian shook her head. "Madame, we agree that peace is the best thing for everyone. I believe you when you say that."

She pointed across the table at Ted, who in the best fighter-pilot tradition was busily carving out the tastiest bits of his portion of roast lamb and eating them, leaving the rest on his plate as sacrifices to his eternal war against body fat.

"I even believe you despise war, Lieutenant. I'm not calling people names or anything like that. However..." She frowned again, then picked up her knife, and sliced herself a few more bites of lamb.

"I accept you're not calling me a bloody-minded militarist, Parliamentarian," Ted said when he finished chewing. "I appreciate the fact you aren't. Would you call the Dracans militarists?"

"It's mighty hard not to," the ex-Governor replied, looking grim.

"What's the latest estimate on their military-related spending? Sixty-five percent of total economic production?"

"With over half of that going into heavy fleet units," Ted added. "The kind of ships you only need when you're going into someone else's space to kick butt and take names. Weapons of aggression, in other words. Almost four times what we spend."

"Almost four times as a percentage, maybe," the Parliamentarian countered with a scowl. "Yet not four times overall. After all, our combined economies are far larger than the Dracan."

"Their money goes further, because they pay beans for manpower and materials from their own poverty-stricken people," Ted responded. "You can't compare our spending to theirs. It's not apples-to-apples. Our economic systems are fundamentally different. However, you can compare fleets.

"We've still got more ships than they do. At least for now. Theirs, however, are newer, faster, and more powerful. Even worse, they're building at a faster rate. In the event of a war, we Navy types can't make promises."

"Of *course* they're building warships as fast as they can," the Parliamentarian replied, slamming down her knife for emphasis. "They're frightened of us."

She turned towards me. "Our systems all but surround theirs. We threaten their key trading points. Look at what we did to Esteppe. How can we raise our heads after such an act of naked aggression? We used nukes there, for God's sake."

A sudden silence descended as all heads turned towards me.

"My father was and still is among the richest and most influential of all Esteppans. This, as he will gladly tell you, meant that during the days of the Autarch he was in many ways less than nothing. Only the military mattered. If he hadn't been well-connected and had a genius for certain areas of technology, my father and I would have been judged worthless civilian mouths. As an easily replaceable infant, I'd have been euthanized at once. He would've been drafted into the planetary labor service like everyone else and then eliminated at the first sign of resource shortage." I sighed.

"Father regrets that he ever cooperated at all with the Autarch, more than he's ever regretted anything in his life. He wishes that he'd gone to the camps instead of trying to save Mother. He loved her very much so everyone says and I believe. He also tells me that I should be thankful every single day that I'll never know what it was like to live on Esteppe during the darkest period of the Autarchy." I looked down at the tabletop.

"I'm so grateful to men like Commander Knight and his dead brothers that it's difficult for me to express. So is my father. That's the simple truth."

"Hear, hear," Governor Wiston declared, half-raising his glass in salute.

"I'm not defending the Esteppan Autarchy," the Parliamentarian objected, her voice now an angry hiss. "I'm not, but it was a war of aggression. We had no business attacking Esteppe. They hadn't done anything to anyone."

A brief pause followed as the waiters came by offering dessert. Everyone ate some sort of hot pudding. I was served nothing at my request.

"They were a threat," my fellow pilot explained once the servants were out of earshot. Now it was his turn to stare down at the tabletop. "Their planet was every bit as much a danger to peace as the Dracans. They were an autocratic dictatorship. Even worse, they were an autocratic dictatorship with a military too powerful to ignore. Besides, they showed tendencies toward aligning themselves with the Dracans whose Emperor is every bit as much a rotten bastard as the Autarch ever was. Don't delude yourselves for a moment on that score."

He looked up, his eyes intense and full of fire. "Democracy and self-determination are worth something, Parliamentarian. In fact, they're worth one hell of a lot, as our young friend here just so eloquently explained. Sometimes things get a little messy, I'll grant you that. Sometimes we get a little pushy, and all the 'i's' don't get dotted just right, but where would we be today, if we hadn't fought Esteppe? If we had to face a second potential enemy in our rear area, one poised at our jugular and armed with a very sharp knife? Bowing and kowtowing to every single threat that the Dracan Emperor might issue, that's where. Because we'd be strategically dead, totally out of options. Worst of all, our enemies would know it."

"We'd be morally in the right, is where we'd be." the Parliamentarian replied, her voice rising. "Morally and ethically in the right, at complete peace, and not caught up in the middle of the biggest arms race since—"

"My," Governor Wiston declared in an overly-loud voice, leaning forward and sniffing at his pudding. Unlike most of the rest of the meal, it was apparently something he could eat and enjoy like everyone else.

"My, oh my, Churilla pudding. How long has it been, dear, since we've enjoyed a fine Churilla pudding together?"

"Months, my love," she answered, eyes aglow with affection as her hand gently squeezed his upper arm. "Maybe even years."

"Well." the rabbit continued, still speaking in a loud voice. "What a shame it'd be to ruin it with sour talk then." He picked up his silver spoon. "Nothing worse than sour talk over sweet food," he continued, meeting everyone's eyes, one after another. "Especially on Game Night. Right?"

"Right," the Minister of Agriculture agreed, picking up his own spoon. "I couldn't have said it better, Governor."

"Okay," Ted agreed, nodding and picking at his dessert. Not that he could eat much of it anyway, with his strict diet regimen.

"Sure," the Parliamentarian agreed, nodding and reaching for her own silverware. "I'm supposedly all for peace, after all, and I'm outnumbered here anyway. I'm not outnumbered out in the precincts and you people know it."

"Maybe you're outnumbered," the agriculture man replied. "And maybe you're not. But we're not going to settle *that* here and now, either. So, let's eat and enjoy. The governor's right. This stuff smells *delicious*."

Chapter Eight

Everyone had to make their own way to Dewey Stadium for the big game. Dinner beforehand at the Knight's was a separate event. The commander's mansion was less than a mile from the stadium, probably that was part of why the meal was so well-attended. Like most of the guests, I opted to walk.

Churilla might've been a temperate planet overall, but the single archipelago that made up well over ninety-nine percent of the planet's habitable land was located barely north of the equator, dead in the tropics. Thus, except at higher elevations the heat was quite oppressive. It was almost midnight, however, by the time that dinner was over, so that the temperature outside was downright pleasant. Balmy, almost. And, as would most certainly not have been the case in my native New Orleans, no annoying insects buzzed about. I closed my eyes and tried to remember what a pleasant late-night summer walk had been like, back in a real body with actual nerve endings instead of just simulated ones. But, the harder I tried, the slipperier the memories became.

"Hello, Thomas." an unexpected voice said from behind, catching me in mid-reverie. I froze in place for a second, teetering as I first lost my balance and then tried to regain it via slow-acting simulated synapses. Fortunately, the man who'd so startled me was as familiar as anyone could be with my situation. In an instant his powerful right arm was at my shoulder, helping me steady myself. "Sorry," he muttered, holding on for a moment so as to make quite certain that none of my gyros had tumbled. "I didn't mean to startle you."

"Father Murton." I replied, taking a little stagger step to set things right again. "I'm fine. It wasn't a mechanical issue. You just caught me daydreaming, was all."

"Ah," my longtime tutor replied, straightening out my tuxedo jacket and smiling up at me fondly. Father Murton was best described as dwarflike, short, rotund, bearded, and powerful. He'd been with me ever since Father had been arrested and held on suspicion of crimes against humanity, back on Esteppe. After the acquittal, he'd decided to stay. I couldn't remember a time when he hadn't been around.

"Imagine that, my little Tommy off in dreamland, and it's not even time for Social Studies."

I grinned, feeling something warm and happy spreading itself inside of me. It was a feeling that hadn't changed at all, mannequin body or no. "Soon I'll be in engineering school, you know. More math, less social studies. Yay! I'll be able to focus on the important stuff."

The priest shook his head in mock frustration. He held doctorates in both history and theology, and this was an old joke between us. "The how of things changes every decade or so…"

"…but the why of things never, ever changes, because fundamental human nature is a universal constant," I recited, completing my tutor's absolute favorite dictum. "Thus, the why is far more important to understand than the how. It's much more important to understand the fundamental character of our species than the details of our creations." I smiled again. "Are you going to the game?"

"Yes," he nodded. "Of course. Missing it is unthinkable, it seems. Last week some of the local clergy invited me to a pre-game dinner over at St. Mary's, and I accepted which is rather a pity, even though I enjoyed their company very much. Is it true Governor Wiston and his wife made an appearance this year at the Top Banana's dinner? I was invited there too, you see."

"Yeah," I confirmed, nodding enthusiastically. "They sat right across from me." I cocked my head to one side. "Why didn't you tell me that there were anthros on this world?"

"Because they're the only two," Father Murton explained. "That I know of, at least. And, from what I hear they're somewhat reclusive these days. I considered it most unlikely that they'd come out of hiding. Though I'd have gone far out of my way to make *their* acquaintance, I assure you." He smiled. "Not for the first time in my academic life, I have to admit to a stab of professional jealousy. Wiston is a historian of note. Even Dracan scholars have been known to applaud his works on pre-FTL times. And his wife is a painter, sculptor, and above all concert pianist. Alicia could tour the known galaxy if she wanted, and fill every concert hall and art gallery with admirers along the way. But instead, she stays here."

"Really?" I asked. "They seemed pretty important. Everyone listened to them."

Murton nodded. "Don't let their titles or lack thereof fool you. Spence might only officially have been governor of this one island, but at the time there weren't any settlements anywhere else. He was de facto chief of state of the entire planet during Churilla's toughest times. Even all these years later, he could easily win any election in which he chose to run. Both political parties here live in continual terror of him doing exactly that. Thus, each does whatever they can to placate him behind the scenes.

"His wife practically made a hobby out of holding down various cabinet posts for decades. I think she finally managed to collect them all. Mrs. Wiston could probably run for president against virtually anyone and win in her own right." The priest turned and looked up at me. "Alicia Wiston, the politician, was considered successful and effective at everything she ever turned her hand to, just like her husband. Even by her enemies, of which both she and Spence made a good number. They're not exactly the sort to suffer fools gladly."

I let my mouth open slightly, then closed it. "Wow."

"Wow indeed," Father Murton agreed grimly. "The whole story isn't widely known off-planet. Society is still too leery of the gengineering thing. People elsewhere read Spence's books and listen to Alicia's music, and are enraptured by their depth and brilliance. Yet, almost no one knows they're anthros. Indeed, a lot of planets actually censor the fact."

I frowned. "But... You're saying that gengineering works, that it *does* create smarter, more capable people."

"Making cyborgs creates better fighter pilots, too," my teacher replied, shrugging. "That's inarguable. However, the right and wrong of it, that's another issue entirely. As is the societal impact."

Just then we came to a corner. When we rounded it, Dewey Stadium was revealed in all its minor-league-level glory. "Where are you sitting?" I asked my tutor.

"I've got a Navy pass," he answered with a smug smile. "As a former chaplain, I rate one. "

"Cool," I replied. "Come and sit with me, then? Please? I'm supposed to be with the Bananas, but I want to be with you, too."

Father Murton nodded. "Of course, I imagine you're having quite a long night of it." His smile faded. "Where's Dr. Layton?"

"Around." I shrugged. "He's been schmoozing VIP's all night long. I kinda lost track."

My tutor nodded and sighed. "Figures." Then he turned to me and grinned. "It's traditional to make bets on Game Night," he said. "Or so my clergy-hosts informed me. This one night a year, I'm allowed to wager shamelessly. So, I'll bet you that Navy wins by thirty."

"Forty." I countered, grinning again. "They'll win by forty."

"Loser has to say ten Hail Mary's for the sake of both of our sinning, gambling souls," he confirmed, solemnizing the wager with a shake of my hand. "Now, let's get inside and cheer ourselves hoarse."

Chapter Nine

"Ladies and Gentlemen," the loudspeakers announced, right on schedule. "Welcome to the annual hyperwave broadcast of the Army-Navy game, live this year from the Space-Navy Academy at Pearl Harbor, Hawaii."

"Yay," cried everyone sitting on our side of the empty field. "Boo," answered the green-clad men and women in the other stands. The crowd was plenty excited, even though there wasn't much of anything for them to see. It was impossible to broadcast video over hyperwave. There wasn't enough bandwidth. Even just this one sportscast would hold up normal traffic for hours.

The announcement seemed to have been the signal to commence drinking. Suddenly a waiter was at my elbow with a tray.

"Beer," he asked politely. "Wine? Mixed drink?"

"No thank you," I replied before Father Murton could intervene. It was difficult to judge the age of a mannequin, I supposed. Just about everyone else in the stadium seemed to be saying "yes." Everywhere I looked, servants and vendors were working their way up and down the bleachers with full loads on their shoulders.

Army was the first to score, and there was wild exultation on the other side of the field. Wright Wilson, a rookie, intercepted a Navy pass on the first set of downs and ran it all the way into the end-zone. As the green-dressed fans across the field cheered their hearts out, the blue-dressed folks I was sitting with sat in icy silence. Meanwhile, as we listened to the crowd go wild on distant Earth, a large mule wearing an olive-drab blanket was paraded back and forth in front of the stands.

"That's a tradition," Knight explained to me in a sidelong whisper. "When we score, they do the same thing with a goat. You wouldn't believe how far back it goes. It'll be a shame, in a way, if they ever figure out a way to televise this thing." He gestured at the mule. "Look at him prance, the bastard. I bet he's got a wad riding on Army himself."

Then the game was on again, and this time there were no quick scores to break the tedium. It was two yards and a cloud of dust, over and over and over again. Three downs and punt, three downs and punt.

Suddenly the crowd roared. It was Navy's turn to snag a wayward pass. Hikaru Watanabe made the grab, then he lateraled the ball to Dan Soaring Eagle, who charged almost all the way to the goal line before being tackled by the Army quarterback. What a play. Now I understood why everyone who could possibly do so gathered in one place to listen to the game together.

Between the energy of the crowd and the skill of the Earth announcers, it was almost as good as being there. I leapt to my feet and bounced up down with all the rest, until this time I *did* manage to tumble a gyro and Father Murton had to catch me to keep me from collapsing altogether. Fortunately everyone else was too preoccupied to notice. I hated gyro-tumbles. The reset took three full minutes, all of which I spent unable to distinguish up from down and pretty much helpless and nauseated.

While I was out of sorts, Navy scored and then set up for the point-after. I was just finishing my reset when Navy faked the kick and went for the two-point conversion. Dieter Klein snatched up the ball, tore across the field looking for a hole...

...and suddenly, just as my internal systems returned to a fully "green" condition, the stadium PA system emitted a painfully high-pitched screech and went silent.

"Godamnit," Commander Knight roared, shaking his mug-encumbered fist and sprinkling me with beer.

"Absolutely," Father Murton agreed, thus, I was certain, earning himself a large self-imposed contrition once he realized specifically what it was that he'd just agreed to. "Of all the lousy, stinking times... "

"We're sorry," a new voice announced. "Please be patient. We're experiencing technical difficulties."

"Goddamn army's in charge of the feed this year," a new voice roared out from the enlisted bleachers off to our right.

"Ground-pounder idiots can't get nothing right," another agreed.

"Hey, Navy," a loudmouth from across the stadium replied. "Blow it out your ass."

"My," observed a fighter pilot me who I didn't know. "What clever repartee."

"About what you'd expect from the infantry," his seatmate observed. He was a Space Marine, dressed in deep blue. "Keep in mind, these are the people whose entire tactical manual reads 'Hey diddle diddle, right up the middle' over and over again. If it was any more complicated than that, their officers couldn't figure out what to do besides stand around with their thumbs up their asses. Much less the men." He stood up and extended his middle finger. “Blow this, army.”

“Belay that,” a gruff voice ordered, and suddenly I saw that there was a group of gray-headed admirals seated down at the far end of our row. “Right now, captain, or else I’ll have to make it my business to find out who your CO is.”

“Sir, yes, sir, ” the marine snapped, though he didn’t look happy.

The minutes dragged passed. Soon, we’d missed a large chunk of the game.

“Come on,” a voice from the enlisted men’s section roared. “Please, for the love of god, can’t you at least give us the score? Think of all the halftime pools.” No one answered.

Then, someone in their working, undress uniform walked up and gathered the gaggle of admirals together in a little huddle. Everyone else strained to hear what was being said, but the background buzz of conversation was too thick to overcome. Finally, they stood up.

“All right, Pete,” one of them agreed. “You’ve convinced me. Do it.”

“Aye-aye, sir,” a second man replied with a formal salute formal.

We were almost in the front row, and apparently Pete, whoever he was, remained in excellent physical condition despite his gray hair. Effortlessly he vaulted the railing and strode out onto the field-- dress-mess uniform, sword and all. Instantly the combined MP/Shore Patrol security detachment coalesced on him. Then they almost as quickly backed off again as they realized who they were dealing with. Without slowing down the admiral shaded his eyes and searched the far-side bleachers. Apparently he made eye-contact with whoever he was seeking because the next thing he did was to make a “come here” gesture. Soon the admiral and a general were standing all alone out in the center of the field, right in between the mule and the goat, shouting, pointing back at their respective CO’s, and waving their arms at each other.

“What in the world?” the marine wondered, shaking his head. “*I* can’t get a little excited, but *they* can go out there and scream at each other in front of the whole effin’ world?”

“Shut up,” Knight countered, not even turning around. His eyes were narrow, and his face grim. “You’re drunk.”

“I’m all of that, sir,” the Marine agreed, sighing. “And more.” Then he raised his arm for a vendor. “Hello? Beer here, or is the army in charge of that, too?”

Suddenly the arm-waving ended, and the general kicked at the ground angrily. Then he nodded and gestured back towards his own stands. A young officer wearing a staff aiguillette strode out, then someone called him back before he made it to midfield.

"Oh my god," Knight whispered. Despite the bright lights, I could see he was growing pale, ,.

Just then, the staff officer came jogging back out, this time equipped with a wireless microphone. "Testing," he said a little breathlessly. "Testing, testing." Then he handed the mike to his general.

"Ladies and Gentlemen," the high-ranker said. "No one is sorrier than I, but tonight's festivities must be terminated."

The anger crowd roared, but the general raised his hand and relative silence was restored. "The signal's been lost at the Earth end," he explained. "There's nothing anyone here can do. Please, exit the stadium in an orderly fashion. There's no reason for anyone to panic. All leaves," he added almost as an afterthought, "are cancelled. All military personnel are to return immediately to their duty stations. All reserves are activated." He handed the mike to the admiral.

"Same goes for the Navy," the Admiral said. "All shore leaves are cancelled, all reservists are to report to active duty. Military Readiness State Alpha is declared. Everyone is to report to their duty stations immediately. The fleet up-ships in four hours, hack."

Chapter Ten

It wasn't nearly as easy to leave Dewey Stadium as it had been to enter. Now everyone was in a hurry, and the distressed beer-vendors were blocking the aisles in frantic, last-minute appeals to rid themselves of their sudden surplus of product, but the customers were no longer in a buying mood anymore. At least the officers near me weren't. Even Father Murton looked worried. A continual buzz of frenetic conversation surrounded us and one couldn't help but pick up the odd phrase here and there.

"...state of Fleet-Opposed-Invasion? What's this shit?"

"...Bananas lofted a full CAP out of Dole not ten minutes ago. Every single standby bird."

"...heard from the Nexus Squadron in two hours. Not a word."

"...must have snuck a fusion bomb into Pearl or that's what Earth Orbital Two claims. I have a brother in the army. They picked it up over the hyperfeed while they were trying to get the game back ."

"...Second Army Headquarters in Nairobi, too? Geez, they must have let security go completely to shit back home."

The closer we got to the exits, the more things slowed down. As we slowed, the more arguing and shouting took place. Father Murton's face grew grimmer.

He motioned me to lean over so that he could speak into my ear. "Where are you parked?"

I pointed. Sometimes having a built-in compass could be a good thing. "About a mile and a half, that way. On the street," I added, beginning to understand where all of this heading. "Where I'm not blocked."

"Good," my guardian replied, nodding. "My rental is all the way at the back of a big church lot. It was jam-packed for Game Night. I'd be hours getting out. Besides, no one can drive your rig but you. It'll still be there, where mine might not be. So if you don't mind, I'm riding with you."

I nodded. "Of course."

Then he reached down and took my hand. “Don’t let go,” he commanded me, as if I were a little child again. “Please, don’t take this the wrong way. But you’re not as agile you once were, and you’re prone to tumbling gyros. If we once get separated…”

“Right,” I agreed.

Just then a pair of Polecats flew overhead. I couldn’t see them through the roof, of course, but the ear-splitting engine note was unmistakable. My mouth dropped open a little. I’d studied their operational patterns for my mock attack. They wouldn’t be over the city unless…“Father,” I yelled, dropping to my knees. “Get down.”

His mouth fell open too. Then he realized that I probably knew exactly what I was talking about. What an inviting target a stadium jam-packed full of military personnel might make. In an instant he was kneeling as well. “Everyone,” he boomed out. “Take—”

Then his words were cut off by the shriek of an aircraft-type I’d never heard before, so low and close as to be deafening to anyone who couldn’t simply dial-down their hearing the way I could. I fell forward, then felt my tutor land on top of me. Almost no one else dropped. They were still in a state of shock. The banshee shriek of the enemy ‘hopper grew to an insane howl, then suddenly dropped away to nothing but a sonic boom as the Dracan finished his run.

“He didn’t drop,” someone cried out. “Thank god. He—”

“NO,” I screamed out, my own voice half-mute in my turned-down ears. “Stay down. It takes time for—”

CRACK-CRACK-CRACK-CRACK-CRACK.

The Dracan’s cluster-bombs interrupted me, detonating savagely one after the other over the open field outside. It seemed to go on forever, like an endless snare drum roll. How big were Dracan cluster-packs anyway? No one had ever told me.

Then it ended, and I realized that I was still alive and unhurt in the darkness. Somewhere along the way the lights had gone out.

“Father?” I whispered.

“I’m all right,” he answered, climbing to his feet and slapping the dust off of his tuxedo. Somewhere in the distance, someone screamed. Loudly. Lots of someones.

“Thank god we were indoors.”

I nodded. Cluster munitions were designed to spread lots of little fragments and kill people in the open, not penetrate structures. Most of the thousands still outside, those who’d waited to enjoy one last beer, perhaps or for the exits to clear, were now dead or horribly mangled. Cluster bombs were ugly, dirty weapons. Every pilot I’d ever met hated dropping the things, even in practice.

"Father," a new voice rang out. A tall figure in an army uniform forced his way through the crowd. A doctor, I could tell by the caduceus embroidered in gold on his sleeve. And a Colonel. "Father, come with me. We have wounded outside. Hundreds of them."

My tutor clenched his jaw, then grabbed my hand again. "I can't," he answered. "Sorry. You don't know how sorry, in fact, but I've got other duties."

The doctor's eyes narrowed. "He's a big boy. I see that he's not normal, but—"

"I'm sorry," my tutor replied. "If you knew the whole story, you'd be on my side. I give you my word of honor, sir. It's a United Systems security issue. There's no time to explain."

The crowd moved towards the door again, despite the fact that little rivulets of blood began to flow in from that direction.

"United Systems security my ass," the doctor replied, his face turning into a full-blown sneer. "We've hundreds of wounded and dying. What could possibly be more urgent? In all my days, I never thought I'd see—"

"Come on, Thomas," my teacher interrupted him, wrapping his arm around my waist and pressing me towards the door. There was only another ten feet or so to go. "Ignore him."

"Coward," the physician shouted, shaking his fist at my mentor. "You rotten, stinking, yellow-bellied piece of filth."

I false-gulped and nodded, the swallowing reflex still worked despite being utterly out of place in my new body. Then I let my tutor guide me through the chaos.

The door itself would be the worst, I decided as we edged close. Two unmoving bodies lay just inside of it, right in the middle of the ever-expanding puddle of blood. One was a man, and the other a woman. Both had taken dozens of fragments to the front of their bodies. At least death had been instantaneous. The priest and I had to walk right through the blood-puddle and then step over the female body. Except that I couldn't step over it. My hips weren't designed for long enough paces. For a long moment, I stood and blocked the flow, until the man behind me gave me a little shove.

"For god's sake, kid." he urged me. "Piss or get off the pot."

"Come on, Thomas," Father Murton said, understanding my situation. "It's all right. She's not feeling anything anymore."

I nodded and pressed my lips together, then placed my left foot directly in the center of the gaping wound that had until very recently been a woman's living belly. Steadied first by Father Murton's hand and then that of a total stranger, I transferred my weight. The corpse shifted a little, but not enough to make me lose my balance. Then I was past her and outside.

If anything, conditions were even worse there than they'd been in the stadium's lobby. Instead of just two bodies there were dozens, and many wounded besides. One of these was a souvenir-salesman. He crawled in circles, bleeding from where his eyes had been and still dragging half his merchandise with him wherever he went. No one had even tried to help him yet. Nor were Father Murton or I, apparently.

The priest maintained an iron grip on my wrist, dragging me along just as quickly as he imagined my servos would tolerate. He guessed right because he'd been living with my mannequin body for as long as I had. It took everything I had in terms of concentration to keep picking my feet up and putting them down again just as quickly as the linkages allowed.

We passed the wreckage of several busses, some of which had been crowded with passengers and now housed only oily smoke and flame. At least things got better as we moved farther away from the stadium. It had been the only target bombed so far in the immediate area.

The quickest way to my car was to go past Commander Knight's house. When we rounded the last corner, he and his sons were visible several blocks ahead of us, jogging steadily towards home. Jimmy was having a hard time keeping up. I felt something ease a little inside of me. If my new friend or his family had been hurt in the bombing, I don't know what I would have done. It was almost dawn by then, and, with my bad eyes, I could just barely make out their facial features as they made the hard left up their own driveway.

Then, the Dracans made it much easier for me to see by lighting up the entire eastern horizon much earlier than predicted by the astronomers. Apparently the fireball itself was well below the curve of the planet.

"Dear god," Father Murton whispered in awe. "A nuke."

I was near enough to being a fighter pilot that my reaction was a bit different. "There went Del Rio," I observed. "The Dracans nuked it just like I did. I wonder if they got any Rapiers off first? I sure hope so. The Top Bananas are about to need all the help they can get."

Chapter Eleven

Our hotel was adjacent to the naval air station. Father Murton and I scanned the horizon ahead of us for pillars of black smoke the entire time we traveled, but we never saw any. Whatever little tricks the Bananas played on the attackers after Del Rio was taken out must've proven effective. The CAP pilots had done their job, at least for the moment. Either that, or a recently-dead Rapier battery-commander had earned a medal that he'd never receive. Maybe the Polecats and the missiles had done their part. At any rate, the Dracans had failed to hit Dole Field, which had to be their top priority target.

That wasn't to say we saw no signs of the war during our trip across Churilla City. The radio carried a babble of conflicting rumors interspersed with urgent appeals for all reservists to report for duty at once. There was an air of unreality about the whole situation.

"I can't believe it's actually happened." the radio people said over and over again, no matter what the channel.

Traffic was virtually nonexistent, and no crowds of children begged at the intersections. On every little street you could tell where food was sold by the long lines of women standing outside the doors. What few cyclescoots we saw were mostly ridden by grim men and women in uniform heading towards their mustering-points.

The hotel parking lot was overfull when we arrived. I found a mound of gravel near one side of the building and simply drove my little car right up onto it. At least it'd be out of the way there, and I figured I wouldn't need it anymore anyway.

"I doubt our Skybolt team will be able to leave right away," I observed as we clambered out and half-slid down the steep, sloping sides of the gravel-pile.

"Half of the ground-crew was at the game with us. Some of them might've been hurt or even killed. Who knows where the rest ended up? We didn't have any more flights scheduled. Most of them were excused from work, to go sightseeing or whatever."

My tutor looked at me oddly, then down at his tuxedo pants. They looked considerably the worse for wear between the bombing, blood, and gravel-dust. He slapped at them again, raising a white cloud.

"Come on, son," he urged me, not replying to my question. "Let's go to the terminal and see what's happening there. "

I shrugged and followed. The space-terminal was just across the lot from our hotel. Their ship-to-shore shuttles shared the airstrip with the Bananas. Interstellar ships always took off and landed in deep water, usually miles offshore. All but a very few special-purpose military craft were too massive to support their own weight on land.

Even before we got all the way to the terminal, I noticed something usual. Between the Eagle Line's red-liveried civilian 'hoppers and the gaggle of military passenger-haulers used to run sailors back and forth between Dole Field and the fleet's floating sea-base, there were always six or seven 'hopper-shuttles sitting lined up alongside the tarmac, either unserviceable or just not in use. Now there wasn't a single shuttle to be seen anywhere. Not one. A big crowd clustered around the outside of the terminal. I hadn't noticed it when parking because the building's entrance was on the far side.

"Look," someone cried, pointing at us. "Earthers."

How they could tell from such a distance, I didn't know. Somehow, we could never hide it. Suddenly we were surrounded by a jostling, eager mob.

"I'll buy your tickets," a smiling young man declared, shoving a fistful of large-denomination notes in my face. "First class, I bet. Half a million?"

"Six hundred grand," an elderly woman declared. She wasn't waving cash, but if her clothing and general demeanor were any guide, she was easily good for the amount." A million-five for the pair, if you're in adjoining cabins. Cash money."

Suddenly the jostling increased, and someone was fishing in my pocket. "Hey," I yelled, trying to strike out with my too-slow arm. Slow I might be, but if I ever gained a solid hold, I could break any normal human in two. Electric motors were nothing if not high-torque. "Stop it."

"Our tickets are bio-keyed," Father Murton explained as the crowd thickened and our forward progress slowed to a crawl. "We couldn't sell them if we wanted to."

"My baby," a young woman cried out, thrusting forward. She raised her child for us to see. "I have a little girl. You know what the Dracans will do. Please, take her with you. Her name is Christine. Christine D'Angelo."

"Gah," little Christine squealed, pleased at all of the attention. "Ma-ma."

My tutor winced, then almost broke down. Like me, he knew the stories were true. Our enemies routinely used starvation to coerce captive populations, and children were typically the first to die.

"Hide her away," he advised, looking away. "Run for the countryside, all of you. There's no way here. You should be organizing a defense and stockpiling supplies, not—"

"Hey there," a shore patrol officer interrupted from off to the right, raising his baton threateningly. Several squad mates materialized behind him. "What's going on here?" He shaded his eyes, peering into the crowd.

"We're just honest businessmen," the smiling man with the wad of cash declared, backing away from me.

The military cop looked Father Murton and I over. "We've been ordered to keep a sharp lookout for you two. Are these people bothering you, gentlemen?"

"No," I answered, meeting the pocket-diver's eyes and watching them drop in shame. "Not at all."

Father Murton followed my lead. "This woman, the one with the baby. She's trying to get off world. Can you help her?"

"Right," the shore patrolman replied, frowning again. "I've told her three times now about the evacuation program set up by Parliamentarian M'bele, just down the street a little ways." He pointed. "Lady, if you hurry, they might still be able to accommodate your kid. Why you're wasting your time here, I haven't a clue."

"Because she wants a ride off world herself," the old money-woman declared flatly as the mother glared daggers at her. "She's hoping to find someone too softhearted and softheaded to be willing to separate an infant from its mother. Even though three infants can travel for one adult." Then she sighed. "I'm a selfish old twat, but at least I'm honest about it." She pointed to the cash-man. "Those bills are all counterfeit, as well."

"Really?" The Navy guard raised his eyebrows. "It's just as well that counterfeiting isn't any of my concern, then. Perhaps I should call the regular police?"

Suddenly the big smile faded. "I'll be moving along now," the man said, turning and walking away just a tad too briskly.

The old woman smiled and spoke again. "I can see there's nothing more to be accomplished here. I'm going home now, to make what preparations I can. It's what I should've done to begin with." She looked up at the Navy man, then over at Father Murton and me. "I'm sorry to have troubled you."

"It's a trying time," the officer agreed, bowing slightly. Then he turned to us. “Gentlemen, some very important people want to see you. May I offer an escort?”

Chapter Twelve

It was clear that Mr. Shore Patrolman had his orders and the escort-offer was merely a way of being polite. It soon became equally clear these orders included not letting either Farther Murton or me out of his sight for an instant once we were located.

The terminal was nearly deserted. Inside a cluster of frightened-looking people gathered in the center, sitting together and clutching at their luggage. One of the ladies nearest to us nodded politely. I had to think a moment before realizing that she'd occupied the cabin two doors down from mine on the outbound voyage. I nodded back and smiled, then someone else in a uniform came in our direction.

"Thomas," the elderly man greeted us, hand outstretched. It was Captain Langley, of the liner *Argus.* I'd sat next to him at the Captain's Table many times on the way out, and liked him. "Father Murton, I'm *so* glad you both made it out. I'd heard you were at the stadium." His eyes wandered to my tutor's bloodstained pants and then politely looked away.

"Yes," my tutor answered for us. "We were lucky indeed."

"Most of your staff is here," he continued. "My purser has accounted for all but five. You'll have to see him for the names, of course. I have *so* much to keep track of just now."

We both nodded in reply. "Of course," Father Murton said aloud.

"We'll be boarding in a couple of hours. All launch windows until then are reserved for the military and the evacuation 'hoppers." He frowned. "You'll be sharing your staterooms, of course. Probably with children. Many of them. I'm terribly sorry."

"I'm not," my tutor replied, clearly meaning it. "Pile them in." He smiled and wrapped an arm around my shoulders. "I have experience at nursemaiding."

The captain nodded, looking relieved. "Good, I'll put that experience to good use, you can be assured. You have no idea how few of the other passengers seem to appreciate the gravity of this situation."

"Speaking of gravity," I observed. "I don't imagine there's much of anything good coming out of the Orion Nexus just now."

"Humph," Langley snorted. "That, son, is an understatement. I've been allowed access to military pippers"

"Right." I imagined what they must look like in my mind—a torrent of red pouring out of the Nikita Points, surrounded by at most a few small blue specks. "Given that, how do you plan to get out?"

Langley smiled, the first genuine display of optimism or mirth I'd seen all day. "That, son, is highly classified."

I blinked. "Classified?"

"Yep," the merchant skipper replied, turning to pour himself a cup of coffee from a nearby pot. "I can't discuss it any further. Now, if you'll excuse me... "

We said our good-byes quickly. Langley had more than enough to do. Besides, our Shore Patrol 'escort' was showing impatience.

"You're supposed to go to Conference Room A," he said, pointing to a little hallway I'd not even noticed when entering, located behind the Immigration and Naturalization desk. "Please?"

"Yes," my tutor acknowledged, displaying good grace. His mood had improved considerably at the knowledge at least some of the children would get away.

The corridor turned first right and then left as it meandered back into the guts of the building. Soon everyone I saw wore a uniform. The Navy was borrowing office space in the underused facility. Judging by appearances, they'd probably been doing so for some time.

Conference Room A was a fairly modest affair from the outside. It looked ordinary to me, except the windows were plastered-over with black construction paper. Three staff officers of various ranks sat in a decorative row just under the windows, waiting for their superiors.

A male secretary with more length-of-service stripes on his sleeve than anyone else I'd ever seen sat at a desk located just outside the conference room's entrance punching information into a keyboard. "Thomas Longo? Father Ephraim Murton?"

"Yes," we replied as one.

The petty officer might have smiled a little, improbable as the prospect might have seemed. It was hard to tell for sure. "Captain Wan is eager to see you," he said, not looking up from whatever he was doing for even an instant. You can leave them here with me, Toby. I don't reckon they're going anywhere."

"Right," the officer in charge of our 'escort' replied. "See you later, gentlemen."

"Bye." I waved and smiled as nicely as I could with my artificial body. They'd been polite, at least, and had saved us from dealing with a nasty crowd.

"See ya," the Shore Patrolman repeated, smiling too.

There weren't any seats available, except right beside the staff officers. I wasn't physically tired despite having been up all night, hiking several miles, and being bombed. Artificial bodies were like that. However, Father Murton was pretty old, and his knees hurt him sometimes. So, we didn't ask permission before sitting.

Black construction paper might be adequate for preventing anyone from seeing into Conference Room A, but it wasn't particularly effective at containing sound. Or at least it wasn't very effective for someone with my ears. They were better than my eyes. I could crank their sensitivity up just as easily as I'd turned it down during the air attack.

"...have to protect Churilla City," a female voice insisted.

She sounded familiar, though I had to think about it a few seconds before I realized it belonged to the same Parliamentarian I'd sat beside at dinner just last night. Parliamentarian...what was her name? Sara something?

"That's where the bulk of the population lives," she continued. "If we're to have any kind of hope for a reasonable evacuation, we need to concentrate our air cover there. Once panic sets in... "

"That, and the stinkyworks," a deep male voice interjected, using the local slang term for plastic-making plants. Churilla had little industry except for plastics. "The stinkyworks account for more than half of our jobs, Captain and three-quarters of our off-planet revenue. If they shut down... "

"So you can see what our priorities need to be," a third voice continued after the deep-voiced man finally trailed off. "We need standing fighter cover over the heavily-populated civilian areas, the greenhouses, the rail network, the road network, all seven hydroelectric dams on Churilla Island, one dam each on South and North Island, and the stinkyworks. We can't afford to let anything get through to any of these targets." There was another pause. "I think that about covers it."

"Me too, sir," replied a man I suddenly understood must be Captain Wan. Presumably, he was the local head of naval air. I'd never met him because he was supposed to be on long-term medical leave.

"I suppose it'd be all right for me to divert a few assets to cover the fleet as well, while it prepares to space? And the air base itself?"

"Not if it interferes with protecting the civilian targets," the Parliamentarian barked. "The children come first."

"That's an order, Wan," the higher-voice man emphasized.

"Aye-aye, sir." the captain replied, through what I imagined must be clenched teeth.

What military idiocy. First priority was to protect the air base. If it were hit, there wouldn't be any cover for anything else. Without the fleet to command the Nexus...

Wan didn't appear perturbed at all. "I'll have fighters orbiting Churilla City in two hours," he said, opening the conference room door. "All you have to do is to get Admiral Jones to countersign the order. He's my direct superior on air-defense matters."

The Parliamentarian, an admiral, and two men I didn't know emerged, followed by a captain who must have been Wan. He was an round-faced man, with piercing black eyes. Obviously he was no longer on a fighter-pilot diet, but his frame remained lean from a lifetime of counting every calorie.

"Admiral Jones?" The officer who'd been giving Wan his orders scratched his chin. "I don't recall ever meeting an Admiral Jones."

"Davey Jones," Wan explained, smiling. "Everyone in the Navy knows him, sir or so it sometimes seems. He's a very busy man, and could be almost anywhere. If you and your staff were to ask around, I'm sure you could find him."

"Right," the admiral replied, pulling his coat into adjustment. It didn't seem to fit quite right. The rings on his sleeves were wavy, I noticed, denoting him as a reserve officer. He turned to the staff officers, who'd stood as soon as the door swung open. "We'll do that, then." He nodded at his lackeys. "Charley, Clifford, Megan...Let's go find this Admiral Jones. We've got important work to do."

Chapter Thirteen

"I can't believe you actually did that to an admiral," Father Murton said as he and I sat down together in front of Captain Wan's desk.

"He's a political hack," Wan replied, his lip curling. "Besides being an idiot, Admiral Lutjens is also Churilla's Minister of Information. Until being offered an admiral's uniform to wear on pretty days, he was strongly opposed to such a large military presence here. So, the geniuses in the Admiralty decided to buy him off." Wan smiled. "His staffers are the same empty suits who work in his office on weekdays. Did you notice that one of them was wearing his ribbons upside-down?"

"You could still get yourself court-martialed," Father Murton warned. "A little advice from a retired chaplain who's been around the block a few times."

"Not likely," Wan countered, his eyes narrowing. "First, he'd have to figure out how exactly how to file the charges. I sincerely doubt that either he or his people are up to handling anything that complicated." His smile faded, then his eyes narrowed. "Problem is, Lutjens is the senior functioning military officer on the planet now. That damn stadium attack took out far too much of the brass. It's amazing that he hasn't figured it out yet. Once he does, though…" Wan shrugged, then sat in his big leather swivel-chair. "The fact is, I don't know that the battle's going to last long enough for that to matter."

My tutor nodded and leaned forward. "It's that bad?"

Wan sighed and looked down at his desktop and then flipped a switch. Suddenly the wall behind him transformed itself into a three-dimensional map, or pipper. Sure enough, the situation looked just as I'd imagined. A sea of red flowed across the sky, with only a few blue destroyers hovering near the fringes to break the monotony. Our own fleet was planetbound.

"Why haven't the heavies spaced?" I asked.

"Lack of manpower, mostly," Wan answered. "The Dracans couldn't have chosen a better time to attack. Only a third of the fleet was at full-strength. We're playing merry hell protecting the ferry-'hoppers. One's been shot down with over four hundred sailors aboard. No survivors. There's spare-parts issues, too. Almost a quarter of our warships are lame. Not that it's going to stop us, mind you. Eventually they'll fly one way or another, and we'll simply have to hope that our engineers are up to improvising.

"Anyone who's shorthanded is going to have to find a way to cope. We've got a drop-dead launch target"—he glanced at his clock—"three hours and nine minutes from now. At that point we're hitting space, ready or not. It can't be put off any longer." He pinned us with a steely stare. "You understand that this is all top secret stuff," he added. "Loose lips, and all of that."

I nodded agreement. There could only be one reason why he was sharing all of this with us. I raised my hand and pointed—awkward with metal fingers, but it could be done.

"What's that little group over there?" I pointed. "The one with the big negative vector? Are those carriers?"

Wan's eyes narrowed. He hadn't expected me to be able to read vector-arrows. "Yes," he replied after a moment. "Two light carriers with escort, moving fast as hell. The Dracans blasted them through the Nexus about ten minutes before they hit Earth. That's where the air-raids came from."

I cocked my head to one side, studying the arrows. "It's impossible to translate a Nikita point at anything like that kind of vector."

"My hat's off to the murderous, goddamned, baby-killing Dracan navigators," Wan said. "Apparently, no one told them it's impossible. It must have taken them weeks to build up that kind of velocity. With surprise on their side, they cut through our guard-squadron like butter, ran in balls-to-the-walls, and hit us before we could react." He sighed.

"At least they're out of the battle now, decelerating. Even better, the Bananas managed to hold their own. That's not good news for the Dracans."

"How are the Bananas doing?" Father Murton said.

"Twenty-percent losses." Wan shrugged. "If I were the Dracan Supreme High Muckety-Muck, I'd have hand-picked every last pilot aboard those two light carriers. Probably the fighting so far has been their elite versus ours." He shrugged again. "Kills are about even. As to be expected, considering."

I winced. "Twenty-percent is unsustainable. No one can win a prolonged air battle with twenty-percent losses per engagement."

"Don't I know it," Wan replied, leaning back and putting his feet on his desk. "There's not going to be a prolonged air battle, son, is there?"

I pressed my lips together and shook my head. "No." I pointed at the chart again. "That big red mass there—it's made up of battleships, heavy cruisers, and heavy fleet carriers. Troopships, too."

"Six carriers," Wan agreed, nodding. "Five heavy battlewagons, one of them an *Imperial Throne*-class, brand-spanking-new. Eleven cruisers, five of them heavy. More escorts than we can count. Every time a scout gets close enough to give us an estimate, it's vaporized before it can get a solid figure." He sighed. "You're a smart kid."

"We can't fight that," Father Murton agreed, looking pale. It appeared the reality exceeded his worst nightmare.

"Nope." Wan looked me in the face. "We can't. It's inevitable. We're going to lose this planet. First aerospace supremacy, then the surface itself. So, the Navy's going to do the smart thing. The fleet's bugging out."

I nodded. They were shorthanded, outnumbered, and in need of parts. Living to fight another day was indeed the proper move. "You want me to help cover the retreat."

He nodded. "Bingo." He looked me up and down again. "In a lot of ways, son, you've had it easy. You've done all the fun fighter-pilot stuff, but not any of the boring, miserable work that goes along with it. You haven't even had to diet, and you'll never know how much the rest of us envy you that distinction." He frowned.

"Son, being a successful military man of any stripe is more about character than anything else. Character and inner-toughness. You're smart, and you can fly. I'll grant you both of those. But, are you *tough* enough to stand up to an aerospace battle? The real thing now, not a game."

"I think he is," Father Murton replied. "He's an Esteppan, remember. Esteppan culture is at its base a warrior society. He's not been given everything, Captain, no matter what you may think. Thomas hasn't led a useless, spoiled rich-kid life. He cut himself badly enough to need professional medical attention while learning to fight with a knife when he was nine, and he was a skilled lasegun marksman at eleven. He was once quite a promising young skimmer-racer, which is hardly a sport for the weak of heart. I rather envy him his upbringing, in fact. I was a fat city kid."

Wan nodded, then turned back to me. "Retreat is an inglorious operation at the best of times. Acting as the rear-guard to a retreat is probably the most dangerous and thankless military operation in the book. The odds are good you won't make it, superplane or no. Knowing this, will you fly for me?"

"I will. Father always said that how a man behaves when he knows he's sure to lose at something important is the best measure of his character. I wouldn't want to let him down even though I'm plenty scared."

"You approve?" He looked to Father Murton. "You're his legal guardian, and he is underage."

Murton's lip curled. "I approve, but, we need another signature. Doctor Layton is his other guardian."

Wan smiled, but this time the expression was icy. "You let me worry about that. I'm well-known for the respect, even near-awe, that I hold for men appointed to positions of responsibility for purely political reasons. Like Admiral Lutjens, for example. As for Doctor Layton, we've already met."

He reached out and shook my hand. "Welcome aboard, Thomas. Somehow, I feel you're going to make me proud to have served with you. There's just something about you." His smile widened.

"Don't worry that you're afraid. We all are. It's nothing to be ashamed of." He snapped off his pipper switch, then gestured at the now-blank display wall. "Personally, every time I take even a quick glance at that damned thing, it scares the living bejesus out of me."

Chapter Fourteen

"...and the heavy-gun ships are helpless inside an atmosphere," Knight continued as we walked across the tarmac towards the Top Banana ready-room. "Their armament can only function in a vacuum."

I nodded. This was all kindergarten stuff, as the commander had explained before beginning, but he had to be absolutely certain I understood.

"Yet the fleets are useless without ocean-bases. They require frequent maintenance and heavy repairs. Even more, they consume molecular batteries and other supplies by the trainload. It's not practical to supply a fighting fleet in orbit. So much energy is consumed just lifting stuff and you need so many shuttles to do the lifting that it's economically impossible. So, planetary bases are essential. The fleet sits and floats, idle until needed."

I nodded again. The ready-building loomed ahead, and we didn't have much time left. "That's why the carriers are vital for offensive warfare," I interrupted. "They can launch fighters, either space-fighting thruster birds or antigravity 'hoppers for down low. You can't capture a planet until you control its atmosphere. Once that's lost, though, it's only a matter of time until the defenders are forced to yield. That's why fighter units like the Bananas are important. So long as the fighters control the air, the planet is safe."

I smiled. "The Dracans don't have any dual-purpose 'hoppers yet that can fight both low and high, like the Skybolt can."

"That we know of," Knight observed.

"That we know of," I agreed as we stepped up to the door. I reached out to open it, but Knight placed his hand over mine.

"You can still back out," he explained, looking hard into my eyes. "Right up until the moment this door swings open. You're just a kid. It was literally only yesterday you were lying on the floor playing vid-games with my Johnny. No one would think the less of you. Including me."

I shook my head. "My father would disown me if I turned you down when you need me so much. He'd be right to do it, too. Father Murton, just a few minutes ago, referred to my home planet as having a 'warrior culture'. Well, maybe he's right and maybe he's wrong about that. So far as I can see, every culture is a warrior culture—certainly all the ones still alive are."

I shrugged. "I don't know much about that kind of stuff. It's way over my head. All I'm sure of is that I could never look in the mirror again if I didn't fly with you guys. In fact, I'd rather die than not fly with you."

Knight smiled. "Well," he said, clapping me on the shoulder. "That's good enough for me, Tommy. You're old enough to know your own heart. Or wise enough, rather. That's a very important difference."

The smile faded. "You're about to become part of a terrible time and place in human history, and you'll be expected to do and experience truly awful things. No oath sworn, no matter how binding and powerful, is ever enough to enable a man to withstand the ordeal of mortal combat. Instead, the strength has to come from within. "

I nodded and smiled a little, then Knight patted me on the shoulder, turned the knob, and pushed me through the door.

Chapter Fifteen

The ready-room's interior looked more like a college rec-hall than a military installation. Pilots lounged about everywhere, and colorful, sometimes lurid, pinups plastered the walls.

"Attention on deck," someone called out.

Before anyone could move Knight spoke. "Belay that for the duration."

"Aye-aye, sir," answered a young officer I didn't know. "Thank you."

"Don't mention it," Knight replied. "Any coffee? I'm parched."

The same young officer pointed at a spitting, hissing coffee-maker. "Just now brewing, sir." He looked at me. "Thomas, right?"

"Yeah," Knight confirmed, stepping across the room. He removed the coffee-maker's urn and replaced it with a battered stoneware mug that bore the logo of the Top Bananas.

"Some of you have already had the pleasure. He's in, gentlemen. I'm vouching for him and so is Captain Wan. Do what must be done."

Out of nowhere, people threw little white things at me from all directions. They felt almost like snowballs when they hit, but they weren't cold. Bananas, it took me a moment to realize. Little pieces of banana, thrown hard enough to hurt.

"Ow," I cried, raising a hand defensively. "Geez!"

Then the ritual was over, and Knight smiled down at me. "You're a Top Banana now, kiddo, now and forever. Nothing can ever take the honor away from you."

"You're welcome in the squadron ready room so long as there's a Top Banana squadron in this man's Navy," another added. "Which will be forever, by god."

"Hell yes," added another. "To all our parties."

Commander Knight produced a pair of cloth banana-emblems from his shirt pocket and handed them to me. "Normally I'd tell you to sew these onto your uniform right away, but as things are, we don't have time. Too, you don't have a uniform. Still, take them. By long tradition, any flier who wears these patches never buys his own drinks at any military base anywhere."

"It's a great fringe benefit," said one of the larger men in the back row. "Though on our diet, it doesn't come in quite as handy as one might imagine."

I nodded and accepted the badges, even though I was still too young to drink. "Thank you." I nodded and smiled to everyone, feeling all warm and happy inside. "Thanks to you all."

Knight's smile widened as he nodded an acknowledgement, but it faded away to nothing as his eyes drifted to the big electronic touch-screen at the end of the room. The thing was a nearly-incoherent mass of handwritten scribbles, except where one entire corner was devoted to a continually-updated pipper. Nothing had changed significantly since we'd left Wan's office. Certainly, nothing had changed for the better. Knight, however, wasn't looking at the pipper.

Instead, he walked over and pointed at a list of hand-scrawled names. "What's this shit?"

"We've lost three more," Lieutenant-Commander Porter confirmed. "One's a deader, sir, Macky Fisher. The other two, Jean Caulley and Fats Dinger, are missing. Maybe they punched out, maybe they didn't. No one's sure yet." He pressed his lips together. "We had to scramble the reserve flight again."

"They got bounced while on fleet-defense," Knight's son Ted volunteered. He looked away. "We didn't have a chance to tell you. The Dracans didn't get through, and no bombs were dropped."

Knight sighed and shook his head. "Jesus," he said, absorbing the bad news. "All right, you guys. Let's hold a proper briefing. We've got a mission to fly."

The atmosphere in the room was subtly different. No one moved, but everyone was all business.

"Find a seat," Ted said, materializing at my elbow. "Here next to me, if you like."

I sat. The elder Knight waited while I settled.

"All right," Knight said. "The fleet's launching at seventeen hundred hours. It's not just rumor this time, and there'll be no cancellations like before. This time, it's for real."

No one said a word, but somehow I sensed an increase in the level of tension.

"Fleet-Opposed-Invasion has been cancelled," Knight continued, his eyes wandering around to meet those of his pilots, one by one. "We can't fight this battle. It's over before it's begun. So, the heavies are bugging out. "

"Shit," someone murmured in the back.

“They *have* to,” Knight continued remorselessly. “The ships and men are going to be needed badly in days to come, to fight battles in places where victories might still be possible. We’re staying. Our job’s to cover the retreat.” This time, no one said anything.

“It’s a suicide mission,” Knight said, his voice even and controlled. “Impossible, even. There’s six heavy fleet carriers filled with Dracan fighters out there. Our orders are to resist to the last man and to the last Polecat. These are *good* orders, given the situation.” His smile had a wicked edge.

“They’re not half good enough, but I’m going to win, not just resist. Who’s with me?”

A sudden chorus of growls filled the room.

“I am.”

“Me, sir.”

“We’re the Bananas, ain’t we?”

Knight surveyed the room again and turned to the situation board. “Gold Flight’s on CAP?”

“Sir, yes, sir,” Porter replied.

“All right,” Knight continued, still looking at the ops board. “They rearm the minute they land and revert to standby status. I’m sorry, but they’ll have to sit this one out. That leaves Green, Blue, Red, and the Staff flight, with a total of...twenty-four all-up birds. Plus, of course, one Skybolt.” He turned to Porter. “Have them armed, serviced and topped off immediately.”

“Aye-aye, sir.”

His fierce smile impressed me, and, satisfied, he turned back to his pilots. “People, we have two dozen Polecats, one Skybolt, about an hour to plan things out, and all the friggin’ targets in the universe. What fighter pilot worthy of the name could ever hope for anything more? Let’s make this fur ball one for the history books.”

Chapter Sixteen

An hour and ten minutes later, we had a plan and I was being mounted into my 'hopper. "It's all right, Tommy," Johnny Repp whispered into my aural nerve. "It's going to be all right."

"Thanks," I whispered back, glad that Johnny was still around. His voice was like balm on raw nerves. Presumably, he'd been watching my biosystem needles flutter. For that matter, I was grateful to everyone who'd stayed. Without Skybolt-experienced ground-crew, the Navy guys would've taken forever to figure out how to mate the four big standard-issue torpedoes to my 'hopper.

"Thanks to all of you. I can't believe you passed up a ride home on the *Argus* just to help out." A slight pause followed.

Only Johnny had a mike. "The boys say that the honor is theirs, Mr. Longo. How could we ever look your father in the eye again if we didn't help you out?" There was another pause. "Besides, we watched them load the refugee kids onto the shuttle 'hopper. She landed only a few yards away. That helped quite a bit. What a sight. We'll never forget it."

Some of the kids, I knew, left only because Johnny and the rest had given them their places. I tried to nod, then remembered I was wearing my Skybolt-body and clicked my intercom twice instead.

"You're good people, all of you. If I have my way, you won't be forgotten."

A new voice interrupted me. "Banana Five, this is One."

"Five," I replied, feeling self-conscious. I'd had little excuse before now to use the air-to-air frequencies. My simulations had all been run alone. I was used to *evading* Polecats, not cooperating with them.

"Five, all is optimal. I repeat, all is optimal. Condition is orange."

"Orange," I acknowledged. "Roger." That meant the fleet was powered up and takeoff was imminent. The Bananas would be airborne in a minute or two at most. All except me. I was a Top Banana too, now, I reminded myself. Me. Who'd have ever thought it?

"Thanks for painting the Banana emblem on me, guys." I turned my port wingtip camera inwards towards my fuselage and admired the little yellow logo on my nose.

"It was nothing," Johnny assured me. "We had to get the paint out to do the insignias anyway."

I nodded, then ghost-smiled to myself. Dad's company logo, by no chance at all, had been exactly the same size and shape as that of the United Systems Navy. The same colors, too, though differently arranged. I smiled at my ride's new roundels and worked my elevons a little in self-admiration. The difference was subtle, but important.

"So long as the check clears, that's the main thing," I answered. Churilla had paid several times the asking price for my Skybolt. Now, it seemed a bargain.

My radio came to life again. "Five," Commander Knight's voice crackled. "This is One. We're rolling."

I clicked my mike-circuit twice. I knew the commander was busy. No more acknowledgement was required. For a time, my part of the plan consisted of nothing, but sitting and waiting. It should have been simple, yet somehow I felt mine was the hardest part of all.

"Wow," Johnny whispered into his mike,

Then I felt it too, a deep, low-frequency vibration running up from the ground and into my undercarriage. It must have been the fleet, operating a thousand or more high-capacity thrusters all at once at full throttle, not far offshore.

"You should hear this, Tommy. In fact, I'm going to try to record it for you. It's the most awesome sound I've ever heard in my life. Like the sky is so full it's going to burst."

I clicked my mike again, and toyed with my canards. My audio-inputs when I was a 'hopper were of low quality. In fact, I was deaf as a post to normal sounds. Airplanes didn't need ears. Then suddenly, I heard one thing I needed to hear again. *Otto*, I thought. *Play Father's farewell message.*

Acknowledged, my simpleminded computer-companion replied. Then, just a second or two later, the audio-video playback began.

"Thomas," my father said, smiling into my mind. "I'm so proud of you, and so very grateful as well."

"We all are," my eldest brother Sven declared from over his shoulder. He was an aerospace engineer. Just like I hoped to be someday.

"If you hadn't volunteered for brain-separation surgery," Father continued, "the Skybolt project would never have gotten off of the ground. For if I had not set the example by having my own son brain-cored, who else would be willing?"

He smiled again. "I wasn't surprised at your courage, Thomas. You've always had more than your share. However, the dedication and energy with which you've learned your new trade has been...phenomenal. What a remarkable young man you're becoming. Your mother would have been very, very proud."

Somehow, I felt what should have been a tear trickling down my cheek, but it wasn't, quite. Would she have been prouder still to know that I was a Top Banana now, about to go into battle? I certainly hope so, though I could never know.

Sven took over. "Thomas, my brother, I swore months back that if you did this thing, you would have earned my gratitude forever—the entire family's gratitude."

He smiled. "When you get back and are fully restored to health, Father and I hereby promise you your full share of the business and its profits, to do with as you like. You can go back to skimmer racing, if that's what you want. Professionally, full-time.

"For the rest of your life, you will never want. Or, you can finish school and take your rightful place at our side as our partner. No matter what you choose, we shall not criticize." His smile faded.

"I swear to you that this one thing that you are doing is enough to earn your share forevermore. No one may rightly ask anything of you ever again."

The camera panned back, revealing my other elder brother Dean sitting in his powerchair between the other two. He was smiling and waving as best he was able.

"Hi, Tommy," he gurgled. "Hi. Hi. Hi."

I felt another non-tear flow down my non-cheek. Dean had been tortured by the Autarchy at age three when they suspected Father had been in touch with United Systems spies. They'd damaged his brain, on purpose, but Father hadn't. Even though he had spoken with spies.

"HiHiHi, Tommy," Dean repeated, bouncing up and down in childish enthusiasm. "HiHiHi."

"Come back to me, my most beloved child" Father urged, looking directly into the camera, and thus into my eyes.

He reached out and embraced his other two sons. "Come back to me so my family might all be together, and my heart made whole once more. Please don't take foolish chances.

"The Skybolt is just another antigravity hopper. It will either sell or it won't. If not, then so be it— life will go on. The fault will not be yours." He smiled. "Come back soon, my son. I miss you already, and you have not yet even left."

The screen went dark, and for just a moment I closed my non-eyes and thought about home and Father and Sven and Dean. We were an oddball family, sure enough. The love that we felt for each other was deep and real.

Then someone spoke into my ear again. I realized it had been going on for some time.

"Banana Five, do you read?" It was Knight's voice, twisted and distorted by who knew how many G's.

"Roger, One," I acknowledged.

Despite the G's, the note of relief in Knight's voice was unmistakable. "Move," he ordered. "You're on, kiddo, and the timing couldn't be better."

Chapter Seventeen

It only took a few seconds to raise the blast door, cast off my umbilical, and roll free of the hardstand under my own power. Then it was a simple matter of turning out to sea and hitting the throttles just as hard as I could. After that, everything was blue again.

I turned my attention to the pipper. It was more crowded than I'd ever seen it before. Even in the craziest simulations I'd ever run, the sky hadn't been half so full. The fleet was rising, all right. It was currently at angels fifty and climbing steadily in a spherical defensive formation. In the very center were two large blips. They represented the *Argus* and the old battle-cruiser *Andrea Doria*. Above the formation, forming a protective umbrella, were the rest of the Top Bananas. Above them all the Dracan fighters in the universe tried to force their way through to our still-helpless ships. So far, it looked like the Bananas were holding their own.

I frowned. The Dracans had lots of large blips in their armada now. More even than they'd had when I'd attended the briefing. Half a dozen or more of them looked larger than the *Argus*. One in particular was huge. I'd never seen anything like it. The *Imperial Throne* herself. As we'd foreseen, there wasn't a single thruster-fighter anywhere in the sky. Yeah, what need had the Dracans for thruster-fighters in the battle? It'd take the Polecats ages to work their way out into deep space, their engines losing power all the way. If thrusters were needed, there'd be plenty of time to launch them later.

My Skybolt was long past transonic when I encountered little pockets of turbulence. At the speeds I cut air, what felt like little zephyrs were in fact the tornado-like vortices left behind by the fleet, enough to totally destabilize or even crash a lesser 'hopper. The Skybolt's entire design philosophy was centered on raw oomph. Tornadoes weren't even close to a fair match for my power-to-weight ratio. Out front, the needle-nose barely wavered.

Then I looked at my pipper again, and realized it was time.

"Hey diddle diddle," I transmitted. My voice sounded calm and even.

I wondered if this would still have been the case had I been forced to speak from an actual mouth. They tended to go dry in moments of sheer terror or so I'd read.

"Right up the middle," Commander Knight verified. It was good to know he was still alive. Fighters were flaring and dying every few seconds, though fortunately many more red ones than blue. "Godspeed, son."

I smiled with nonexistent muscles, then clicked my microphone circuit twice and pulled my nose up, up, up, until I was climbing dead-vertical. My torpedo sights locked on the single huge enemy blip that took up half the sky.

Chapter Eighteen

Before this battle I hadn't wanted to make suggestions in the ready room. Who was I, after all? A sixteen-year-old kid and only an honorary squadron-member. Nobody, in other words. I wasn't even in the Navy. No one had thought to administer the oath. Nobody else had come up with anything that even remotely looked as if it might work. Worse still, it soon became obvious that none of my fellow pilots really understood, even after my demonstration, what I could and could not do.

"Putting a wingman on me would just slow me down," I protested at one point. "I don't know the Thach weave," I said at another.

More out of frustration that anything else, I offered an idea of my own. "All I really know is how to penetrate defenses. It's what I've done over and over again. Air-to-air is just something I have to do sometimes on the way in. I avoid it whenever possible."

"This whole mission is about air-to-air," a young Banana countered.

"Maybe," I replied, "and maybe not." I paused, thinking about something that Captain Wan had said to me. "Think of the bigger picture. All of the elite Dracan pilots are probably on those two light carriers. The ones headed out-system, scrubbing off speed. They're out of the battle."

"Thank god for it," Knight answered. "They were too damned good."

"They're the leaders," I explained. "The quick thinkers. The ones who react correctly to new situations. What's left with their main fleet are the dullards, relatively speaking. Left leaderless, to boot. When I studied air combat, they taught me over and over that decisiveness is a key element to success. Are these guys likely to make the right decisions if we pressure them?"

"Decisiveness," Knight agreed. "That and sheer bloody-minded aggressiveness under virtually all conditions." He leaned forward, eyes narrowing as they met mine. "What do you have in mind, son?"

"Something from the army playbook," I answered, looking down at the tabletop. My cheeks would've been beet-red had they not been made of rubber. "At least, that's how a marine once described it..."

Now faced with the massive Dracan ship, I had to pull it off. It had seemed so simple, as a dry sterile concept. Shooting skyward and glowing like a meteor in reverse, I wasn't nearly so confident. Every pipper in the Dracan fleet had to be focused on me. I moved at five times the speed of anything else. My high-performance antigravs raised a hyperwave racket to shake the ether with an intercept course for the enemy flagship. Every last Dracan fighter-controller must be staring at my pip, and reaching for their microphone switch. I certainly hoped so.

It wasn't hard to pass through our own ships. I'd elected to tear right through the heart of the United Systems sphere. In an eye blink, I passed the *Doria*. I noted her starboard batteries were in the process of training outboard so she could fight her way clear.

Some trigger-happy idiot fired at me despite the briefing and others joined him. I twisted and dodged the laser-bolts. It would be far worse among the Dracan fleet. It'd would be worse for my flight to end via some jackass gunner who hadn't gotten the word. Then I reached the ongoing fighter-versus-fighter battle.

As planned, I flashed right on through without pausing, though I altered course by a few degrees to direct a couple of laser-bolts at a single Dracan fighter tailing a Polecat, a difficult high-deflection shot. To my surprise, the Dracan flared and died.

"Thanks, kid," Ted Knight replied.

Then I was through the fighter actions as well and rising, rising, rising so hard and fast that if I didn't find a way to slow down before getting too far from the planet I'd escape the system entirely and drift forever among the stars. The Dracan fleet was far above the top of the atmosphere. They hovered there waiting to ambush our ships and blow them of space with their larger and more numerous guns. Their combat superiority was total.

The last thing they expected was a counterattack.

For about the hundredth time, I checked my torps. They were hot and normal. I potentially carried the fate of four huge, expensive spacecraft under my wings, the cost of each of which might well exceed the gross annual product of more than a few planets. Now, there wasn't a single fighter in the sky between me and them.

My antigravs were growing a bit sloppy, but normal when I ventured into the blackness, away from the planet-sized mass my power-system needed as an anchor to operate properly. I was still much livelier than any thruster-craft ever built. Things could get a lot worse before I'd have real problems.

A few Dracan laser-bolts began to come my way. Fired by more able and alert gun crews made them dangerous. I dodged and weaved a little. No actual limbs had to move to transmit my control-commands so I could react more quickly than any gunner, no matter how competent. He could , of course, always get lucky.

More and more laser-bolts came at me until I whirled and twisted at the heart of a many-sourced vortex of fire. The sweat would have been pouring off of my forehead if I still had one. However, the Dracan fleet still held their majestic, perfect formation.

"Come on," I muttered sub-vocally. "You've *got* to react. You've never seen anything like me before. I'm too much of a threat to ignore no matter how strong you are." I virtual-frowned, then decided to emphasize my dangerousness by firing a missile.

"*One,*" I thought, recentering my pipper for an instant on the mother of all battlewagons, the largest ever built by anyone anywhere. "Fire!"

The missile streaked smoothly away, and I went back to zigging, weaving, and dodging. It wasn't so hard now because my missile distracted the gunners and the navigation officers, I realized with glee. The great ship was yawing out of formation, away from the missile and away from the *Doria* and *Argus* and everyone else in our fleet still rising steadily into space behind me. With any luck, she wouldn't be in position to get off a single salvo.

I pulled virtual lips back from my lips. "Sheer bloody-minded aggressiveness," that was how Commander Knight had put it. Now I proved him right. Like a machine, even as my original missile struck the huge spacecraft' and exploded in a blaze of nuclear glory, I turned towards a second battlewagon which, following the example of its larger cohort, swung out of line as well. Without me even having to fire a shot.

About then the Dracan fighter-controllers went totally nuts, ordering their fighters away from the surviving Bananas and into fleet-defense mode. Those Dracan pilots foolish enough to obey such an insane order didn't live long. To turn away from an enemy as skilled as a Top Banana in mid-dogfight was perhaps the most certain death possible in an aerospace battle. With any luck the Dracans were doing exactly that, in droves. That was Commander Knight's problem, not mine, and I left it in his capable hands.

A gaggle of thruster-fighters belatedly launched from one of the carriers, but not many. I was at just the right time and place. With a mere thought I willed myself behind them and bam, bam, bam, bam. Four Dracans died before they could even orient themselves to the combat swirling so unexpectedly around them. It was murder, pure and simple. Thruster fighters stood no chance at all against a Skybolt, or at least not a Skybolt so near a planet.

Chaos, once initiated, propagates exponentially. In this case, it worked against the Dracans as intended from the get-go. In seconds, the once-orderly formation-filled sky had transformed itself into a mass of dodging, weaving ships desperately seeking to avoid collision. This was normal in battle, but only for the smallest of craft, like my Skybolt. Now, however, the improvised dodging and weaving was being performed by sluggish, hard-to-turn capital ships of many thousands of tons burden, while, behind me, our own fleet rumbled by just above the atmosphere at flank speed.

They didn't quite get away clean. As I continued to aim myself at various ships and threaten them with my torps and caused them to take increasingly desperate evasive action, I saw at least two United Systems destroyers struck and crippled by energy-blasts from the Dracan escorts. The *Imperial Throne* got off a full broadside as well. It exploded the cruiser *Houston* in a single, all-consuming fireball. Surely every spacer aboard was killed, but *Doria* did the fleet proud, pumping five salvoes into a much-heavier Dracan battleship one after another, leaving her powerless and adrift.

I didn't see much of the naval battle because I had to concentrate on my pipper. My 'bolt still had a ferocious outbound vector built up, though I'd shed as much of it as I felt I could safely manage while weaving and dodging. If I did nothing, in seconds I'd pass within easy range of the slow, barely-armed landing ships packed with troops for the invasion. The things weren't even armored. It was the job of the Dracan fleet to defend them. Said fleet, however, was currently preoccupied with not ramming itself.

Commander Knight and I hadn't dared plan this far ahead. Frankly, "Hey Diddle Diddle" had already taken me farther than either of us had ever dreamed. I was supposed to have died long minutes ago. Yet here I was, not only alive but still not hit, still successfully dodging and weaving, and still carrying three perfectly-good nukes.

What a terrible shame it'd be to let them go to waste.

The landing ships were thrusting away from me for all they were worth. It appeared they'd noticed my rather spectacular approach. Not that it did them any good. They were sitting ducks. I lined up and fired once, twice…

Then some idiot Dracan gunner got lucky. The hit was halfway inboard on my right wing. I felt a stab of pain, then went spinning so hard the universe became a blur.

"Gee overload." Otto cried. It was the first time I'd consciously noticed him the entire flight. "Gee overload. Systems damage. Starboard antigrav out."

I stabilized using the emergency thruster and fired the port antigrav to compensate, scrubbing off more velocity lest I commit myself to the sublight interstellar-tour thing. "Shit," I cursed aloud, wishing I could slam a fist into something. "Goddamn it."

I was a lame bird now, hardly able to outrun a thruster-fighter. Half the antigrav power would generate only a ninth the thrust. Without the raw power that was my reason for being, I was useless.

In the distance, a fireball swelled, to be joined by a second an instant later. The troopships, probably. Well, my mission had been to provide a distraction. I figured I could count that as accomplished. Now it was time to run for home.

There was no way in the universe that I wanted to accept combat in my lame state. I swerved far towards the galactic south before thrusting for Churilla and tried to put as much space as possible between me and the Dracan battlefleet as I could reasonably manage. All I wanted was my nice, safe hardstand. If I never flew aerospace combat again, it'd be too soon for me.

As I came about I was treated to a wonderful view of the *Doria* and *Argus* thrusting hard for...Where?

I would've blinked if I'd had eyes. Instead, I reset my pipper to see if the electromagnetic effects from the hit I'd received might have disoriented me. Everything came back up hot and normal. I had my directions straight. The fleet wasn't headed for any of the Nikitas. Instead, it moved away from all of them.

Why? It didn't make any sense at all that I could see. Without Nikita points, interstellar jumps were impossible. That was why the Nexus was so vital to begin with. Sure, some Nikitas were a little unstable, expanding and contracting with traffic volume, for example, and sometimes fading out altogether for weeks and months at a time. They even moved, though never very much. So, why not use them?

Maybe there was another Nikita Point in the system? One that'd been kept a closely-guarded secret?

Even as I watched, the fleet began stringing out into line-ahead Jump formation. Yes, I silently screamed. Yes. Yes. Yes. They were going to get away after all.

Then the big battleship I'd torpedoed earlier seemed to take notice as well. It had emerged intact from all the confusion, and its captain was beginning to head back into the battle. The vessel's giant guns swung towards the *Argus*.

I had to do something. I rammed my mental throttles forward and my lame bird responded as best as it could. I looped sloppily around, lining up the big ship so that she was caught right between me and the

Doria, whose big guns were still blazing away.

The big ship attempted a counter-maneuver. My earlier hit had been far from enough to kill her, but I could see where a patch of plating had been melted and some of the sensor-masts were missing. There was no possibility of maneuvering out of such a box with a battleship, so instead her resourceful captain did the next-best thing. He rotated her, swinging her wounded side away from the threat of the battle-cruiser's heavy guns and directly towards me.

I didn't have time to think. Pure instinct took command. I throttled my remaining on-line antigrav all the way to Full Emergency and plunged in to the attack as fast as I could. The laser-bolts thickened up again. This time I had far less to dodge them with. One struck home right on top of the muzzle of my own cannon. The hit silenced the weapon, but its rugged mount prevented further damage. Then a second round struck me deep in the vitals, shutting off all but emergency systems and leaving me drifting powerlessly on my last vector.

That was that. It was time to eject. I was lucky to be alive. My nose was swinging towards the battlewagon. My weaponry circuits might still be active. A heavy-caliber laser-bolt struck home just as I mentally ordered the missile to fire.

The torpedo zoomed off an instant before the stub-wing it had been mounted on spun away, completely severed. The automatic systems took over from there. Nausea struck as the dying Skybolt performed its last service for me, ejecting my survival-capsule so high over Churilla that the entire archipelago was a green smudge against the blue sea only half-lit with night falling.

The last thing I saw before passing out was a bright, bright light. Whether it was the battleship blowing up or my own Skybolt exploding, I never expected to live to find out.

Chapter Nineteen

When consciousness finally returned, it was so dark that I first thought my optical systems had failed. I figured my gyros had tumbled as well. Everything was topsy-turvy, and I wished for the thousandth time that Father could've worked out some sort of solid-state gyro-substitute capable of operating in close-proximity to an antigrav. There'd been nothing available, so I was forced to live with the all-mechanical substitute. My non-stomach heaved and lurched as I ran my reset sequence over and over and over again. Everything kept coming up green, yet "up" and "down" were wandering all over the place.

Perhaps an hour elapsed before my head cleared enough for me to remember I'd bailed out of my Skybolt. It took even longer before I grew dimly aware of the fact I must've suffered a truly epic blow to my titanium skull. My gyros worked just fine, but I was afloat somewhere well out to sea.

My corklike false head danced this way and that with every wave. My survival pod was designed to float. I should even float face up, all else being equal, but all else clearly wasn't equal. With each swell I bobbed and rolled and tumbled.

The survival pod was designed to keep my brain alive for a month without servicing. Knowing the way Father always did things, I'd probably last a good forty days or so. If I had to spend the whole time tumbling, I'd as soon it was over with now. I'd never been more miserable in my entire life. I wanted to vomit worse than anything in the world, but I didn't have anything with which to vomit.

It went on like that for what seemed like hours and hours. I'd drift around a while in misery, pass out, and then wake up unable to remember where I was or why. However, after the fourth or fifth cycle I began to feel sharper. I extended my tripod and played with it a little, until finally I was able to configure it as a sort of crude sea-anchor. It wasn't much, but once locked into position it held my face above water and kept my head pointed upwind. That helped a lot. Now I surmounted each wave in a smooth and predictable manner instead of rolling around like so much flotsam. More correctly according to my rapidly recovering mind, jetsam. Flotsam was the residue of a shipwreck, while jetsam consisted of stuff that had been deliberately jettisoned from a ship. My ejection had been planned and deliberate, so technically I reckoned I was jetsam.

Somehow, I felt a lot better after figuring that out. After all, who wanted to be flotsam?

It wasn't until then that I thought to do a full systems-check, which by rights should have been my first action upon regaining consciousness. Everything was in the green except for my escape gear. The parachute and heat shield were gone, of course. My built-in locator-beacon was firing. Two of the medical indicators were in the yellow, but a quick check showed that the core readings were trending the right way. Presumably I'd suffered a concussion, and was improving.

The dark, overcast night revealed no stars. I couldn't make out the single tripod-leg that should have been in my field of view. Apparently I was under a solid cloudbank.

The night dragged on and on, seemingly endless. At last I sighed and turned my vision inward, to where Father had long ago added a very elementary video-game capability to my interface. He'd originally done it to help me through the long periods during my first days of adjustment when I hadn't been able to do much. He knew boredom always depressed me.

So instead of staring into the blackness, I flew a pretend-fighter for a time, getting myself killed many times over along the way instead of just the once. Many times in a game was a lot better than once for real. Being a shot-down pilot was boring.

About an hour later, dawn broke and I established there wasn't even a speck of dry land to be seen in any direction from my sea-level viewpoint. So much for rescue.

Then, I heard an antigrav in the distance. Carefully saving my video-game, I had an all-time record score going when interrupted. I turned my attention to the real world around me.

My survival-pod ears were every bit as good as those of my mannequin-body. Ears were cheap and easy to make. It was superhuman eyes that broke the bank.

At first the 'hopper was a long way off, so far that sometimes it seemed to fade away. Then, it grew louder on a dead-intercept course. Surely, the pilot had picked up my automated distress signal. My tripod-feet were designed for compactness and light weight, not for swimming. Still, I managed to kick myself upright for an instant and fire my one and only flare.

POW!

The recoil drove me all the way under for a moment before I bobbed back up the surface, and, by the time I'd gotten face-upright again, the firework had exploded far up in the sky, leaving a huge cloud of colored smoke hovering above my location.

The engine grew louder more quickly after that. For a moment or two I kicked and cavorted in glee. I didn't inhabit a survival pod often, but being only about three feet tall—not to mention having three spindly legs and no arms—was different enough from human-normal that it offered fun. Paddling like a machine, I lifted myself as far out of the water as I could only to realize too late that the motor I was listening to was *not* that of a Polecat.

Blam. Blam. Blam. Blam.

The enemy fighter flashed overhead well in excess of Mach one. The shots went wide, but the sonic boom seemed to rip the heavens apart. I'd never been shot at before, except when I'd been a fighter-plane myself. This was scary.

The Dracan rolled hard left, performed a show-off Immelman, and then came back for another pass. I hit the off switch on my locator beacon, even though it was too late. Then, instead of trying to rise out of the water to wave, I surface-dived as he came past.

Blam. Blam. Blam. Blam.

His cannon fired again. My aural sensors under the water muted the sound this time. His laser-bolts didn't like water much. In only a few inches of water they transformed themselves into puffs of steam. The sonic boom, however, was another story with the improved sound-transmission capabilities of water. It kicked me like a mule in the gut I no longer had.

"Ooof," I gasped through my speaker grille.

Then I bobbed about on the surface again, and the Dracan did a second Immelman. I didn't like that. Because he was taking the time for showy maneuvers meant he wasn't worried about the Top Bananas. He lined up for his third pass, I prepared to duck underwater again.

Suddenly a Polecat emerged from the low-hanging clouds behind the Dracan.

"Yes, "I screamed aloud, waving a tripod-leg awkwardly in delight. "Yes. Yes. YES."

Even as I watched the Navy fighter's guns flamed, and suddenly the Dracan was a ball of greasy smoke. It was just that quick.

The Dracan hadn't been working alone. Three more enemy fighters emerged from the same cloudbank that the Polecat had come from, accelerating hard. My savior in the Polecat was doomed. They had him boxed. Whichever way he turned, a cannon waited for him. Laser-bolts ripped into the 'cat's fat, rugged-looking fuselage. An explosion followed and a second greasy-looking cloud of smoke spread itself across the gray, soggy sky. The Dracans didn't hang around to sightsee. As one, they turned and flew off towards what my internal compass identified as north.

If they'd loitered even ten more seconds, they'd have seen the big orange Navy parachute pop open five hundred feet over my head.

Chapter Twenty

It was a pure stroke of luck for a pilot to come down so close to me. My squadron mate landed less than a quarter-mile away. I watched his life-raft inflate. The images came as a series of still-shots each time I crested a wave. He appeared to have a lot of trouble climbing into it. It must have taken him twenty or thirty waves. Once he got there, he didn't paddle. That worried me.

It hadn't made any sense for me to try and swim while I was so far from shore I couldn't see it, but crossing a measly quarter-mile was a different story. My legs weren't designed for the task. However, they never grew tired. It took me several hours of three-legged kicking, but at last I made my way alongside.

"Hey," I cried out. "Ahoy the raft."

The pilot looked up, startled. His head turned this way and that, searching the horizon far beyond me.

"No," I exclaimed. "Down here. Thomas, the Skybolt pilot. I'm a brain box now, because I bailed out."

This time the pilot followed my voice. "Jesus," he muttered, looking down at me. Then, moving very stiffly, he extended a paddle. "I can't stretch much further, kid. Can you latch on somehow?"

I tried to gulp, but didn't have the muscles. I could now tell he was hurt. What I'd thought were scorch-marks on his g-suit from a distance were bloodstains.

"I think I can." I extended a tripod leg and tried to hook the paddle in the crook of a "knee." It took me several tries before I managed it.

"Good enough," the pilot said, pulling me in. I only weighed a few pounds as a survival spider.

It should've been easy for him to haul me aboard. Instead, we had to work together, coordinating his feeble efforts with my clumsy ones for many long minutes. By the time we finished, the pilot was exhausted.

"There ya go," he said as my braincase finally teetered inboard. "Jesus, but that was hard work. "His eyes closed, and in a moment he passed out.

I nodded, examining him carefully. *Lieutenant Eaglish*, his name badge read, though the Top Banana emblem just above it was smeared with crimson. Eaglish's whole right side was puffed up and subtly misshapen. His right lower-leg ballooned out over the top of his boot. Even the side of his face looked as if had been punched repeatedly. The right eye was swollen closed.

Flesh and blood did not respond well to hypersonic bailouts. This was one of the major selling points for the Skybolt. My survival spider was safer and more effective than the Polecat's ejection seat. Lieutenant Eaglish hadn't enjoyed the best of luck when he'd hit the silk.

I didn't know what to do for him. None of my airmanship classes had covered anything like first-aid. I was supposed to be flying simulated combat, not the real thing. Even worse, my spider didn't have manipulator arms. All I could think of was to use one of my foot-discs as a fan. So, I lay back on the raft's soft rubber floor and waved a foot back and forth in front of Eaglish's face.

I fanned for many hours, almost until dark. All that time Eaglish lay full in the sun, and I couldn't figure out a thing to do to shade him. The raft had a survival kit aboard, but I didn't have the fingers necessary to open it. At times I grew so bored I fired up my video game, but then I'd feel guilty I wasn't doing everything I could to help my fellow pilot. His skin turned an angry red where it was exposed, but somehow seemed paler than ever.

Near sunset Eaglish half-smiled, then moaned a little. "Shit." He tried to sit up. "Honey, I just dreamed—"

"It's not a dream," I said, half-folding my legs into my 'sitting' position. "We're really at war. You just shot down a Dracan, then got flamed yourself. You bailed out. Along the way you saved my life. Thanks, by the way. "

Eaglish looked at me for a moment and then flinched away. "I...Who are you?"

He tried to stand, but made the raft dance. "Mary? Where's Mary? Ow! Shit, that hurts."

Having no arms, I couldn't touch Eaglish to reassure him. "Mary's not here," I said, "though I'm sure she's worried about you. "

"Who are you?" the lieutenant snarled, drawing his survival knife with his left hand. The sheath was on that side so Eaglish was a leftie. "What're you doing here? Where the fuck are my children?"

"Easy, now," I said, growing frightened. Eaglish's knife most likely couldn't kill me outright, but it might cripple me so badly death would be just a matter of time. "Easy, Eaglish, everything's all right. No one wants to hurt you."

"You fucking Dracan bastard," Eaglish screamed, lunging forward on his good left leg. His blade sizzled through the air less than an inch from my rubber nose. "You fuckin' Dracan monster, where's my wife?"

I backed up until I was at the extreme end of the life raft. "Eaglish," I wailed. "It's all right. I'm not a Dracan. I'm with the Navy. You're hurt. Out of your head. Please, let me help you."

It was no use. Eaglish lunged forward again. I ducked and Eaglish's right leg collapsed under him and tossed him overboard.

"Fuck," he screamed out, splashing. "What's going on? What the fuck am I doing?

Maybe the cool water had revived him? I hoped so. "Lieutenant Eaglish?"

"Yeah, kid," he responded. "Jesus. I mean, god, but I'm sorry. My head…it hurts something awful."

"It's all right," I answered, smiling as best I could with my disembodied face. I extended a tripod-leg. "Grab this."

Eaglish reached out with his good arm. He had dropped the knife. Try as he might, he couldn't quite reach my leg. Even worse, the stiff wind pushed the raft downwind faster than it pushed Eaglish with his lesser sail area and greater drag. He tried to swim, but didn't manage well.

"Try the paddle," he urged.

I nodded and reached over to the other side of the raft. The five feet long paddle still lay there. Exactly what I needed, but, how was I to pick it up?

I tried and tried to grasp the thing, but couldn't. Even my mouth wasn't fully functional. My jaw moved a little when I talked, but, the speech-servo wasn't powerful enough to support the paddle against gravity, much less the paddle with Eaglish attached to it.

"Hurry, kid," Eaglish's voice urged me.

"I can't pick it up," I cried, frustrated. he was already too far away for me to use it.

"Jesus," Eaglish said. "Try tossing me the rope. "

It was the same story all over again. My feet ended in three circular rubber-tipped pads and weren't good for much of anything besides being walking. I lay down on my back and tried to grasp the rope's end. The result was the blackest of black comedy. I was helpless.

"Jesus," Eaglish repeated. "You're drifting away. Help!"

"I can't do it," I wailed, wanting to cry. "I can't."

"God help me, PLEASE," my fellow pilot yelled out, his voice hysterical. "Mary, where are you? I don't want to die here alone."

Frantic, I worked a spider-leg under the grab-rope that ran around the perimeter of the life raft, then bent both knees until I was doing the nearest imitation possible of grasping the thing. I flipped the rest of my body over the side of the raft, and grimly began kicking towards the sound of Eaglish's voice with my remaining legs.

"I'm coming," I cried out as loud as I could. "I'm coming, Lieutenant. Just as fast as I can."

"Mary?" he demanded. "Where are the kids?"

It grew dark soon after, but Eaglish remained at a constant bearing. It would have been a harder swim without the compass in my head and impossible with legs that grew tired. Then, not long before dawn I felt the raft nudge into something solid. It had to be Eaglish.

"I'm here," I cried in triumph. "I'm here. Climb on in. I'll keep pushing to give you something to work against."

Eaglish didn't answer. He hadn't spoken in a long time now.

"Come on. You're a Top Banana, the best there's ever been. You can climb back up into the raft."

Again only silence.

Part of me already knew. It couldn't have been any other way. Just to make certain I changed my kicking-angle and spun the raft around so that I ended up next to where Eaglish floated limp in his lifejacket. I reached out with a tripod-leg and wrapped it around the flier's waist. His flesh was cold and lifeless.

"I'm sorry, so very sorry, especially after you saved my life. I tried and tried and tried..."

Tears I couldn't shed hung in memory. I unwrapped my leg and let Eaglish's remains float free. Soon even his little flashing light would be out of sight forever.

"I tried, really, I did."

I rolled into a ball and mourned for hours. Dawn came before I wrenched myself back into the raft proper, using my grip on the line as leverage. There was no end to my grief. Eaglish would be with me for the rest of my life, no matter what. I'd tried, yes. I'd done my best. In war, trying wasn't close to good enough.

Chapter Twenty-One

I floated for three more days after the lieutenant passed away. The second day it rained and misted all day. Tiny droplets kept landing on my camera-lenses, and I didn't have anything to wipe them off. Often, I couldn't see at all. I had nothing to do except curl up into a ball and think about things I'd rather forget like how many kids Lieutenant Eaglish might have had, what had happened to the rest of the Top Bananas, and what my chances for survival were.

Father had done a good job on building my container. I wasn't sunburned, dehydrated, cramped—not any of the things that usually went with spending days in a drifting raft. Yet what were the odds of anyone finding me when I couldn't even turn on my beacon without being strafed? Dying in comfort was better than dying in abject misery. If I could, I would have shuddered thinking of Lieutenant Eaglish's death. I didn't want to die at all.

By dawn of the fourth day, I'd set eleven new records on my silly internal videogame. I'd also decided that if by some miracle I survived my rafting adventure, I'd advise Father to put video games into the skulls of all his brain-cored pilots. The game was all that kept me sane.

I was just getting to work on trying to set record number twelve when I noticed something odd. The horizon, which had been uniform all around me for days, was a little off-color, dead downwind. It was brownish, the same color I saw in all directions from the center of Lake Pontchartrain back home.

The color of land.

After so much sensory deprivation for so long, even a slight color change on the horizon created a tremendous sense of excitement. I stood as high as I could in the raft, adding maybe three feet to my height above sea level. Nothing new revealed itself. For hours I stood bolt-upright staring at the brown sky-stain and trembling at the wonder of it all. With agonizing slowness the discoloration resolved itself into a jagged line of broken hills—typical archipelago terrain.

By sunset I saw bright green hills with pioneer algae busily breaking down the naked rock into useful soil. When night fell, I could see a single steady artificial light coming from somewhere about halfway up the hill, the first artificial light I'd experienced since ejecting. Wonder of wonders, around midnight a train wended its way through the hills as its wheels kicked up little blue sparks. A train? Wonderful!

It wasn't full light when my raft piled onto a wide, sandy beach. I weighed so little the raft had hardly been drawing any water. My feet barely got wet as I stepped out in the darkness. Almost at once I tripped over a long, cylinder-shaped object.

A tree trunk? Here? That made no sense. There wasn't enough soil yet on Churilla to support a wild-growing forest. Food-crops were still grown in hyper-efficient greenhouses. Yet there it was, a palm-tree trunk as bold as life and twice as big. I shook my head, shrugged, and moved inland.

The palm tree, it turned out, was no freak. Before I traveled fifty yards the rising sun revealed I was hiking through a virtual forest of the things in a forest of the sort one found only on worlds like Earth. Churilla's tiny land areas had been nearly barren until humans arrived on the scene. Only a few pioneering breeds of native dry-land algae existed. These few had preferred wet areas like bogs.

I looked down at where my three disc-feet were squishing along. This was a bog all right. Perhaps someone had been trying to establish a 'wild' ecosystem in native soil? It made as much sense as anything. Still, I was relieved to see when the tree-canopy broke the uplands were indeed all planted in a uniform covering of soil-making lichen. If there'd been trees in the hills, I'd have counted myself insane.

It was a pleasant walk through the unexpected forest after so many barren days at sea. I electronically whistled a happy little Esteppen folk tune as I tramped along. In a human body I'd be sweating like a pig and attracting clouds of biting bugs. Instead, I was cool, confident, and for the first time in days happy. When I finally came to a path I began to accompany myself with a song.

"Duty is the point of life
and honor is its goal;
Love between a man and wife
and unity of soul."

"Halt," a voice rang out of nowhere, "or I'll shoot."

A single laser-bolt sizzled by not missing me by much. Whoever was yelling at me meant what he said.

I obeyed at once, frozen in midstep. "Don't shoot." My heart would have been pounding at a mile a second, if I still had one. "Please, I mean no harm. "

"What the fuck?" a second voice demanded.

"Jesus," a third agreed.

Suddenly a brush pile shifted, and, for the first time in days, I saw a dark human face. Thankfully, it wore a green combat coverall and helmet. The Dracans wore khaki.

"What the fuck are you?" it demanded, heavy blast rifle at the ready.

"I'm a United Systems citizen," I answered, remaining as immobile as a statue. "A real, honest-to-goodness human being. May I move a little?"

The dark face nodded. "Slow and easy."

I nodded my head and pointed with a tripod-foot at the Top Banana insignias my ground-crew had affixed to each side of my braincase. "I'm a fighter pilot. "I was here to demonstrate a Skybolt. Then the war came, and I had to fight against the Dracans."

I lowered my foot and straightened as tall and straight as I could. "I flew with the Bananas, at the end. The Dracans shot me down. I just floated ashore today."

"Shit," the first voice muttered. I hadn't a clue where it might have come from. "That makes sense, Otis. Remember when that experimental flyboy nuked the missile base, right before game-night?"

"Right," a black man agreed, in a non-committal voice. "Just the day before the Dracans nuked it for real." He leveled his rifle at me. "Hell of a coincidence, that."

"It *was* a coincidence," I assured him. "Honest."

"Those are genuine Top Banana insignias," a new voice offered from somewhere behind me. "Or else damn good fakes. God knows I've had to throw enough money in the kitty to buy the arrogant bastards their drinks. I ought to know them well enough."

"They're real," I assured the mostly-invisible men. "Come and look closer, if you want."

There was a long silence. "It's a trick," the black man insisted, not wavering his gun barrel an inch. "The thing wants us to get close so it can kill us."

"No," I repeated, shifting subtly on my tripod and getting ready to run. "I don't want to kill anyone. I just want to go home."

"Like everyone else," the black man agreed, finally lowering his muzzle a little. "What's your name?"

"Thomas Longo," I said. "My father is Willy Longo, of Longo Gravitonics. "

Suddenly the black soldier's mouth fell open. His gun's muzzle swung decisively away. “Him I’ve heard of,” he said at last. “All right then, Thomas. Welcome to the Third Squad, Second Platoon, Easy Company, Fourth Light Infantry Division.” He stood and extended his hand. “I’m Sergeant N’Dukwe.” I walked over and clumsily met it with a disk-foot. “We’re lost as hell, out of touch with anyone, and haven’t eaten in two days.”

“You say you’ve been flying with the Bananas,” a younger man said, emerging from behind a shimmer-shield. No wonder I hadn’t seen him. “Well, we’re quite a few rungs down from them, I’m afraid. Us grunts are fighting a much lower-rent sort of war. I’m Private Mendes, from Pampas.”

“Thomas,” I said, reaching out and shaking Mendes’s hand as well.

I’d demonstrated the Skybolt on Pampas. It was a beautiful planet, and I’d liked the people I’d met there very much indeed. “I’m starting to get the idea there’s enough war going around for everyone.”

Chapter Twenty-Two

The Third Squad, Second Platoon, Easy Company, Fourth Light Infantry Division had been ordered to keep a lookout on the coastal road. It was still obeying those orders four days after they'd been issued, even though nobody had seen an officer since.

"This wasn't where our division was supposed be," Sergeant N'Dukwe explained as we sat around the lunchtime fire. There wasn't any food to cook, but a fire seemed to be mandatory nonetheless. "Out here in the ass end of nowhere like this."

"We trained for the mountains," Private Ahkmed agreed. "Me, I don't miss them. Up and down and up and down and up…"

"Our supplies were pre-located there," N'Dukwe explained. "All our food and shit. Transport's been a real bitch from day one. The Dracans shoot up anything that moves, except the trains. We think they're saving those to use. Everything's fubared all to hell. I mean, look at us," he said, waving his hand to include the rest of the group. "Hungry as shit, and nothing worthwhile to do."

"Where were you supposed to be stationed?" I asked, feeling vaguely guilty that I wasn't hungry, and wouldn't be right up until the very moment I dropped dead for lack of nourishment.

"Up in the Kammhuber Pass," Mendes answered. "Where the big fight's just *got* to happen. Everything on the main island goes through the Kammhuber—rail lines, pipelines, the highways. It's the economic chokepoint for the entire Archipelago."

He sighed. "The Fourth Light Division always covered the southern approaches during drills, while the Churilla Brigadiers covered the north. It was hillier up their way, see? More difficult terrain."

As it happened, I didn't see. In fact, I knew nothing about strategy at all except for aerospace stuff. I nodded anyway though, to be polite.

"Who changed the plan?"

"Some bugfuck admiral," N'Dukwe answered, his lips curled in disgust. "He's sending little bits and pieces of units here, there, everywhere. What a moron. Why can't he stick to playing with starships?"

I gulped. "The admiral... Is his name Lutjens?"

"Yeah," Mendes answered, smiling. "That's the bastard. Rumor is he's a political type, totally without a clue."

"Usually the army and Navy have enough sense to each mind their own knitting," N'Dukwe added, his frown intensifying. "But this clown thinks he's god's gift to the strategic sciences."

The sergeant shrugged. "Now he's the senior officer on the planet. So what can you do? There's no place for appeal. If he's stupid enough to throw his weight around, he's stupid enough to throw his weight around. No one's gonna stop him."

Something tasted very bad in the mouth I didn't have. "The Navy," I said, "seemed to be doing its best to ignore him or it was the last I heard."

"Smart Navy," Mendes answered, raising his battered coffee mug in salute. At least the coffee hadn't run out yet. "I wish our officers were that bright."

I shook my head and turned away. I might only be a kid, but even I knew that men like Captain Wan didn't grow on trees. Then again, Wan was the ex-CO of the Top Bananas. That probably helped, too.

"Anyway," I said after a long, long silence. "What's the plan?"

Mendes lowered his mug and shrugged to N'Dukwe, who suddenly looked as if his stomach pained him. "We've been ordered to guard this coast road…" he said.

"We're starving, Sarge," the private countered. "We've been out of touch for days." He pointed at me. "We ain't seen a fucking thing, but the fighter-jock, here."

"You want us to have to eat our boots, Sarge?" Ahkmed asked. He didn't look very happy. "How many more days can we go?"

N'Dukwe shook his head again, looking confused. Then he turned to me. "What do you think, sir?"

I blinked. "Excuse me?"

"You're in charge here," N'Dukwe explained, smiling for the first time since I'd met him. "You may be a flyboy, but you had to go through officer-school, right?" He leaned back. "What are your orders, sir? By rights it's your call."

"I…Uh…I mean…" My head spun.

"Yeah," Ahkmed agreed, slapping his blast-rifle's stock in triumph. "He must be an officer. Even though he doesn't have any insignia." He cocked his head to the left. "Are you a lieutenant, sir? Or still just an ensign? Either way, you're in charge." He pointed his thumb at N'Dukwe in obvious relief. "Not him, anymore."

I looked over at Mendes. He was the brightest of the bunch and the one most likely to understand. “I'm a c-c-c-civilian.” I spluttered.

“You can't be a civilian,” the young man from Pampas explained with exaggerated patience, “not if you were flying combat. Only serving officers can be pilots in the Navy.”

My head spun again. “Well, no. Yes, I mean. But...”

“In wartime there can't be any buts,” Mendes continued, his eyes boring hard into my own. *Please*, his lips added silently.

I closed my eyes and thought just as hard and fast as I could. N'Dukwe wouldn't take responsibility for anything. He seemed to recognize he was out of his depth, though he couldn't quite admit it. Mendes seemed capable, but what could a mere private do?

I tried to take a deep breath, forgetting I had no body, and then worked my jaw nervously instead. “You've been here how long?” I wanted to make sure.

“Five days,” Mendes replied, his eyes still locked with mine. “Five hungry, useless days.”

I nodded. “How long has it been since you heard from your own officer?”

“Four days,” N'Dukwe replied. His eyes appeared eager too, I decided. Beseeching, even.

I shook my head and sighed. “All right, then.” I said, thinking of Captain Wan. “I'm an officer, all right.” I looked at Mendes. “What do you think we ought to do?”

“Move out,” he answered without hesitation. “Towards the Kammhuber. It's only about twenty miles from here. Try and make contact with the division.”

I nodded. It sounded sensible enough to me. “Then that's what we'll do.” I lowered the frequency on my external speaker a bit and chose my words to sound as mature as I could manage. “We'll leave in twenty minutes. I see no reason to waste good coffee, and there's plenty of daylight left.”

“Sir, yes, *sir*,” Sergeant N'Dukwe said, and this time his coffee mug rose in salute.

“Twenty minutes,” Ahkmed confirmed. “I'll be right back. I need to pick up some gear.” He closed his eyes for a moment as if to pray before getting up and leaving.

Then Mendes smiled and clapped me on the shoulder. “It'll all be fine,” he assured me. He left to follow his fellow private.

“Right,” I agreed, sounding more cheerful than I felt.

Maybe it would all be fine in the end, I decided as the Pampan strode away, whistling. Sure, they'd eventually prosecute me for impersonating an officer. That was the bad news. There was good news too. I was still just sixteen. So they'd have to try me as a juvenile.

Chapter Twenty-Three

"So all the supplies have to move through the Kammhuber," Mendes explained as we strode up the steep, naked ridge. His power-frame and my servo-motors created an interesting tempo with him having two legs and me three. "We knew before the war ever started that nothing was going to move by sea. It's too easy for a 'hopper to blow a ship out of the water. Nothing's moving by air anymore either. Not on our side at least. So, that leaves the roads and rails."

I nodded. "You guys have to eat."

"Eat, drink, repair, and recharge our equipment. An army needs a million things." Mendes smiled.

He'd been accepted for officer training though the Dracans had arrived before the final paperwork went through. "We can't exist without the Kammhuber. The old German General Staff used to have a saying. They were the first purpose-educated General Staff, and still maybe the best ever assembled. 'Amateurs,' they used to say, 'talk about weaponry. Professionals speak of logistics.' That means the study of supply-flow is the root of all military strategy."

His smile widened. "Take Manstein's 'sickelschnitt', the 1940 German attack on France. If you look at the French logistical base—"

"Can it, will ya, Mendes?" Sergeant N'Dukwe interrupted. He'd probably never even considered bucking for officer. "I'm getting a headache, listening to all this strategy shit. How about you maybe use that oversized brain of yours to figure out how to score us some chow instead?"

Mendes sighed and looked at me. I shook my head and turned away. Sure, I was pretending to be an officer, but only when N'Dukwe needed me to be one it seemed. The rest of the time, he still wanted to be in charge. I'd already decided that I didn't like him much.

For a long time the four of us marched. The ridge we climbed seemed to go on forever, and not a plant in sight to break the monotony.

"So," I said, "explain to me again how the soil farming works. I'm from Earth and Esteppe, and we didn't have anything like it in either place."

"You were lucky, then," Mendes replied, looking glum. "Even this planet is lucky relatively speaking. My home world had no soil at all when the First Colonists landed. It takes fairly advanced forms of life to create usable soil, and we didn't have any. Just algae. Even the atmosphere was primitive back then. You could barely breathe it—not enough oxygen. It's better now."

I looked up at my new friend. "But...I saw green everywhere when I flew over it."

"Only in the long-colonized areas," the private explained. "Then, only on the Great Plain at that. We didn't have soil, no. At least, we had a great sea of dust to work with. Some Earth plants grew in that right away."

He waved his arms around, indicating the steep, rocky slopes. "Here, they had no dust seas to work with. Most of the terrain is too steep. They did have a good variety of sea-life established, some of it even able to survive a little ways inland. That's where the coastal forests come from. The colony's early ecologists established an earth-swamp biome there. I imagine the earth life drove everything else out without even breaking a sweat."

Mendes kicked at one of the endless sea of half-rotten stones at his feet. It, like all the rest, was covered in green fuzz. "This is tailored lichen, see? Just like ours back home. It breaks the rock down, and then what's left runs down the mountains and into the creeks, ending up in the coastal swamps. They're probably growing measurably every year."

"Except that the locals mine trainloads of mucky shit out of them," Private Ahkmed added. He didn't talk much, I'd noticed. "That's what goes in the greenhouses to feed everyone. Someday, when there's enough, they'll make actual farms."

"Right," Mendes agreed, smiling again. "That's how it works. Soil is an easy thing to take for granted, but on most colony worlds, you have to fight for it."

I nodded again and then looked at my feet so I could place them with the greatest precision possible. The rocks were growing bigger again, and, while it was unlikely, I would or perhaps even could trip and fall in such a way damage myself. It was a long way back to the repair shop in New Orleans. Besides, Sergeant N'Dukwe was scowling again, and I didn't want to provoke yet another of his bad-tempered outbursts.

We'd been walking for two days, steadily climbing then descending most of the way. The others hadn't had a single bite to eat. The miserable heat must sap their strength. I suspected if not for their power-frames, my comrades would have long since collapsed. After leaving the coastal swamp, I saw nothing to look at but an endless assortment of greater and lesser lichen-coated rocks and ledges. Unless you counted the numerous Dracan contrails filling the sky above us.

They had to be Dracan because at times I saw more contrails than Churilla had total aircraft before the invasion. I'd felt a little ill the first time I'd seen so many enemy craft with not a single Polecat in the sky to oppose them. That was the state of affairs now. Defending the fleet's escape had become the Banana's swansong.

"Custard pie," N'Dukwe muttered to himself after a long time. "Hush puppies. Okra. French bread."

"Hot fudge sundae," Mendes answered back, sounding a little miffed.

He didn't like this game, I'd come to realize. Sadly, N'Dukwe hadn't achieved no such insight. If he had, he'd chosen to ignore it.

"Spaghetti and meatballs. Enchiladas. Garbanzo beans," Mendes continued.

"Shit," Ahkmed said. "Shit, shit, shit."

The climbing lasted for hours. Mendes found a little cave while on point around noon, and we all huddled together in it for a while. There was nothing left to consume, not even coffee. N'Dukwe lit a little fire anyway. For the first time ever at one of our rest stops, no one spoke at all, not a single word. Then we set off and climbed again.

"I suggest, sir, " N'Dukwe said after we'd been on our way again for perhaps an hour, "that we make camp on the far side of the crest line. When it's light in the morning, we can reconnoiter the valley."

I nodded. I was an officer again which meant N'Dukwe was having a hard time deciding. "Excellent," I agreed, even though I had my doubts about our making the ridge crest before dark. This was by far the highest we'd ever been forced to climb, and our pace was slowing with every mile.

"Are you sure this is Kelly's Ridge? "

He shook his head, which was understandable enough. When the division had been redeployed at the last moment, everyone had been required to exchange their old map data for new. The new, however, had not managed to arrive in time to be doled out. Another fubar.

"I think the Kammhuber is four ridges in," he replied in a tentative voice. "When we get to the top of this one, we'll have crossed three. After dawn tomorrow, with any luck—"

"Halt," a voice suddenly called out from nowhere. We complied, but I half-tipped over. "Freeze, motherfuckers."

"Sergeant N'Dukwe," our squad's leader cried out. "Sergeant N'Dukwe, Third Squad, Second Platoon, Easy Company, Fourth Light

Infantry Division. If you guys have a password, we sure as shit don't know it. We've been out of contact for almost a week."

There was a long silence. "You," the voice barked. "The head on stilts. What the fuck are you?"

"N-N-Navy pilot," I stuttered back. Not the proper time for complicated explanations. "Ph-ph-physically modified for flying."

"We haven't eaten since I don't know when," Mendes added. "Christ, look at us. We haven't seen any Dracans, but do they look half as sorry as our asses? Somehow I doubt it."

"Humph," the voice snorted. "You're raggedy-ass soldier-boys, all right, though not quite the sorriest I've seen here of late. You're right. The Dracans are prettier, at least until they've been in combat for a few hours. After that they get all bloody and shit, just like everyone else."

A shimmer-shield faded, revealing a soldier behind some sort of heavy tripod-mounted blaster. He wore a heavily-singed dust-covered dark-green uniform of a marine.

Then a second shield faded a few yards away. "Navy pilot, eh?" a new voice asked.

This man was a marine as well, though far neater in his appearance. An officer I saw once he stood up and walked forward to meet us.

"We mere earthlings have been told to keep a special eye out for you swabbies, even though the word is that there's nothing left on-planet for you to fly." He eyed my odd body up and down for some sign of rank, then clearly gave up. "Well," he said, extending his hand in a noncommittal gesture for me to shake. "Welcome to Outpost Olympic, sir. We're as far forward as it's possible to get these days. I'm Lieutenant Hickam."

I reached out with a foot-disc and awkwardly completed the greeting. "Thomas Longo." I artificially lowered my voice a bit.

I had one last thing to do while I was an officer instead of just a teenager. "These men saved my life, Lieutenant. Like they said, they haven't eaten in days."

Hickam blinked. He'd recognized my slightly-scorched Top Banana insignia. They had what I was beginning to understand was their usual effect.

"Sir, yes, sir," he snapped. Then he turned around towards the top of the ridge. "Baker," he shouted. "Go get Jonesy and have him fire up three ration-packs for these army types. You hear me?"

The wind blew uphill. Rather than try and shout against it, Baker merely waved his acknowledgement. Then the lieutenant turned back to me.

"We're not exactly rolling in grub ourselves, sir. Supply is totally fubared. There's practically no ammo, either."

"The army too," N'Dukwe offered. "Everything's fubared everywhere. Christ, the Dracans must own us by now, we're so fubared."

Hickam's eyes narrowed, but after the slightest hesitation he allowed the defeatist remark to pass. Probably, I reckoned, he was considering the source.

"We're holding firm here at the Pass," he countered. "The Dracans have tried to land behind us twice, and both times we've wiped out their footholds. They're running wild on the other islands, sure enough. The base facilities they need most are here, and we still hold them." His smile was icy.

"They control the sky now, but our air defenses are working better than anyone ever expected, so they have to stay high. Even better, the Dracans can't seem to muster the kind of overwhelming ground strength they need to force the Pass. At least they haven't so far."

Hickam looked at me. "We hear rumors that one of you Banana-boys pasted a couple of their troopships." He raised his hand to his helmet in a sort of mock-salute. "If so, then by god you swabbie bastards have earned all those free drinks.

"Nothing's really happened on this flank yet, but over on the right where the army boys are stationed, the Dracans keep attacking over and over again in the same places, even though they're too weak to break through. This is a guess, but so far as I can see their long-term plans are fucked."

His smile widened. "The bastards are thrashing about without a clue as to what to do next." He turned to N'Dukwe. "Don't forget, fubarring goes both ways in wartime. In fact, fubarring is the one factor that no military force in history has ever been able to overcome." I smiled a little, then looked down at the rocks nearest my feet.

"Well," Hickam said at last. "Your rations are heating." He pointed up the hill. "There's no mines between the big rock, there, and the little one about halfway up the slope. Don't stray." Then he turned back towards his battlefront and scowled. "Captain Marseille is at battalion HQ for a briefing. He's due back any moment. I'll leave a message about you for him at his tent."

He turned back towards me. "With any luck, Captain Marseille will send you on your way back to an airfield in two hours or less."

Chapter Twenty-Four

Wherever Captain Marseille was, he had to be busy. We never got to see him at all. Instead everyone except me ate a ration pack apiece and then we were sent back to the local field hospital. The docs took one look at my three companions and gave them each a special pass for a second ration pack to be eaten over at the mess tent, shortages be damned.

No one seemed to know what to do with me. At last a colonel wearing medical insignia emerged from the depths of the big tent and thumbed me into what passed for his office, a sort of draped-off enclosure with a pile of empty boxes in the center that served as a desk.

"Name?" he demanded.

I tried to gulp, but couldn't. Would I *ever* get over that sort of thing? "Thomas Longo," I replied.

"Rank?" he continued.

"None," I replied. "I'm a civilian."

The colonel's eyes narrowed. He was a very large man in late middle-age, with a deeply weathered face and a hard, calloused manner. He looked far more like a soldier than any other officer I'd met on Churilla so far.

"What do you mean, none?" he demanded. "You're a pilot or so you say."

"A civilian pilot," I countered.

"Wearing Top Banana insignia?" The colonel shook his head, then his face softened. "I've met very few modified people like yourself," he said, "even as a doctor. Were you totally paralyzed before they did this to you? I imagine it's quite hard, even though there probably wasn't much choice. "

I closed my eyes and then re-opened them. "I'm not suffering from combat fatigue," I answered, trying to sound calm and reasonable. "I'm a civilian. The Bananas made me a sort of honorary member before I flew a mission with them."

Then I had an idea and pointed a disc-foot at my head, "I'd be very grateful if you'd pull those badges off for me. I don't deserve them anyway, not really. I can't do it myself. They're causing all kinds of misunderstandings."

This time it was the colonel's turn to slowly blink. "I... don't know, son. I'll have to do some checking up on all of this." He frowned. "No one here can even do a physical on you. We're not equipped for it. Are you feeling all right?"

I nodded. "All my life-support systems are still green. I've got another twenty days or so before I'll need feeding and a recharge. I'll be glad to have my mannequin-body back. I miss having hands something awful."

The colonel blinked again. "Mannequin-body, eh?" Then he shook his head and stood up. "Wait outside, Longo. I'm not at all sure what we're going to do with you, but whatever it is, it'll have to come from someone higher up the food chain than me."

The colonel's office was right next to the hospital-tent's main entrance. I was bored, so I decided to interpret his instruction to "wait outside" literally. After all, my wait was liable to be a long one. Outside, at least, I could sit and watch the others work.

The field hospital was much larger than I'd have imagined. It consisted of long rows of large tents erected along either side of a paved, two-lane road. Trucks with red crosses came and went in a continual stream, filled with supplies and, sometimes, badly wounded men. Some of them screamed, and I had to look away. I thought about Lieutenant Eaglish, and how much I wished I could have brought him here. That started making me feel sad and guilty, so I decided to look up at the Dracan contrails for a while and see if I could figure out what they were doing.

Strange. For the first time since I didn't know when, I couldn't see any. Perhaps this was because it was almost dark? Somehow, I doubted it. Darkness had never affected me.

A little later, Private Mendes and Sergeant N'Dukwe emerged from the mess tent, half-finished ration packs in hand. They were smiling and laughing.

"I got okra," N'Dukwe explained, "and Mendes got a hot-fudge sundae, just like we were imagining."

"Ahkmed got shit, shit, shit, too," Mendes crowed, his eyes sparking. "Rhubarb pie, macaroni and cheese, hominy. Worst ration-pack I've ever seen."

"Hey," I replied, bouncing up and down on my tripod legs. "I'm really glad you guys got something to eat. Even if it was rhubarb pie."

I looked down at the ground. "I really felt bad that you were hungry when I wasn't."

N'Dukwe reached out and patted my head. He'd never, ever done that before.

"Don't worry, kid. It wasn't your fault." His smile widened. "We heard inside how much damage you Bananas did to the invasion fleet. Holy shit."

"Fucked 'em right up," Mendes agreed. "The jarheads claim they can hold the Pass forever, if they have to. They say they're digging in deeper every day. Plus, tons of reinforcements are flowing in. We're going back to our unit over on the other ridge. They finally moved us back where we were supposed to be to begin with after they finished scattering our equipment and shit all over the fucking planet."

I looked up again. Still no contrails. Odd.

"So," I said, "the marines are getting stronger every day. The Dracans can't establish a base on this planet unless they hold the Kammhuber. Besides, they've lost a lot of troops."

"Shit loads," Mendes confirmed. "Almost half their total ground force got scragged in orbit. Plus a fucking dreadnought, I hear." He shook his head. "A fucking dreadnought. Can you believe it? Here I thought we were losing."

I false-gulped and looked up at the sky again. Still no contrails. I turned to Mendes.

"Practically everything the United Systems has is deployed right here, at an obvious strategic bottleneck. One the Dracans have been halfheartedly attacking for days, Lieutenant Hickam told us. Encouraging us to reinforce, reinforce, reinforce."

I looked my friend directly in the eye. "I'm a pilot, Carlos. What kind of bomb do you think I'd be planning to drop right now, if I were a Dracan?"

Mendes frowned. "We're as concentrated as shit," he said. His eyes widened in sudden understanding. "Biggest fucking target possible. That stupid motherfucking admiral—"

It was already too late. Even as Mendes leaped to his feet in anger, the air-raid siren sounded.

"Duck and cover," a heavily-amplified voice screamed over the ululating wail. "Duck and cover. This is no drill."

Chapter Twenty-Five

Time seemed both to rush past and then slow to a crawl. It was an odd sensation. Not at all what I experienced when I dropped a simulated nuke from a 'bolt. Things felt different when *you* were the one on the ground.

"Come on," Mendes urged, leaping to his feet and running hard towards a nearby slit-trench.

Everyone else in the world seemed to be heading for it as well, some of them trying to put on their anti-radiation suits along the way. It didn't look to me like the hole would be even close to big enough for everyone.

I was perhaps ten feet away when something boomed by overhead, high and fast and Dracan judging by the sound of its antigravs. By then Mendes was well ahead of me. My electrical legs might be tireless, but they weren't fast.

"Christ." Sergeant N'Dukwe screamed as he pounded up behind me. "Christ. Christ. Christ." His eyes were big and round, and his lips were peeled back from his teeth.

The first flash came while I was still ten feet from the edge of the trench, the second, fainter one while I was in the act of teetering over the edge. I landed on what appeared to be a marine nurse. She didn't even seem to notice.

"Fuck, fuck, fuck, fuck!" she whimpered, her skin white and cold. "Fuck, fuck, fuck, fuck..."

The blast wasn't nearly as powerful as I'd expected. First came a long, hard, double-peal of thunder, followed by a sudden breath of unnaturally warm wind. It was powerful enough to trash the hospital tents, I reckoned, but not as bad as some gusts I'd experienced in thunderstorms back home. The sun hid itself behind a thick, dark cloud that resembled a mushroom from further away. Then, it was over.

"Fuck, fuck, fuck, fuck," the nurse continued, the only sound breaking a long, long silence. Somewhere along the line she'd wrapped her arms around me so tightly that I couldn't move.

"Christ," I heard another voice exclaim. "They must've missed."

"Or else we weren't the prime target," someone else said.

"Either way," Mendes observed, "We got off light. By the way, could whoever's standing on my hand please move their goddamn foot?"

Someone grunted, and one by one we climbed out of our improvised shelter. A corporal I didn't know lifted me over the parapet or I might never have gotten out. All around me, people stood around in stunned little groups. The tents had indeed been flattened. No permanent damage met my survey.

"It was an air burst," Mendes opined.

"Yeah," a medical orderly of some type agreed. He wore a bloodstained lab coat.

He pointed first to the base of the huge cloud that now almost blocked the sun and then to the base of a similar cloud a few miles away. "You can see where they detonated, way up high in the sky. Why on earth would the Dracans do that?"

My jaw dropped, and then I closed my eyes in resignation. We didn't use the filthy things ourselves. At least we hadn't used them yet. One special type of bomb had a delivery profile like that.

"Shit," a Marine whispered, reaching the same conclusion I just had. He clutched at his chest, tearing at a little badge with fumbling fingers. "Holy shit."

"Fuck," Mendes agreed, grabbing at his own chest.

At first he tried to unpin his dosimeter, then in frustration he simply ripped it free. I leaned closer and turned up my eye-magnification.

The indicator bar was coal-black. All the way across. Well beyond the point marked 'lethal.'

"Fuck," Mendes raged, first throwing the little device down on the pavement and then grinding it to shreds under his combat-booted heel. He was crying, now. "I'm fuckin' dead."

"Me too," another voice wailed out. "Oh Jesus, save me!"

"Oh, god," the Marine nurse wept, staring down at her own doom. "Oh god, oh god, oh god, oh god…"

Then everyone began wailing, screaming, and smashing things. A combat rifle went off down the street, and I saw a headless body drop to the pavement. A second shot followed and a second man fell screaming and thrashing. Apparently, he'd flinched. It wasn't long before a third shot finished the job.

"The fucking Dracans," N'dukwe screamed to no one. "Fuck the fucking Dracans. Fuck them all to hell."

No one would be fucking them. I now understood deep in my heart, they'd won. It was all over but for the digging of the mass graves. In a day or two, the entire Kammhuber defense force would be dead. In a week, the radiation levels would be down to nothing. In at most a month, the Dracans would be operating the vital rail and road network as if there'd never been any interruption at all.

After all, that was what neutron bombs were did.

Chapter Twenty-Six

For what felt like hours but was probably only minutes, I stood in the middle of the street and simply stared as the world I understood slowly dissolved into something hideous beyond belief. All around me, men and women wept, wailed, or shook their fists at the heavens.

A few blocks away a sort of circular firing squad formed. They aimed and fired. Then the survivors closed ranks and the squad did it again. The second time, there weren't any of them left. Most people, however, suddenly seemed to want more than anything else to leave messages for their loved ones. Everywhere I looked, wounded hospital patients and staff alike sat around either talking into recording devices or scribbling down their words the old-fashioned way. The letters stood no chance whatever of being delivered and their authors had to know it. Somehow, it didn't seem to matter.

"...never told you how grateful I really was, Dad..."

"...raise her a Catholic. It doesn't matter anymore what I think..."

"...kill them all for me, David. No mercy. Kill them all..."

Every once in a while, one of the letter-writers would finish their note, carefully seal it in an envelope, and then blow their own brains out.

"Hey, Longo," a familiar voice called out.

"Yes?" I asked, swiveling to face my friend. Mendes looked a little better now, pale and sweating, but rational. Except for the fire in his eyes.

"I'm gonna go do a Dracan before I go," he explained. "More than one, if I'm lucky. I'm not gonna just fuckin' die in this war, and not ever have fired a shot. I'm gonna kill me one, and kill him slow if I can. You hear me?"

I nodded slowly. It sounded like as good a plan as any. I'd have killed any number of Dracans just then myself, slowly or not.

"You're a good kid," the private continued. "You've already done your part of the fighting." He raised his gun slightly. "You want me to do you before I go? Make it clean, like?" His eyes narrowed. "Or are you radiation-hardened?"

I looked down at the ground. A few days before I'd been in near-proximity to multiple thermonuclear discharges. Just the "noise" from my Skybolt's antigravs at full power generated higher background readings than what I was picking up now. How could I do my job and not be radiation hardened?

"I thought so," Mendes answered, nodding slowly. Then he laughed and shook his head. "I'm glad you're going to make it, Thomas, really I am but I wouldn't go around advertising the fact just now, if I were you. Not everyone is likely to be so understanding." He reached into his pocket and pulled out an envelope. "Please?"

I nodded, even though I wasn't sure how I could possibly manage to carry anything. "I'm so sorry, Carlos."

For just a second, Mendes's eyes hardened into balls of iron. Then he looked away for a moment before speaking.

"I'm glad you're going to make it," he said. "Somehow, I get the idea that you're a lot more important than you seem." He stuffed his envelope into a sort of pouch-thingie, then used a little necklace he'd been wearing to secure the pouch to the narrow area between my braincase and drive-motors.

"It's been good to know you, kid." He managed a smile, and even thumped the top of my casing affectionately. "I'll be seeing you around."

Chapter Twenty-Seven

I don't recall much of what happened the rest of that afternoon. It rained for a little while, rain my built-in instruments told me was radioactive as hell.

During the storm, the marine medical colonel who hadn't known what to do with me crawled out from under the big collapsed tent and ran around screaming at everyone, trying to restore order. "We have patients to care for," he reminded his people. "There were surgeries in progress."

Eventually most of the medical types seemed to remember their duties. As I walked down the road gunshots were sounding under the canvas. Not that I was able to stay on the road very long.

Soon one truck after another whizzed by, jam-packed with panicked troops and traveling too fast. The second time one of these almost hit me, I figured out I better off by myself. So, I headed cross-country. I was still close enough to the road to see when one of the overcrowded vehicles missed a curve and overturned. A lot of screams filled the air, but no one came to help.

I remember steady walking, keeping my head down in the failing light and putting my three feet down one after another after another to avoid the eternal rocks and trying my best not to trip and damage myself more. I couldn't anything do for anyone, unless you counted delivering Mendes's letter. Not a thing.

Near dawn the next day, others began to sicken and die. I had only the most remote idea of where I was and avoided roads anyway as much as I could. I decided to slice diagonally down the slope of Kelly's Ridge and down towards where the valley met the sea. With any luck, I headed away from the Dracans. I hoped to find another patch of coastal swamp there and closer to Churilla City this time. Perhaps I would find some people as well. Just as the sun rose, I came to another rear-area base of some kind, this one much smaller than the hospital. It looked to be a supply depot.

"Hello," I called out, trying to attract the attention of a guard. I stood and waved a tripod leg, but that didn't do any good either. "Hello."

Silence didn't signify good news, I decided after a time no one would reply. I circumnavigated the little tent city, maintaining a distance of at least a hundred yards or so at all times. I was almost halfway around before I found the garrison, all lying near a foul, reeking slit in the ground. A latrine? No one was moving, and I thought them all dead until finally one of them stirred.

"Fuck," he muttered, staggering to his feet. "Not again."

"Yeah, again," another replied lifelessly. "We're gonna shit ourselves to death."

I couldn't help but look at the man's droppings. They were watery and blood-red. His pants were stained with the stuff and he didn't bother wiping.

"Oh, god," he cried out as the cramps wracked him. "This hurts *so* bad."

Another man crawled over to the trench and vomited. His secretions were blood-red, as well. I turned away and started walking, sickened beyond anything I'd ever felt before. White-hot rage exploded in my phantom-chest. *God damn the Dracan Empire.* I screamed inwardly. *God damn the filthy, murdering, bastards. God damn their strutting Emperor, God damn their slavish masses, God damn their competent, able generals. What the fuck was the use of it all, anyway?*

I trudged down the long, continuous slope of rubble. I'd fought, the marines had fought, the Top Bananas had fought, everyone had fought. We'd taken out a dreadnought, for Christ's sake, and two troopships against all odds. We'd lost.

Everyone in the world was either dead or dying. I wanted to cry, wanted to weep, scream, kick things and break the necks of every fucking Dracan in the universe. We'd lost. We'd fucking lost.

No matter that we'd fought so hard, no matter that good people were vomiting their guts out, no matter that the fleet had gotten away. We'd lost. All it had taken was a single Dracan fighter and two flashes in the sky and, hey presto, dead marines, dead and dying, wherever one cared to look. Just that easy.

Not if I'd been in the sky. Not if hotshot pilot Tommy Longo had been at the stick of his super-fighter, playing the coolest video-game ever made. I'd have blown every last Dracan out of the sky, would've dodged and weaved and twisted and...

I would've nuked the fucking Dracans just like they'd done to us. Just like I'd killed thousands of them aboard the two helpless troopships. One instant they'd been alive, breathing, hoping, and dreaming. Just like my marine friends. The next...the next...the next...

They floated in boundless space, breathing vacuum, kicking, writhing, and dying in the deep cold black.

So, how was I better than the Dracan pilot who'd nuked *my* people? How much blood was on my hands? It'd been *so* much easier when I hadn't seen the target's-eye view of things.

"God damn it," I screamed aloud, looking up at the empty blue bowl of the sky. "God damn all of this shit to hell. What the fuck was I supposed to do? Let them land and kill off anyone they liked? Let them walk in and run things however they want? Let them fuck up this planet like the Autarchy fucked up Esteppe? Let them turn people like my brother into vegetables, to slaughter innocent people, to use this planet as a base to fuck up even more planets?"

War sucked. All I had to do was close my eyes and I could see Lieutenant Eaglish's little flashing light fading in the distance. Under my feet I could feel the half-gutted corpse of the civilian woman who'd been cluster-bombed back at the Army-Navy game so long ago. I knew that circular firing squads and blood-shitting wretches would inhabit my nightmares for the rest of my natural life, no matter how long or short that might be.

What was worth that? What could *possibly* be worth doing that to anyone?

Had the whole universe gone mad? It'd all seemed so simple, not so very long before. Now everything was all twisted. The Dracans were wrong. Yet how could my slaughtering thousands of troops in an assault ship ever be right? People had a right to fight back, yes. Yet what could possibly be gained by using a neutron bomb?

My mind went in circles on those questions for hours and even days. Outwardly, I appeared a calm, cold machine. Internally I raged, screamed, and cursed like a marine against whatever pitiful excuse for a god had let things be this way.

"It's not fair," I screamed to the tops of the mangrove trees. I'd long since reached the swamps I'd sought, but no people. "It's just not fucking fair we have to live in such a fucked-up universe."

"I've often agreed, Thomas," a voice replied from nowhere. "Perhaps more often than you might imagine."

I spun around, unable to locate the source of the sound. "Who? I mean, what..."

"It's quite all right," the voice continued.

This time I was able to use my microphones as binaural locators. The voice came from the base of a thick thorn bush.

"You're in no danger, son." A moment's hesitation followed. "I'm going to stick my head up. If you're armed, I hope you'll refrain from shooting me? "

I nodded. In point of fact, I wasn't armed at all. However, there was nothing wrong with letting a stranger think I was. "Come on out."

"Right," the voice replied. Then a slight rustling sounded and out of the hedge emerged the lapine head of Spencer Wiston, Founder and former governor, wearing a battered ear-holed campaign hat. My former dinner-mate.

My jaw dropped. "Sir…I mean…"

He smiled and climbed the rest of the way out of the brush. In addition to his battered hat, he also wore thick canvas coveralls adorned with what looked like a thousand pockets, and a huge antique-style scoped cartridge revolver slung in a crossdraw holster across his chest. The rabbit's left arm was heavily bandaged, but he didn't seem at all handicapped by the fact.

"It's okay," he declared, extending his right hand. I met it with a tripod leg. "I wasn't exactly expecting you either, son.

"Right," I agreed, feeling more than a little dazed. That dinner had been so long ago. It felt like a million years.

The rabbit looked up the slope, and his eyebrows rose. "Did you come from…?"

I nodded slowly. "Uh-huh."

"They're all…I mean…"

I nodded again and looked down at my feet. "Yes."

Wiston's eyes closed and he bowed his head. "I see."

"It's all over," I whispered. "Everyone died for nothing."

The rabbit examined me with a searching gaze. "It's never for nothing, son."

I shook my head. "We've lost, don't you see? We've lost the Kammhuber. All the combat troops are dead. At least most of them are. The Dracans own the sky, and they own all the Nikita points. That means they own everything."

Wiston cocked his head to the left and then back to the right. "You're wrong, dead wrong. You ought to know it. You're a bright enough boy by all accounts."

I blinked and looked up at him. I wept inside, though my body couldn't show it anymore. Weeping like a baby.

"All the army people think it's over. How can they all be wrong? How can you be right and everyone else be wrong?"

"Because I am," the rabbit-man replied. He pointed at his chest. "The Dracans don't own this, Thomas. They don't own my heart. I suspect they don't own yours either or I'm a much worse judge of character than I'd ever imagined. You know what?"

"What?" I felt about eight years old.

"They're not going to, either. Not now, not tomorrow, nor the day after, either. Never. I will not submit. The game isn't over until I win." He smiled and wrapped his good arm around me.

Almost against my will, I snuggled close to him. He was warm and very soft.

"Come on, Thomas. You've had a terrible time of it. A worse time of it than I can imagine, probably. It's all right that you're hurt and bleeding inside, for now."

"It was hideous," I whispered. "People were killing themselves, doctors were killing their patients, and everyone was writing last letters."

"I see," the rabbit replied, nudging me along the forest path.

"And," I continued, rubbing up against him even closer, "I had to watch another ejected pilot die. A Top Banana. It took him hours. I shot down five Dracans. No one bailed out. Not one of them. I must've killed them all." I gasped a little. Somehow, I'd never really thought about that until now.

"Uh-huh," the big rabbit answered, urging me on with a squeeze. "It must have been a terrible thing."

"Yeah," I answered dreamily, letting Wiston guide me beause I had no idea of where we were going. "Terrible."

A long silence came after that as we strode down the path just as if the universe were still at peace. My head snuggled close under his arm.

"Well," he said after the quiet had stretched out for a while. "It sounds like you've had quite a war already, Thomas. Quite a war indeed."

We rounded a corner as he spoke. The path crossed a set of rail lines there. Presumably we'd been paralleling them for some time, but I'd been too preoccupied to notice. Wiston stopped and pulled a little compu-box out of one of his many pockets.

"I wish I could tell you that it's all over. I mean, certainly you've done your part and more."

He frowned and pecked at the tiny keyboard for a few moments. In the distance, I heard a locomotive come suddenly to life. "I fear the real fun may be just beginning."

He gazed at me quizzically. "Thomas, I have very little time just now, and many responsibilities. If you want to go your own way, feel free. No one would ever dream of questioning your honor if you were to turn yourself in to the Dracans. Not after what you've already done.

"They'll treat you well, considering who your father is. The Skybolt is hardly a secret weapon. Everyone knows about it. Your father's even been buying full-page ads. I don't imagine that you could tell the

Dracans much they don't already know or will know pretty soon regardless."

I nodded. If I did that, my war would be over, and I'd never, ever have to look at anyone shitting blood again. It seemed like a remarkably good idea to part of me. But...

"But," Wiston continued, his eyes boring into mine. "If you come with me, well...Things will be damned interesting indeed, I can assure you, though mostly in bad ways.

I've fought rebels before, you see. When I was governor." He smiled. "So, I know all the places to hide and all the really dirty tricks. The kind that actually work, I mean."

Just then the locomotive, drawing a single car, pulled up and obediently halted at the rabbit's side. "You...You can control the trains?"

He nodded and smiled. "Uh-huh. Any time that I like. Better than the Dracans will ever be able to control them, I rather suspect. I wrote the software, you see. All of it, all the way back to the first draft, from the ground up. In fact, I planned out the entire rail system."

His smile widened. "I own every inch of rail on this planet and many other things, as well. There are benefits to being a planetary Founder." He punched at his keyboard again, and the railcar door swung open.

My jaw dropped. "I...Uh..."

"Seriously, Thomas," the rabbit said, leaning forward. "Choose wisely, but choose quickly as well. I must be about my affairs."

"I...Uh..."

The railcar door stood open, inviting. Yet... What Wiston was talking about was guerilla warfare. Anyone could see that. Nasty. Dangerous. Probably futile, as well. No sane odds maker would give the rabbit a chance against the Empire. I had only so many days of nutrient and power left. The Dracans could recharge me. I'd be a prisoner, yes. but a live one, with honor intact. No one could blame me for trying to stay alive. Besides, the war had to end eventually.

"If you come with me," the rabbit said, "I'll do everything possible to take care of you. To even get your other body. My word of honor."

Word of honor. The phrase rang oddly in my head for some reason, though at first I couldn't quite figure it out. Word of honor, word of honor, word of honor.

Then I understood. It was the last word in the phrase that was giving me difficulty, and it was my heart that was having the trouble. Wiston was right. I couldn't give up. If I did, how would I ever live with myself afterwards?

I shook my head hard to clear it and spoke the words that Lieutenant Eaglish, Sergeant N'Dukwe, Mendes, the marine doctor-colonel, and all the others I'd seen die demanded of me. "Of course, Governor," I answered, stepping carefully up into the boxcar. "I'm at your disposal. How could it be any other way?"

My life wasn't my own anymore. It hadn't been ever since I'd agreed to fly combat. I saw that now, formal oath or no. There was no such thing as a limited commitment. A man was either a soldier or he wasn't. The universe might not be fair or even sane, but that didn't mean I had to betray every principle in which I'd ever believed. I couldn't sit by and do nothing while my friends looked over my shoulder from the grave.

The rabbit cocked his head again and smiled. He removed his hat and formally bowed. "I in turn am at yours, Thomas. By everything I've ever held holy, I'm at your service as well."

Chapter Twenty-Eight

We didn't ride the train very long, which was probably a good thing. The car Spencer had chosen for us might've been fairly clean, but it hadn't ever been meant for passenger use. There weren't any windows, and I'd always gotten motion-sickness when riding in anything without windows back when I'd had a stomach. It would've been black as night inside save that Governor Wiston pecked calmly but intently the whole time at his little console.

"Well," he said at last, holding the display up where I could see it. "It's official. They've surrendered."

I nodded and looked at the tiny screen. The lapine must've had very good eyes indeed, for he'd scrunched the whole page down to the size of his ultra-compact monitor rather than just viewing a section at a time. *Capitulation* the headline read in the biggest type I'd ever seen. *Armed forces Unconditionally Surrender Government to Transfer Power.*

It'd been one thing to imagine a full-scale surrender, but it was quite another to be conquered. Especially after having seen so many of my friends die to prevent it. I pressed my lips together in anger. I turned away, feeling a sucker-punch to the gut.

"Thank you." I stared into the darkness. "I...I don't want to read any more just now."

"Right," Wiston agreed, frowning and withdrawing his pocket computer. "I don't blame you. I've little choice myself. I have to keep up with as much about what's happening as possible."

"Of course, I understand." I folded my three legs under me and sat the floor.

Wiston continued to respect my need for privacy as the miles rolled past. For an hour or so, he typed busily, sending and receiving e-mails at a speed I found difficult to digest. He muttered sometimes as he pecked away. Mostly it was unintelligible, but occasionally I could make out the words with my augmented hearing.

"Good old Ralph," I heard him say once, smiling faintly at the screen during a rare pause in his machine-gun typing. "There's a man to be trusted."

Apparently not all of those trying to reach the former governor were of such sterling character. "Coward." I heard him growl once. "Incompetent fool." Throughout, he never hesitated more than a few seconds, but instead typed, typed, and typed like a machine.

"We'll be stopping in a moment, Thomas," Wiston warned me as the train's engine began to slow. "From this moment forward I have to assume the Dracans are trying to track me. So we must leave as quickly as possible. There won't be any station-platform. Will you need help getting down? Please, don't be shy about asking."

I frowned, then admitted that in my current form I couldn't climb very well. "I'm sorry and yes, I'll need you to lower me down."

"No worries," the rabbit answered, smiling. "This railroad didn't build itself, you know. I've swung pickaxes, set explosive charges, dug drainage ditches...In the beginning, we didn't have machines for everything like we do today. The first few miles, I had to build practically by hand. So, I've done my share of manual labor and more. Being governor and a Founder doesn't make me fragile. In fact, I'm quite spry for my age."

I smiled a little. It wasn't easy to picture the dignified rabbit digging ditches, but I was certain that he spoke the truth. His battered hat and worn coveralls backed up every word. The easy, familiar manner with which he carried his revolver bespoke his having lived in a more dangerous time. As for his age, he acted more like my eldest brother, still in his thirties, than a great-grandfather. Gengineering conferred advantages.

When the train stopped, Wiston stabbed a console-button and the door slid open. In a flash, the rabbit-man leaped to the ground. With my slow-moving electrical servos, I was hard-pressed to step to the edge of the car before my fast-moving friend had turned around and reached for me.

"Easy does it, then," he said, snatching me up as if I weighed nothing and then setting me firmly back on terra firma.

We were still in something resembling a coastal swamp, but neater and almost park-like. Trees surrounded us. Instead of growing all crazy like the ones I'd seen earlier, these were planted in rows.

Wiston smiled. "Welcome to my estate." In a flash he was typing again. Obediently, the train lurched once more into motion and rolled smoothly away.

"It's like magic, isn't it Thomas?" Wiston said, smiling. "There's not much in life more enchanting than a train, even in this age of interstellar travel. I was still a small boy when I lived on Earth. Back then I'd spend hours down by the tracks, chasing up and down alongside when the big freights rumbled through." He looked at me quizzically. "I was born in Kansas City."

"I'm originally from Esteppe, of course," I answered. "Now I live in New Orleans. That's what I think of as home." I tried to smile. "We had trains too, but Father never let me chase them."

Wiston smiled and gestured towards a little cobblestone pathway. Obediently, I began walking down it.

"It was a different time," he said softly. "The engines were chemically fueled back then—ancient tech. Once we landed here and got things going, there wasn't any doubt at all in my mind what I wanted to do for a living. As soon as it became economically feasible, I ran track between the original colony at Churilla City and the mines at Tres Haciendas. That's still part of my main line. Some of the rails I laid by hand are still in service."

I nodded, not knowing what to say.

"When you run the railroads, you get to know all the important businessmen. You come to understand their businesses, too. They're your customers. In time, they become your friends and your allies. You learn to trust each other."

I nodded again. Wiston was clearly trying to communicate something to me, something he considered to be important or he wouldn't be wasting time on it, but what? I didn't understand at all. Yet, I didn't say anything, because he clearly thought I was smart enough to catch his drift.

The trees began to open up in front of us, and presently we rounded a corner. The path split there. To the left stood a large white mansion. It was a good three stories high, complete with pillared entryway and a bronze fountain-statue of two anthro-rabbits, both of whom I recognized. To the right sat a medium-sized bungalow-home, ordinary in every way and looking hand-built. By then, I wasn't surprised to see that the path towards the smaller building was far more worn.

"The government built that granite monstrosity for us," he explained, ears low in embarrassment. "It's supposed to become a museum someday after Alicia and I are gone. They keep asking us to move in, so that we can 'put our mark on it for posterity.' We like our little house." He shrugged. "Alicia and I never go up there except to meet with officials and tourists and such."

I nodded again, this time a little bemused. The soil alone on the Wiston estate had to be worth a king's ransom. I'd rarely seen such a rich, well-cared-for lawn. It was probably the only one like it on the planet. The governor's bungalow was smaller than some of Father's servants' quarters.

As we walked across the soft green turf, I wished I could feel the green blades under my bare feet like I had when I was still a kid. Soon I heard piano music. Alicia was regarded as a highly talented concert pianist. She was playing something very complex as we walking to the house—complex and very sad.

Wiston didn't hesitate or knock. He grabbed the doorknob and turned it. "Honey," he cried out like billions of men before him. "I'm home."

"Oh," Alicia gasped. I heard her scramble to her feet, music forgotten as she clattered into the living room. "Thank heavens, Spence." They embraced and exchanged a ritual kiss. "I was *so* worried."

Then she looked down at me. "Thomas? Is that you?"

I nodded, then Alicia turned back towards her husband for an explanation. "He flew combat with the Bananas," the governor explained. "Rather successfully, if the rumors are true. Then he survived being shot down."

His face hardened a little. "Thomas was up at the Pass, hon. The stories we heard were true. I'm back early in part because Thomas was able to confirm everything I needed to know. He's had a bad time."

Suddenly Mrs. Wiston's right arm was wrapped protectively around me. "Oh, my," she whispered. "Is there anything you need? I mean, I'd make you hot chocolate or something..."

I smiled a little. "No, ma'am," I said. "There's not much anyone can do for me."

"That's the saddest thing of all," Alicia agreed, nodding. "Well, as a Top Banana and combat veteran you're officially a hero in this house, Thomas. Anything you'd like, anything at all, is yours. Anything."

I looked down at the ground. "Thank you," I whispered, not really knowing what to say.

An awkward moment passed and then Wiston reached out and touched Alicia's arm. "Have you heard? I know how you are when you're playing. I got it off the planetary net. They've surrendered."

She looked at the floor. "I knew," she whispered. "Couldn't you hear it in the music?"

This time it was Wiston's turn to examine his toes. "It'll be all right. We're down, but not out. There's still the entire United Systems on the other side of the Nexus, and they'd be fools to leave us to the Dracans. Fools and oath breakers alike. If they let the Dracans keep us, the Emperor will eventually dictate peace terms in London. Any idiot can see that."

"Can anyone stop the Dracans, Spence? "Alicia gazed at him. "Even more importantly, will anyone stop them? I'm certain we haven't heard half of everything that's gone wrong yet. This won't be the only military disaster. Wars don't work that way. It'll be a long, bloody road back."

"They'll fight," Wiston answered. "They must. Even if they don't... "

Alicia nodded. "Even if they don't, we'll fight our own little war right here. Of course, Spence, that's a given. You don't make peace with murderers. Period. Ever. No matter what the cost."

The big rabbit smiled his coldest smile and turned to me. "We won't stay long, Thomas. It's not safe for us. Now that the official fighting has ended the Dracans will be after Alicia and I. Personally, I mean. You too, if they suspect you're alive."

I nodded. "Yes, I see."

"So," Wiston continued, "we're going to be doing a little high-speed packing, my wife and I. It shouldn't take us long. We've been ready for this for weeks."

He pointed to a back room. "That's our guest quarters, Thomas. Please, make yourself at home. We'll be on a train in twenty minutes or less."

Chapter Twenty-Nine

It took eighteen minutes by my internal clock. The governor bounced around the bungalow stashing odds and ends into a little rucksack, while his wife went dashing off to the big "granite monstrosity" with the fountain in front of it. Meanwhile I stood in the little guest room, trying to keep out of the way.

"Come on, Thomas," the big rabbit exclaimed as he pulled a revolver and holster slightly smaller than his own out of a bureau drawer and dangled it loosely over his left shoulder. It must belong to Alicia.

"We've got a train to catch."

My host had timed things perfectly. His wife came pounding up as we emerged, puffing a bit.

"I've got it all," she proclaimed, snapping open a little leather briefcase. Official looking documents filled it. "Everything we wanted. Alec was on duty. He figured out what I sought and helped. In fact, he wanted to come along."

Wiston nodded with a smile. "Good for Alec. He was always my favorite museum employee. Not pushy, like the other guards."

I'd stayed quiet for a long time, and hadn't asked any questions. So, I figured I was due.

"What is that stuff?" I nodded towards the documents.

"All sorts of things," Alicia said, dimpling. She fingered through the little folders, one by one. "The Planetary Constitution, Churilla's copy of the United Systems Treaty we signed, the original Founder's Articles—"

Spencer chuckled, pointing down at the Articles. "See? That's my signature right there on top. I was maybe fourteen. My penmanship was awful back then."

I gulped. My face would have gone white, if it had had any blood in it to start with. "You..." I spluttered. "You can't..."

"Sure we can," Alicia declared, grinning as she snapped the briefcase shut and started down the little path towards the railroad track. "We just did."

"We're the government in exile," Spencer explained, wrapping his arm around me and urging me forward. “So we need all the ‘proof of legitimacy’ we can muster. Are we legally elected? No. Do we have actual, real, binding titles? No. Have we sworn any oaths of office? Not for a long time.”

Then, he wriggled his nose. “I just thought of something.“

“What, dearest?” Alicia’s eyes glowed.

She must adore the idea of setting up an illegal shadow government. Especially one equipped with genuine documents.

“When I swore to uphold the constitution and do my utmost for the populace of Churilla as their elected governor, there wasn’t any sunset-date specified. Was there?”

The doe-rabbit pursed her lips. “Not that I recall. Nor for any of my ministerial posts, either.”

Spencer’s grin widened. “Well, then, there we have it.” He tapped the briefcase. “All nice and legal. Kind of.”

“Kind of,” Alicia agreed, her step full of spring and her head held high.

“But…” I spluttered. “But…”

“Governments-in-exile are never legal, Thomas,” Alicia explained, taking pity on me. “Not until their side wins, that is. Then, their actions are retroactively discovered to have been fully legal all along with everything justified by extenuating circumstances. It’s a beautiful thing, really.”

“That’s right,” Spencer agreed, taking his wife’s hand and walking beside her as if on his way to a family picnic instead of a desperate war.

“If we win, we’re a government-in-exile. If we lose, we’re treasonous rebels. Today, Thomas, you’re an illegal guerilla warrior fighting on after a legal surrender, not protected under interplanetary treaty, and liable to execution without trial. I wouldn’t let that get you down.

“Once we’ve won, you’ll be acclaimed as an honorable freedom fighter and Churillan patriot, even though you’re technically not a Churillan except by adoption. Probably, you’ll even get medals and a pension.” He turned to Alicia. “We are adopting him, right? For the duration, at least.”

“Of course we’re adopting him,” she answered, raising her voice against the roar of the approaching locomotive. “How could we not? He’s a hero.”

Chapter Thirty

It was almost dark when the three of us disembarked from our boxcar and Spencer sent the train off on its way without us.

"Right on schedule," he crowed, hustling us off into the thick brush that grew along both sides of the right-of-way.

I thought at first that we must be in the coastal swamplands, but the vegetation looked different somehow. It wasn't as tropical or quite so green. I didn't see any trees. Then I realized we were at the end of a narrow little gorge with near-vertical walls soaring a good hundred feet into the sky. Where there was a gorge, there was almost always a river. I closed my eyes to concentrate, and sure enough I could hear a steady splashing gurgle in the distance.

"We don't have far to go," Wiston said. "Come on, we need to be out of sight in the next six minutes when the next train comes. It'll be a hazmat run with a live engineer."

Alicia frowned and nodded, picking up the pace despite the way the brush caught at her skirt.

"Why are there plants here?" I stared about the gorge. "I mean, I can tell there's a river and a river means rocks and stuff would be halfway to soil anyhow ..."

The governor nodded and smiled. "An old friend of mine started this biome. The gorge was formed by a geologic feature called a 'dike'. That means that a sort of thin soup of basalt flowed up and into a natural crack in the country rock, widening it along the way and then hardening. Basalt is relatively short-lived as rocks go. It weathers quickly when exposed to rain and wind. So all you see today is the empty crack, with a river flowing down it." I nodded.

"Basalt also makes for a fertile soil, once it breaks down," Alicia continued for her husband. "So fertile that, here in this narrow valley and a few dozen others like it, earth life forms grew without much help."

She waved an all-inclusive arm. "Not desirable earth life, mind you. These are all weeds, by Earth standards. Pioneer plants, some scientists call them. The soil is still too thin and fragile to mine it for use elsewhere. So, we have a sort of idyllic little green spot here, patiently developing itself a soil in which to grow, though one too obscure for much of anyone to know about it. Except, of course, my husband."

Spencer's ear-linings reddened. I knew by now that this was a blush.

"Some guerrillas holed up here during my second term as governor," he explained. "A little ways up, the dike branched and created a shallow cave under the gorge wall. The rebels expanded it back hundreds of feet. We never even once suspected they might be hiding out here. It wasn't until after they accepted an amnesty that their secret leaked out.

"There's nothing about it in the official records. What little remained I erased a few days back. Almost no one left alive, except Alicia and I, would remember first-hand."

"Wow," I said, looking around me with new eyes. "The gorge is so narrow that overhead photography won't show a thing."

"Not even infrared," Wiston agreed. "This area's still geothermally active. A hot spring feeds the river, and the ground is warm here and elsewhere. The rebels weren't stupid.

"You should never assume your enemy is less bright than you. They taught me that lesson, in spades. One of them was a satellite imagery specialist on the government payroll. We didn't suspect a thing until the amnesty. I doubt the Dracans will either, so long as we're careful. Like us, they'll probably figure we're holed up in a city or in the coastal swamp. We're tens of miles from either."

"Wow," I repeated. "There's fresh, clean water, too."

"Even fish," Wiston said. "They're part of the biome—spotted bass and other pan fish. I brought a fly rod, for when I need to sit and think. Most important of all, the river will cover our tracks. I'm afraid we're about to go wading."

It wasn't too bad of a wade, though the current was spirited, the water was shallow and large, flat rocks covered the bottom. I didn't have any trouble, despite my flat, slippery tripod feet. I even saw a few of the fish the rabbit had mentioned. Beautiful blue-tinted, hand-sized creatures eyed us suspiciously from behind assorted bits of cover.

The two rabbits had to bend down in order to enter the cave, but I didn't. Once inside, it was almost like being in a house. The walls and floors were smooth and flat. I had to strain my eyes in order to see where they'd been laser-hewn into such an unnatural shape. Everything was dry.

Spencer had stored supplies for weeks if not months, judging by the stacks of things. Five small molecular batteries lined the far wall and would provide enough power to last the three of us for half a decade or more. I glimpsed huge stacks of military ration-cans. Either it was overkill or my host expected a long war. Several rough chairs sat clustered around a large trestle-table. They looked old enough to have belonged to the original rebels. Near the table was an all-electric camp kitchen. The rabbit had also rigged up twin computer workstations.

"Oh, my," Alicia gushed, seeing her workstation was equipped with a simulated piano keyboard and pedals. She fingered the keys lovingly. "You're so thoughtful, sweetheart."

"I know how you get when you can't play," Spencer replied, smiling. "We need you at your best, dear. Not all twisted up and frustrated inside."

Then he turned to me. "The left wall of the corridor is lined with small bunkrooms. The first one is set up for my wife and I. Pick whichever of the rest you'd like. Mmm...Would you be willing to move in next to us? You get first choice, by right of seniority, so it's up to you. Things will grow more crowded later, I'm sure."

"Of course," I answered. "I'd be honored."

"Excellent." Spencer sighed, lowered his backpack to the floor, and turned on his computer. "No time for fishing just now, I suppose. There's too much damned work to be done."

Chapter Thirty-One

Judging by the way my two hosts set themselves about their keyboards for the next day and a half, they faced a ton of work. Despite the fact I was invited to every single meal, I felt a little neglected.

"You're living here with us," Alicia explained when I protested I didn't need to eat. "Mealtimes are when we make plans and share information. For right now it's not critical, but when more patriots join us, you'll find that being present at meals is the only way to keep abreast of things."

"Besides," Spencer added, "I'm no psychologist, but I imagine inhabiting such an odd sort of body must be difficult for you. We're going to be getting you your…what do you call it? Your mannequin body?"

"Yes, sir."

He smiled at me. "Anyway, I've already taken steps to get that back for you. It shouldn't take more than a few days. You have that long before your emergency capsule run out. In the meantime, wouldn't you be better off keeping your routine as normal as possible?"

Maintaining a facade of normality in my life was one of the few things on which Father Murton and Doctor Layton had always agreed. Even in my mannequin body, they'd insisted on that. Crazy at it seemed, they'd even encouraged me to continue dating. So I sat and smiled at breakfast, lunch, and dinner while Alicia and Spencer traded rapid-fire comments about people I'd never met and economic relationships I'd never understand.

Being a guerilla fighter was boring, I began to understand boring in a mind-numbing sort of way one had to experience firsthand to truly appreciate. Spencer supplied me my own computer from somewhere and wired me into the planetary 'net via his secret railroad connection, but how was I to use it?

Voice-recognition was slow and awkward. I'd never been any good at it. So, mostly I spent my time in my little stone cubicle, equipped with a bed I didn't need, a chest-of-drawers I had nothing to fill, and a computer terminal I couldn't really use. I tried to catch up on some engineering classes, but the vocal interface so frustrated me I began to spend my time exploring the surroundings.

Spencer had said I could wander about, so long as I used common sense. "We'll all need to go outside and be alone from time to time," he replied when I asked permission. "We'll go mad otherwise,. Just be careful of the road at the other end of the gorge.

"It's an easy thing for a man to stumble onto without realizing it's there. There's not much traffic on it anyway, but one never knows. Stay close up against the canyon walls as much as you can and try return before dark. If you don't, Alicia will worry."

It'd been a very long time since I'd left home to go play in a creek and been warned to be home by dark. I strode through the short, squat cave entrance maybe not so long after other people. Only a couple of years had passed since I'd spent whole days hiking alone along a muddy little stream that ran into Lake Ponchantraine on Father's estate.

Adults spoke of a couple of years as if it were nothing, even though it felt like forever to me. I'd pretended to be an explorer then, Pierre Laclede or Hernando De Soto exploring up and down the length of the Mighty Missis-sip. I'd hoarded my lunch, pretending to be short on food, and kept a sort of mockery of a journal with detailed notes on the insignificant little gullies that served as "tributaries" to the nameless little stream. Now it seemed so unreal. The games an imaginative boy with too much time on his hands played.

I splashed up and down my new nameless stream, scaring the beautiful fish and silt-clouding the clear, perfect water. At almost seventeen. I was considered a child by ordinary people and was much younger than the ancient Spencer and Alicia. Most kids my age were still at home playing with each other. They pretended to fly fighter planes and rough-housed on the furniture.

Most of them would envy me. I'd shot down five enemy fighters, and I'd blown two real troopships full of men out of the sky. I'd also, judging by what I'd heard, helped bring down one of the biggest superdreadnoughts ever built.

So, why didn't I feel lucky? Or, even much like a kid anymore?

Why couldn't I be happy?

I felt pretty sorry for myself by the time I rounded the big bend in the stream and found myself standing in the open not far from the foot of a highway-bridge. I'd been feeling so sorry for myself that, despite Spence's clear and cogent warning, the road had sort of just snuck up on me. He'd also told me the route was little used and lightly-trafficked. He was dead wrong. Men, mostly in ragged United Systems uniforms with others wearing fresh, sharply-creased Dracan brown filled the right-of-way.

I froze where I was. I didn't look particularly human or like anything else one might easily recognize at a glance. My metal parts were finished in dull, non-reflective colors. Even my rubber-like face was much the scuffed and worn. It had survived a nuclear attack in space, hard vacuum, the subsequent re-entry, days adrift at sea, more days wandering ashore, and a second nuclear attack on land. My false-flesh looked more gray than pink, and its finish had become every bit as non-reflective as the rest of me. A large bush screened me from the road. I wasn't likely to be seen.

No single United Systems soldier in the endless stream even once lifted his or her head to look around. Only the Dracans seemed at all interested in their surroundings, but their eyes were reserved for their prisoners alone. The rest just plodded along in abject misery.

Relieved, I relaxed a little and crouched down behind my concealing bush. Spencer and Alicia would want to know of this. Spencer was paranoid almost to the point of madness about knowing everything that happened for several miles around the shelter at any time. If I went back to get him, the soldiers might be gone when we returned. It was late enough in the day that one of the gorge's walls was in shadow while the road was bathed in bright sunlight. Between that and my unlikely appearance, I decided, no one would see me if I took a closer look. I was probably more likely to get away with it than Spencer himself.

The shadows were kind to me. I was able to close to within thirty feet of the road, where I found a nice natural cavity behind a boulder in which to crouch. The stream of POW's looked endless. It stretched as far as one could see in either direction. The men and women looked worse up close. As well as being hopeless and dejected, they were starving. Rations had been tight among the front-line troops. It appeared they'd been tighter still in the rear areas. I could count every rib on the men whose shirts flapped open in the oppressive heat. The women's cheekbones looked ready to slice through the taut, dull flesh of their faces.

"Water," one of the men cried out as he neared the bridge. He was on crutches, his left foot missing. "For the love of god, let me have some water."

"You will march as ordered," a Dracan screamed, waving his rifle. It had a sort of long knife mounted on the muzzle end.

I'd never seen anything like it before. Our forces didn't have knives mounted on their guns. It looked silly and old fashioned.

"You will march."

“I need a drink,” the man said. “I’ll die if I don’t drink. I won’t hold you up. Promise.” He turned towards the right and the Dracan shoved the rifle-knife into his gut, all the way up to the hilt.

“You will obey orders,” he shouted, almost drowning out the dying man’s own cry of pain. “All orders. At once.”

At first, nothing else happened. No one dared stop moving. Instead, the flow of POW’s broke into two separate streams, one on each side of the corpse. No one stopped even when the Dracan pulled out his blade and wiped it clean on the uniform of the nearest passing prisoner. More wounded troops came trudging down the road, moving slower than those who’d come before. Some had missing limbs, some bore too-fresh surgical scars, others showed no mark of injury at all except mad, staring eyes. An army officer stepped out from the group, dragging his left leg badly. A major.

“These men need water.” he barked. “There’s a stream right here, for Christ’s sake. No excuses. Your planet is signatory to—”

Suddenly the major’s words were cut off by the impact of a rifle butt into his gut. He sort of whoofed and then collapsed onto the road, writing in pain.

“You are insubordinate to a representative of the Emperor,” the Dracan who’d delivered the blow screamed, kicking dirt into the man’s face. “The penalty is death.”

“Fuck you,” the man mouthed, though he still wasn’t able to make a sound. “Fuck you all to hell. I was dead anyway.”

“Sergeant Smith,” the angry guard yelled. His uniform was so plain I hadn’t realized he was an officer. “You will give your bayonet to a prisoner and have him execute this man.”

He raised his head so that as many of the POW’s around as possible could hear. “Your officers have no rank. The lowest of the low, they have no authority over you. Anyone saluting an aggressor officer of the old regime or obeying his commands will be shot.”

Sergeant Smith, if that’s was his name, didn’t take long to act. He removed his stabbing-knife, and handed it at random to a soldier.

The man stopped and stared down at the long knife and then glanced back at the guard. “Respected Sergeant…” he began.

“You, hold the prisoner,” the Dracan officer snapped, gesturing towards two POW’s. “Get him on his feet.”

“It’s all right,” the man lying in the dirt muttered. He tried to gather his good leg under him. “It’s all right, men. I—”

The Dracan kicked him in the good knee. “Silence,” he commanded. He again pointed at the two POW’s. “Pick up this man, and hold him.”

They looked at each other and complied. The wounded POW neither resisted nor spoke as he was levered upright.

Then the Dracan returned his gaze to the prisoner with the knife. "Kill him," he commanded.

"S-s-sir," the knife-wielder stuttered. "R-r-respected—"

"Kill him," the Dracan screamed again, this time raising his own weapon. "Now."

"Private," the wounded major shouted. "You goddamned, motherfucking, worthless sack of shit. Obey the fucking order now!"

"A-a-argh," the private screamed, sinking the knife deep into his leader's chest, his face screwed in agony. It ended quickly. someone had taught him well. I wasn't sure, but I thought the officer had looked grateful for this as he died.

"Good," the Dracan officer declared, smiling and nodding at the private who'd driven the blade home. "Very good. Clean the bayonet and return it to the sergeant. When you have finished, you three may drink all the water you please."

He raised his voice again. "Your officers are powerless and so are those so-called politicians who led you into this disastrous war. You fought on the behalf of your oppressors. You live only at the Emperor's sufferance and that of His representatives. All hail the Emperor."

"Hail," repeated the guards, and not a few of the more crazy-eyed among the POW's. "Hail, Hail, Hail."

Chapter Thirty-Two

"...then he ordered the private to kill him," I sobbed, my head buried deep in Alicia's sweet-smelling fur. My eyes didn't water any more, and I didn't get all stuffy, but I was sobbing for real. It felt good to sob.

"The private didn't want to kill the major, but he did it anyway. If he hadn't, things would've been worse and everyone knew it."

Mrs. Wiston cuddled my head in her lap, while her husband stood over us, fists clenched in rage. "Those...barbaric..."

I'd never heard him at a loss for words before.

"Shh," Alicia urged me, as if I were a small child.

Too bad I wasn't anything like done yet. "Then, the guards let the three executioners drink while everyone else stood and glared at them. I mean, why shouldn't they have drunk? Their getting water didn't hurt anyone else. If they hadn't drunk, the others wouldn't have been any less thirsty. Two of them cried and the third staggered around in shock. They'd had a bad time. The others..."

"It's brainwashing," Spencer explained, his eyes dark and angry. "Divide and conquer. Drive in little wedges wherever you can and hammer them in as far as they'll go." He shook his head and turned back to the holovision.

"Tomorrow I'll have a look for myself. I don't expect I'll find much of anything but a trail of bodies. The Dracans make a habit of leaving those lying about wherever they've been."

We all sat in silence for a while, except for my sobbing, until I'd finally cried myself out. I felt like six years old, but still somehow couldn't feel ashamed of my tears. I'd seen too much suffering of late. Yet the war was still just beginning. Commander Knight had warned me I would see and even do terrible things once I got became involved in it, but I'd never imagined in my wildest dreams how right he'd be.

"...dawn of a new era for the people of Churilla," a Dracan-accented voice said on the holovision. I hadn't noticed it before, because of how important my own news had been.

"A new era of rationality, justice, and social equality for all." I looked up at the screen. A uniformed man with a military crew-cut and razor-thin rust-colored mustache was speaking. He was standing at a very plain podium, reading his speech from a data-pad.

Governor O'Donnel, the glowing letters under his image read. "There is no joy greater than complete and total dedication to the Emperor." At the last word O'Donnel pressed his palms together and formally bowed, as did the slightly out-of-focus honor guard behind him.

"There can be no higher calling in life than His divine service. People of Churilla, I tell you only your aggressor-oppressor leaders need feel the shame of defeat. For ordinary Churillan men and women, there has only been victory. Today, you are free. Ring your church bells, dance in the streets, and rejoice that you too are now numbered among the children of the Emperor."

I blinked, somehow unable to picture the men and women of Churilla City, whose biggest planetary holiday had been Army-Navy game night, celebrating their adoption by the Emperor.

The camera cut to someone else, and I realized with shock I recognized the face. Parliamentarian Sara Fowler, who'd sat with me at dinner the same night that I'd met the Wistons, smiled. Letters formed under her image. *Assistant Governor.*

"The war is over," she began, "and the fighting is behind us. We lament the tragic deaths of thousands of the finest men and women on both sides of this struggle..."

"It had to be her," Alicia snapped, no longer hugging my head to her. "I knew it."

"From the beginning," her husband agreed. "Ever since the day that self-righteous bitch..." His voice trailed off, but his face did not soften.

"...further resistance is not only futile," the new Assistant Governor continued, "but constitutes treason against all the basic principles upon which our world was founded."

"She didn't sign the Founder's Articles," Alicia screeched. "We did. How dare that woman claim to know what they stand for? She hasn't a clue."

"...food for the hungry, productive work for the unemployed, education for all," Fowler continued, "the same goals the best of humanity everywhere has always sought. The Emperor"—she paused to curtsy—"has a vision for Churilla's future, one I have always shared. A vision of a healthy, prosperous populace, unified in purpose and at peace with all. The enemy of the Emperor is the enemy of peace." Fowler smiled, and stepped across the stage to shake the Dracan Governor's hand.

The camera cut to what appeared to be another room, where

someone else I recognized stood at attention—Admiral Lutjens, with his aides clustered behind him. They looked older than they had when I'd first met them, even though it really hadn't been that long ago. Lutjen's right arm trembled continually. The camera panned back to reveal the admiral faced a plain wooden table with a seated high-ranking Dracan facing him.

More glowing letters appeared on the screen. *Admiral Lothar Lutjens, Commanding Officer of the Aggressor Forces* read the script under Lutjen's head. The words under the Dracan read *Lieutenant General Brooke Masterson, Servant of His Imperial Majesty.*

"It's time," Masterson commanded. "You will now sign the instrument of surrender."

Lutjens nodded, then stepped forward. "I hereby make official my abject, complete and total surrender to the mercy of his Imperial Majesty." He took a moment to bow at the mention of His Imperial Majesty.

"In signing this document, I legally surrender my entire command, including all aerospace and land-based units, again begging the mercy of His Majesty." He bowed again.

"Any remaining members of the mercenary forces I once led who remain at large are encouraged to turn themselves in at once. All who do so will be treated with dignity. I also hereby confess the criminal nature of my former resistance against the rightful claims of His Majesty to the planet Churilla and take full responsibility for the many war crimes perpetrated by the men and women under my command."

He looked at General Masterson, who simply nodded. Then, using his left hand to steady the right, Admiral Lutjens signed the document. The camera flashed back to Governor O'Donnel and Assistant Governor Fowler now standing hand-in-hand.

"This has been a traumatic time for the people of Churilla," the governor said, smiling. "Regrettably, there have been many needless deaths and injuries, and much damage to property."

"The bad times are over," Fowler continued. "In the days to come, there will be peace and prosperity and dignity for all, under a new economic order that does not tolerate the tyranny of material wealth."

"Please," O'Donnel added, "Return tomorrow to your places of work, to your ordinary lives. There will be changes, but for now all need peace and harmony and a return to the daily routine."

"If you encounter a uniformed representative of the Emperor," Sara added, curtsying, "show him the same respect you would our beloved new father himself. As I now demonstrate."

"Obey orders when they are issued, promptly and willingly," the

Governor continued. "They are for your own good. Those who disobey orders disrespect the Emperor." He bowed.

"Above all," former-Parliamentarian Fowler finished, "do not tolerate among yourselves those who would not accept their new place in the grand new order of things. Remember, it was the aggression of your former militarist leaders that brought you this war and all the wasteful killing and destruction that followed. A Dracan Internal Security representative will be at every police station in the Archipelago in three day's time. They will deal with the uncooperative. They will also give rewards to those who are especially cooperative."

"Gah," Spencer declared, turning off the set. "Sorry, I just can't take any more. It's all being recorded. We can study it in detail later. For now…"

Alicia shook her head. "I knew it would be her," she said again. "Somehow, I just knew."

Spencer shrugged. "It had to be someone, I suppose. Not that it matters."

He frowned. "Though, I must admit I'd rather it hadn't been someone with whom I've broken bread."

Alicia nodded. "It will be hard," she whispered. "So very hard, but, we knew that."

"Right," Spencer agreed.

He looked at me. "Don't let it get you down, Thomas. Things aren't as hopeless as they look."

"Uh-huh," I agreed, trying to smile a little, though I knew he spoke more to himself than to me.

"In the morning," he continued, "I'll go down and look at the road they used for those POWs. Maybe take some pictures for the historical record."

He sighed. "That's about all I can do for them, mind you. What I can do, I will." Then his fists closed. "In the afternoon, I'll try to figure out what to do about my old friend Sara. Yes, there are other matters that demand my attention. More than I care to think about. This one, however, is urgent."

"We'll figure out what to do about her," Alicia corrected her husband. "Together. I want in on this one."

"Of course, my darling," Spencer replied, taking her hand and kissing it. "How could I ever deny you anything?"

Chapter Thirty-Three

I was a deep-sleeper even before brain-coring. Able to shut my hearing off now, I could sleep through Armageddon. It was almost ten before I awoke the next morning. It had been hard for me to fall asleep because I'd squatted for hours in the dark, legs locked and eyes closed tight. Instead of sleeping, I could only picture the horrible things I'd seen in the last few weeks, over and over and over again. When I managed to sleep, I'd gotten no rest. Instead, nightmares of my disabled brother begging to be bayoneted, Father's estate going up in a big mushroom cloud, and my tutor shitting blood and expecting Dracans to torture and kill while he lived.

Nightmares in my bailout-body wasn't the same as having them in my mannequin-body or even the real one I left so long ago I sometimes couldn't remember what it'd been like. I didn't toss and turn, didn't cry out, and didn't even wake in a cold sweat. Instead, my eyes opened in the cave-black darkness of my little cubicle. I'd phantom-sigh, re-close them, and in a few moments pick up the same horror show I'd just left without having missed a single gore-flecked moment.

I was in a foul mood when I woke for keeps. I frowned and took a moment to groom myself as best I could with a clumsy foot-disk before switching my ears on, trying to avoid reality a little bit longer. When I activated my hearing once again, I wished I'd done much sooner.

I heard voices outside. New ones I'd never heard before.

At once I stood at the door with my left microphone pressed hard up against the wood.

"...need Gonzales for Intelligence. He's reported the news for decades and knows everyone who's anyone."

"No," Spencer's voice replied, flat and cold. "Absolutely not."

"Why, Governor?" the first voice asked. "Please? I mean, you trust me enough to bring me here. I am most grateful for this. You don't accept my advice and won't tell me why." A long pause followed.

"Colonel Russell," Alicia said, "you are correct that we trust you. Today, we're trusting you with both our own lives and Churilla's future.

Spence and I have decided for the duration of this war, there are exactly three qualifications we expect in those admitted to the inner circles." She paused.

"Loyalty, loyalty, and loyalty," Spencer finished for her. I could easily picture his bucktoothed grin. "I bear no grudges against Gonzales, Colonel. None whatsoever. He's probably more competent than Annie Bergman. Alicia and I don't know Pietro as well as we know Annie and that's that. She can do the job, if not quite as well."

I frowned. There wasn't any reason for me to listen anymore. I swung my door open, making a little more noise than necessary in case my hosts wanted me not to see or hear something.

"Well," Alicia cried out as I rounded the corner into the main meeting room.

She rose to her feet. "Good morning, sunshine. We thought you'd never wake."

I smiled back. Morning was always my most awkward time of day. I didn't drink coffee, eat, shower, or do any of the other things ordinary people do to begin their days.

"Good morning, Mr. and Mrs. Wiston."

I saw a misshapen man wearing plain black coveralls. A dark slash of a mustache divided his face, and he looked as wide as he was tall. I looked at him and smiled. Both he and Spencer rose to their feet.

"Good morning, Thomas," the rabbit-man greeted me and smiled. "Thomas Longo, meet Colonel Gilbert Russell."

Wiston's smile faded some. "Colonel Russell once commanded my bodyguard, Thomas. He took a laser-bolt for me, when he was young. That's why he's a bit lopsided to this very day. It nearly killed him."

I started to extend a tripod-leg, but stopped when the Colonel's jaw dropped. "

You?" he said, eyes wide. "You are Thomas Longo?"

I blinked. "Last time I checked."

He closed his mouth and licked his lips. He noted the stained and slightly-charred Top Banana insignia still affixed to my brain-dome.

"I am honored." He spoke in an awed voice and stepped forward. He bowed to me. "Sir, I am at your disposal."

Not sure how to respond, I looked first at Alicia and then at Spencer for guidance.

Spencer finally rescued me. "Word's getting around, Thomas. About the troopships and the dreadnought, I mean. The five fighters too."

"I've never met a fighter-ace before," Russell said, straightening and extending his hand. Reflexively, I shook it.

"Everyone on the planet is talking about you, sir. Everyone. Do you realize that you've killed more Dracans than any man alive? Probably by a factor of a hundred or more?"

I would have blushed if I still could. "I…uh…"

A terrible suspicion dawned. I looked Spencer in the eyes. "You didn't tell everyone…"

He grinned. "You're a hero, son. I told you you'd be getting a medal. Today, your story is in every e-mail box on Churilla."

My jaw worked. I wasn't a hero. I was a…a…

"Come now," Alicia said, approaching me and wrapping her arm around me. "It won't be so bad."

She sighed and looked at the ground. "Times are very dark, Thomas. All people see is defeat, everywhere they look. People need heroes, especially at times like these. We'll be asking them to do hard things and make terrible sacrifices."

She gave my head a little squeeze. "You've been brave and successful as well. People will look at you and what you've done and find courage in their own hearts. They'll stand a little taller, and be a little prouder. Some, Thomas, will go to their deaths thinking of you and making you their example."

"We need you as a hero," Spencer added. "I'd have made you into one even if I had to lie through my teeth to do it. 'In war,' Napoleon said, 'the moral is to the physical as three is to one.' He was dead-right. I didn't have to lie, Thomas, because the truth serves us just fine. The honest-to-goodness truth is that you are a hero. A very brave young man indeed."

I shook my head. "That major yesterday morning," I said. "The one who ordered the private to kill him. He was a hero, not me, only no one will ever know."

"Maybe," Alicia answered, squeezing me again, "and maybe not. We're working on that."

"The bodies were gone when I got there," Spencer added. "The Dracans must have picked them up so the civilians wouldn't see. I got pictures of the bloodstains."

He picked up a little camera from the table. "As soon as it's safe, I'll spread them as well, along with what your report." His eyes narrowed. "Because you're a hero, Thomas, and because of who my wife and I are, folks will believe us."

I sighed. This was absurd beyond all reason. It went against everything I'd ever learned about how a person ought to live their life. I wasn't any better than anyone else. My accomplishments, such as they were, weren't anything that a million or more others might not have managed in similar circumstances.

Worse still, I'd done things better, more worthy men would have refused to do at all. I didn't want to be a hero. I wanted to get far away from this place, this planet, and this filthy, unholy war, as far as I possibly could. I wanted off by myself. Maybe in a few thousand years, I might forget what I'd seen and done. I could be happy again.

Maybe.

I looked at Alicia's hopeful oversized eyes and Spencer's equally oversized yet somehow harder ones. Lastly, I looked at Colonel Russell still smiling in obvious pleasure at having made my acquaintance. He'd once taken a laser-bolt for Spencer. I imagined the Wistons were about to ask far more of him for the sake of Churilla than he'd ever given before.

Had he really gained strength from my so-called example? Did the Wistons or anyone have the right to ask more of me than I'd already given? I had seen the Dracans. After I watched that unknown major yesterday, I felt the need to act. Any complaints would sound so petty, after he'd given his life.

A man like the colonel deserved the very best performance I could deliver, nothing less. "It was an honor serving with the Bananas. They deserve most of the credit, not me."

The colonel's eyes shone again. "They were heroes too," he declared. "All of them."

"Thomas," Alicia added a tear trailing down her cheek—she, at least, seemed to understand—"I'm certain they're very proud of you."

Chapter Thirty-Four

Alicia and Spencer were gengineered. It was obvious just from looking at them. It became more obvious when I watched them work, either individually or as a team.

By noon, they'd finished with Russell, who was to recruit first a small full-time security and counter-espionage group for the cave to be followed by an operational sabotage squad, and then an entire army. The Wistons seemed to know as much about creating a guerilla army out of nothing as Russell did, perhaps more. When they spoke, he listened, taking notes and nodding.

We took lunch with Vanessa Pooks, an attractive young woman who was an expert in improvised weaponry. I had to go through the whole introduction-thing again, and Ms. Pooks's eyes shone just like the colonel's had. The Dracans had killed her father at the Army-Navy game. She hated them all.

We spoke of extemporaneous explosives over our salads, and flame throwers while sipping coffee. Again, the Wistons experts on everything but the most trifling details of design and knew where to get everything.

"Fulminate of mercury will work if nothing else is available," Spencer offered at one point. "It'll cause corrosion, but in all honestly the slug-guns will probably be used for a short time, just until we can arrange for something better. Talk to Billy Anderson at his stinkyworks, no one else. I'll let him know you're coming. He can help with propellants too."

"No," Alicia interjected in a later conversation. "Plain dynamite is adequate for car bombs. There's no sense trying to get fancy. Modern explosives may be more deadly per pound and safer to handle, but you can stuff plenty of dynamite into a car. Besides, we can manufacture the stuff by the hundredweight in two weeks or less. Spence has already 'lost' most of a trainload of dynamite-makings in transit, so we're pretty much committed. A primitive car bomb now is worth ten high-tech ones later. The fragmentation effect does the killing anyway.

"Would you like a chocolate-chip cookie, dear? They're surprisingly delicious, considering they've been in a can for so long."

I found it amazing to watch. They never slowed down. Instead, they made snap decisions on obscure matters one after another like machines. These were fur-covered machines that smiled and laughed and were equipped with long ears and poofy tails and were head-over-heels in love with each other. It made my head hurt when they snuggled up close and settled on a thing that would cause the deaths of hundreds, maybe even thousands.

I wondered if Spence and Alicia had been in charge when the Dracans arrived, would Churilla have fallen so easily? Would it even have fallen at all? They were far more competent and resourceful leaders than Admiral Lutjens and probably more competent and resourceful than the admirals who'd died in the initial stadium attack as well.

Gilbert Russell and Vanessa Pooks were not fools and were powerful leader-figures in their own rights. Yet, they deferred to Alicia and Spence like obedient children to their parents, unquestioningly and without resentment.

What if everyone were gengineered, like the Wistons? What might humanity accomplish then?

When Vanessa left to sneak her way back to the railroad tracks for the train already arranged for her, the Wistons took a short break. Spence sat and read an old-fashioned leather-covered book, *The World Crisis, Volume Two* was its title. Meanwhile, Alicia sat and toyed with her electronic sketchpad. Having nothing else to do, I sat and looked over her shoulder. She didn't seem to mind.

I soon realized Alicia's sketching-style was as complex as her piano-work and as distinctive. Where most artists begin with rough outlines, Alicia at first drew what seemed to be dozens of random lines that made no sense whatsoever to me. Then a hand appeared, a leg, a foot, an arm. They weren't connected to anything. Instead, they were randomly scattered across the page. Then she drew in a torso and everything came together.

"The three monkeys," I whispered.

She smiled and moved her hand so I could see more clearly. "Yes, or the three Assistant Governors, more like."

She began drawing again. *See no oppression* the caption over the first monkey now read. Of course, the monkey looked a lot like Sara Fowler. *Hear no screams* the second monkey's caption read. *Speak no truths* read the third.

Alicia raised her tablet for her husband's inspection, The finished work looked it had taken a skilled artist weeks to produce. Yet Alicia had sketched the thing in fifteen minutes or so.

"What do you think, Spence?"

"Not bad," he allowed, looking up from his book and then setting it down with reluctance on the table. Break time was over. "For a first effort."

She sighed, then blanked her screen. I rather hoped she'd saved the drawing because I'd liked it very much.

"Spence, that woman is dangerous because she's competent, much as I hate to admit it. We've got to act."

The governor nodded. "She's already got relief efforts underway and making promises about jobs programs in the very near future. The Dracans have set up three free soup kitchens in downtown Churilla City, and are putting the homeless in the big mansions."

He frowned. "It's all meaningless, of course. The jobs programs will be slave labor while the ones who sign up for relief will eventually be liquidated as useless mouths. For now, while the war's still on, the Dracans are playing it smart. It's hard to gain popular support for a revolution against a government that's meting out what appears to be economic justice."

Alicia sighed. "It's the planet itself that's the root problem, you know. Not enough dry land. Not enough mineral resources. The population grew far too fast."

She shook her head. "The only reason this world was colonized in the first place was to create a base to protect the Nexus. The price is poverty, and, we'll pay that price forever. The underlying economic problems are insoluble, short of enforced birth control."

"That isn't going to stop Sara from making promises to the contrary," Spencer replied, his face grim. "Very popular promises indeed."

He sighed in resignation. "The real problem is her competence. She was popular in the barrios long before the Dracans arrived."

His face hardened. "She's got to go. That's long-term priority one."

Alicia nodded, satisfied. "We'll make it our first big operation, and we'll do it in a way the Dracans can't hide. Very public so we get the maximum possible mileage from it."

Spencer sighed. "I can't argue with you, dearest, though I'd very much like to."

Alicia tilted her head to one side. "Why is that? It's a perfectly legitimate assassination. She's a quisling. Anyone can see it."

"I..." He frowned. "I'd just rather start this affair with something other than killing a Churillan. That's all."

He sat in deep silence for a moment. "Maybe we can work this into something bigger. Still the first operation, but only part of it. I'll have to ponder on it."

He picked up his book again. "You keep at the artwork, won't you, honey? I'll forward that first one out on the 'net tomorrow. Sign it, if you would. That will let the people know we're alive and resisting. Meanwhile, I've have to do some serious thinking. I do my best thinking with a good book in my hands."

Chapter Thirty-Five

It was almost suppertime before anyone else arrived at the cave. This time, I thought I recognized the voice giving the password.

"Father Murton?" I asked before Alicia could reply.

Cursing my slow-moving electric legs, I strolled across the cave instead of running despite how much I wanted to. "Father Murton?"

"Thomas?" My tutor's voice was husky with emotion. "Oh thank God."

For an endless awkward moment, we faced each another in the little stone anteroom, wanting to hug but not quite able to figure out how. Father Murton solved the problem by simply taking my head in his arms and squeezing for all he was worth.

"Thank God," he repeated. "Until yesterday I thought you were dead."

"No," I answered. "Not quite." I looked up and met the priest's eyes. "Aren't you...supposed to be off-planet? I thought you were aboard the *Argus.*"

"No," Murton sighed. "How could I, when there were children left behind? I didn't say anything because heaven only knew you already had plenty on your mind without worrying about me." He grinned and released my head.

It was only then I realized others had arrived with him. Johnny Repp and the rest of my bio-support team or most of the team. Frank, the RN and general-helper-outer, was missing.

"Hi, guys," I said. I didn't want to ask about Frank. I'd heard far too much bad news to have false expectations.

"Hiya, Tommy," Johnny said. His grin was as wide as ever, but seemed subdued somehow. "Are we proud of you!" He looked over his shoulder, and the rest of the team nodded agreement.

He met my eyes, and the smile faded. "Frank was too, Tommy. He got killed in a bombing raid back at the base. Before he went, he asked us to tell you he was grateful to you for bagging those ships. If we ever met you again, that was. He was sure you were still alive, when the rest of us had pretty much given up hope."

I nodded again and bowed my head in respect. "I liked Frank. He stayed behind when he could have gone. Just like the rest of you."

"Part of those ships you killed belong to him," Father Murton said, his eyes cold and hard.

He turned to Spence and Alicia, who waited in silence along the back wall. "Thank you both for contacting us," he said, inclining his head. "We've brought everything we need. We're in full agreement with your terms. None of us are leaving for the duration. We know too much, and the risks are too high. Perhaps we can make ourselves useful in other ways, besides keeping Thomas in proper working order."

Spence nodded and smiled, stepping forward he extended his right hand in greeting. "Thank you for coming," he replied warmly, his eyes sweeping wide to include the entire team. "All of Churilla is grateful for your help. We're at your disposal."

"No, Governor," Johnny replied, removing his battered old fishing hat in a gesture of respect. "We are at yours."

"And how," added Jim Williamson, from the back. He was a micro-electrician specializing in servomotors, and a good one. "You're killing Dracans or, you will be soon enough."

Spencer smiled. "Excellent. Can we offer you dinner?"

"No," Johnny replied for everyone. "We ate in the boxcar."

He stepped across the floor and took me by the chin, examining my face and the readouts at the base of my throat. "We've got a lot of work to do. Thomas has been trapped in that escape capsule much too long already. The sooner we get to work, the sooner he'll have hands again."

He smiled at me. "Are you looking forward to having hands again, Thomas? "

I rolled my eyes at him. "I dream about them sometimes."

Johnny took off a backpack that appeared to be mostly full of tools. "Let's see if we remember how to do this. Governor, have you got a spare room we can use as a workshop?"

Chapter Thirty-Six

It was a tremendous break for me that my so much of my support team survived intact. Experienced cyborg techs didn't live on all planets. Especially cyborg techs who were trained in my fathers Esteppen techniques. The local medical people might have kept me alive, but even if they succeeded, they wouldn't have known how to keep my nerve-connections sufficiently healthy to be reconnected someday. I'd have remained a brain-core for life.

Johnny and his staff had brought me my walking-around body, as Father called it, the one that allowed me to feel at least somewhat like a human being part of the time. The government had insisted Doctor Layton be part of the program to verify getting brain-cored hadn't ruined my sense of humanity or anything like that.

At least I didn't have to worry about sitting through his "counseling" sessions anymore or have him telling me to do things I knew Father would never have asked of me. Layton had shipped out on the *Argus*, the sole member of the Skybolt team to do so.

"He believed his report on your mental state was absolutely essential to the security of the United Systems," Father Murton explained to me during the first day of enforced immobility.

My brain was still growing and developing and it didn't like all the tricks being played upon it. Between sometimes having a 'hopper for a body, sometimes a car, sometimes three legs, well... It was understandable enough.

I'd lived in the survival capsule for much longer than was healthy, and my brain had begun the process of rewiring itself for its new body. Now I had to be de-wired. While the process was painless, it was annoying and time-consuming in the extreme. I pressed my fully-restored and repaired lips together in frustration. I was trying to grasp a little block of plastic in my right hand and failing miserably. It was as well that Layton wasn't around. He always frowned and took long notes when I had body-trouble. It made an already bad situation worse.

"Steady, there," Murton urged as my fingers first brushed up against the block, then shoved it clean off of the improvised bedside table.

Father Murton had always been the one to work with me during the most frustrating times, either he did or the now-dead Frank. I let myself flop back on the mattress while the priest went fumbling after the dropped block. I hated being helpless.

"How did Frank die?" My tutor straightened up, toy in hand. "I mean…Did he suffer?"

My mentor looked away, and I knew he was debating whether or not to tell me the truth. At last he shook his head, shifted uncomfortably in his chair. and put the block down well outside of my reach.

"It was ugly, Thomas," he said. "Very ugly. I don't think it's right for me to tell you any more. You don't need to know nor does anyone else. Some things are better left not discussed."

I nodded slowly. "Father?"

"Yes?" he replied, leaning forward a little. He could always tell when something was especially important to me, even better than my real father could.

"I…" The words wouldn't come, now that I wanted to speak them. "I mean... I liked Frank. You know that."

The priest nodded.

I shook my head. "But…it's almost like it doesn't matter to me that he's died. In my heart, I mean. I feel so cold inside. Like, like…" I pressed my lips together again. "Almost like what Dr. Layton was afraid of. Like I'm not human inside anymore."

Father Murton closed his eyes and then re-opened them. "We haven't talked seriously since we've gotten back together. Not really. It's my fault, I suppose. You see…" A single tear crept down his cheek. "I've seen so much, Thomas. Given so many Last Rites. Bandaged so many, many wounded."

He frowned. "I know…I mean…Governor Wiston told me you walked out of the Pass."

"Yeah," I agreed, looking away. "I did."

"It must've been horrible. Before that, there was the battle. I've seen tapes, Thomas. They filmed the whole thing from a dozen different angles to study later. All the people shooting at you. It must have been awful."

He leaned forward again. "Do you need to talk about it?"

I knew in my heart it wasn't the battle. That had been nothing. I still felt bad sometimes about killing so many people. The truth was that the whole thing still felt to me like just another demonstration flight, a big video game in the sky. It was everything that happened afterwards that I didn't like to think about, the raft and Lieutenant Eaglish, Mendes and

Sergeant N'dukwe, the mass-suicides at the Kammhuber… How could I even begin?

I couldn't, I realized I couldn't talk to Father Murton, because as good and as loving and as willing he was, he hadn't been there. He hadn't listened to Eaglish call out for his wife, hadn't heard the wails of anguish as everyone had looked at their dosimeters and known that they were goners, hadn't had to see the animal come out in Gonzales when he'd gone seeking Dracans to torture. There was so much to tell I couldn't even find a place to begin.

Our lives had taken different paths over the past few weeks, so different I wasn't sure they could ever be brought back together. The ugliness I'd seen, I now understood, had frozen my heart. I'd been like a clean white towel soaking up vomit and now I was so full of filth I could never be made clean again. I was barely seventeen and already used and ruined. Better if I remained silent. Better if I went to my grave without smearing sour vomit on everyone around me. Some things should stay without discussion, and good people like Father Murton were better left unstained.

Once I'd been warm and sensitive. I couldn't mourn for Frank because I'd turned hard and cold inside. The war had reached inside me and ripped the very heart out of me. Someone I knew and liked was dead and had died wretchedly, and I couldn't make myself care. A wave of guilt crashed through me. It wasn't being a brain-core that made me inhuman, it was war itself.

Then Father Murton surprised me by speaking. I'd almost forgotten he was present. "It's called the thousand-yard stare. Combat veterans get it when they've seen too much. You've got one of the worst cases I've ever come across, Thomas. You had it just now. Even the Wistons noticed and they're worried. You seem to want to spend all of your time alone, brooding."

He smiled with knowing sadness. "It's not enough to get your body working again, Thomas. Not by half." I blinked and tried to interrupt, but Murton kept right going. "You've had a hard war already, son."

He reached out and took my half-functional hand. "I fear you have a still harder one ahead of you. A longer one, certainly."

Sighing, he shifted in his chair. "I've seen many things Thomas, many bad things. I know it won't be easy for you, but can't you at least try to tell me what it was like?"

I sighed and stared at the ceiling. I knew he was right. It might even help me feel better. Yet putting words to it all would hurt so much.

Like as falling off a horse had hurt me when my Father had taught me to hunt I reminded myself. Like it'd hurt when I'd cut my finger playing with the knife he'd given me. That hadn't stopped me playing with knives or riding horses. That was why my father had let me hurt myself in the first place, I suddenly understood. I was understanding all sorts of new things of late.

Did that mean I was growing up? If I was, shouldn't I act like it?

"I...I guess I never really thought much about dying before the battle," I began, laying my head back and closing my eyes. "I guess I was too young and stupid back then to be afraid."

Chapter Thirty-Seven

I spent a lot of time talking about what had happened to me over the next few days, as my tutor and I persuaded my reluctant brain that I only had two legs again. At first, I was afraid I was overloading him with ugliness. He grew pale and haggard, and sometimes tears crawled down his cheeks. At least it didn't hurt me as much as I had feared it would.

I felt more like a machine than ever in some ways replaying what I'd recorded without experiencing the associated emotions. Father Murton warned me that'd come later when I least expected it. Talking made me feel better.

I also quit having awful nightmares, but they didn't entirely go away. Everyone went out of their way to be nice to me. The governor personally wired up a bedside terminal for me with a mouse that operated directly off my tongue-nerve inputs. my support-crew helped him, but it was a nice thing for him to do as busy as he was.

Spence also sat down with me almost every day he was in the cave to talk about this and that. He knew a lot about history. Sometimes we talked about Ancient Earth and why peaceful, civilized people fought wars they would have preferred to avoid. Other days, we talked about Churilla. No one knew more about Churillan history than Spencer, except maybe his wife. They'd lived through all of it.

Alicia came every morning to visit, though she wasn't as chatty as her husband. Instead, she brought in her keyboard or sketchpad, and played or drew for me. I didn't like classical-style music very much, but she seemed not to mind. Instead she played New Orleans classics and lively ditties that I suspected she was composing on the spot. If so, I hoped she recorded them, because some of them were very good indeed. As much as I liked her music, it was her visual art that really drew me.

"I hear you were on a life raft," she'd begin, drawing a little oval and clicking the 'yellow' button to fill it in.

"No," I'd correct her. "I didn't start out on one. It belonged to another

Top Banana."

"Right," she agreed, blanking the screen and saving the raft for later. Then she drew a rough sketch of my survival-capsule body. "Is this how you floated?" she'd ask.

Pretty soon she'd created a whole comic-book panel-set of my adventures to date. I'd never seen a comic book drawn so beautifully. I learned every time I told my story it came easier. So, I didn't really mind. All in all, Spence and Alicia were wonderful people. Even better, they were interesting people, in the same way that Father's unusual life had made him an interesting person.

I learned more about art from sitting and talking to Alicia than I had in eleven years of school and more than I'd ever learn in any college. I absorbed all kinds of stuff from Spence about supply-and-demand, fixed resources, the cold equations of realpolitik, and the ins and outs of political power. No one else had ever explained realpolitik to me. I couldn't understand why not, when realpolitik explained so many other things about history and had killed so many people. The term was over three hundred years old.

Why didn't anyone ever talk about it? Was it because it was so ugly? Did they think they could somehow protect me from it? They couldn't even protect their own societies. Why hadn't I been told the truth?

By the end of the first week after I got my body back, I was able to totter about the room a little. I still fell down a lot. By the end of the second, I could manage without too much stumbling, though it still took me a lot longer than it did a normal person. I spent most of my time sitting now, instead of lying.

Once every day or so, Spence or Alicia would politely knock on my door and bring in a new gift from some Churillan I didn't know. "This certificate is signed by all the workers at my good friend Harvey Benford's stinkyworks," Spence would say, holding up a framed handwritten document. "They wish you a speedy recovery and want to thank you for what you've done for their homeland. Each of them took their lives in their hand to sign this. Each and every one."

I never knew how to properly respond to all the little gifts. Sometimes it was chocolate I couldn't eat, now worth more than its weight in gold on the black market. Other times it was flowers that had traveled too far and were wilted when they arrived. Always the gifts came with dozens, sometimes hundreds of well-wishing signatures on them.

I worried Spence and Alicia were taking a terrible risk by accepting the things. When I raised the subject, the governor laughed and explained that he'd be taking a bigger risk by appearing ungrateful. Besides, he had a pretty good security system in place. My only regret was that I couldn't send 'thank-you' notes. While sending e-mail was safe enough at our end, woe be to the Churillan caught with an individual note in their inbox. So we limited ourselves to mass-mailings.

Still, once I was up and walking halfway well, Spencer and Alicia began parading me in front of their associates again at every opportunity. They'd even come up with something resembling a uniform for me. I didn't like wearing it, since I wasn't really in the Navy. Father Murton assured me under these special circumstances it was all right. In fact, it was his personal lieutenant-commander's rank badges that were sewn onto the collar right next to my own stubbornly-stained Top Banana emblems. They also had me wear a whole chestful of ribbons, but they didn't mean anything anyway so I figured that was all right, too.

I was never involved in discussions in any substantive way, but whenever possible room was made for me at the table. "You're the face of the United Systems, Thomas," Father Murton explained to me one day after I'd sat through three hours of deadly-dull debate on whether to sabotage xylene production. Until that day, I'd never even heard of the stuff.

"You remind them that the fleet is coming back someday, and, when it does, there'll be a day of reckoning. You're the face of hope as well as the face of heroism. So the rabbits need you to help boost morale."

He sighed one of those sad ones. "Are you following the news?"

I nodded. "They're rounding up all the intellectuals."

"All that were stupid enough to turn themselves in," the priest agreed, shaking his head. "They're 'registering' all the doctors, all the lawyers, all the teachers. The ones they don't need won't come back from the registration centers. All the Dracans want left here is a population of sheep to man the stinkyworks and support their own fleet."

I frowned. "Sara Fowler's saying it's so scarce human resources can be reallocated fairly. So everyone can have a doctor, and so the rich won't have all the best teachers anymore."

"Don't believe it for a minute," Murton answered, shaking his head. "It's always the same thing, over and over and over again in history. This stunt has been pulled a thousand times before, by a thousand quislings like Fowler who are either duped into playing along or go willingly. Kill off the potential leaders, and the rest of the populace gives less trouble."

He shook his head. "Those who can will run to the barrios. God knows there's no place else to hide. Try and blend in. The Dracans will be expecting them to do exactly that. I can only wonder how many will make it, with Sara Fowler having so influential there."

I frowned at him. "The Wistons want to assassinate her. They discussed it the day you got here."

"I'm not surprised," my tutor replied, frowning and looking away. "They're not the only ones. Even before the invasion, I heard a lot of..."

He shook his head and sighed before meeting my eyes again. "Thomas, let's not discuss this assassination thing any further. I've already said enough Hail Mary's for one war. Don't tempt me into thinking more violent and sinful thoughts about that woman. Please?"

Chapter Thirty-Eight

It was all talk, talk, talk, I thought as the endless discussions continued. What industries to leave alone. How much to interfere with the rail system. How often to send out new propaganda. Talk, talk, talk from the moment I woke in the morning until I went to bed without a break. On bad days I thought boredom was more likely to kill me than the Dracans.

I wasn't the only one who fretted. Sandy Golden, the young lady Spencer had brought in to relieve him of most of his hacking duties, appeared to feel the same way I did. "All we ever do is plan," she complained to me one day as we waded down the little stream outside our hideout just before sunset. A big meeting had been cancelled due to the Dracans making unexpected railcar inspections, so we had a little time to kill.

"No one ever actually *does* anything to the Dracans," she said. "They're raping Churilla, while we sit and hold conferences."

"The planning's important," I countered, even though I didn't believe it. "We can't afford to make even one single mistake or the whole underground will collapse."

"I know." Sandy picked her way through the shallows.

With bare feet, she had to be careful. My feet were bare too, but it didn't matter if I stepped on something sharp.

Sandy wasn't all that much older than I was. However, she had an extraordinarily gift for computers, Spencer had explained upon her arrival. He'd known one of her professors, who spoke glowingly of her abilities. Her brother had died defending the Pass. Even better, because she had no formal certifications or professional history, she wouldn't be missed.

"It seems to me that we ought to do something."

I frowned. The fact was that Spence and Alicia wanted everything in place before doing anything spectacular. Building a successful insurgency wasn't a job accomplished overnight, Alicia was fond of saying. Besides, we hadn't been idle. A few car bombs exploded at

Dracan bases and a small quantity of food destined for a Dracan barracks had unsuccessfully been poisoned. Resistance fighters had died committing these acts, and the Dracans had shot innocent hostages in retaliation for the attempted poisoning. To date we hadn't done anything like the kind of things I knew we could. Instead, we sat and talked.

I kicked at a little underwater pebble. Despite the fact my foot wouldn't move very quickly anymore, the rock rolled several feet along the bottom just as it would if propelled by muscles instead of servomotors. I'd kicked it in the same direction the current was flowing, creating an illusion of normalcy.

"Easy," Sandy cautioned, grabbing my arm. "Be careful of your gyros." Father Murton had warned her about my stability problems.

I sighed and shook my head. "It's all right. They're not that delicate.""

It felt *good* to have Sandy clinging to my arm, even if she was a little on the pudgy and nerdy side. With my clunky, grotesque artificial body, after all, I was hardly a prize myself.

She smiled and gripped tighter. "We can't afford to take any chances. "I'm supposed to be watching you."

"You're doing a good job of it," Spencer said as we rounded a large bush.

He was fly-fishing, taking a little R and R of his own. It was difficult to be alone at rebel headquarters even out-of-doors. There were too many of us living in too little space, and the situation would grow much worse before it got better. My entire support team, for example, shared a single room.

"Hi, Sandy. How are you, Thomas?"

Sandy colored, but still not release my arm. "Hello, Governor." She made a little curtsey.

All the Churllans did that with Spence and Alicia, even their closest friends, though the rabbits asked them not to. I supposed people from Earth might feel the same way about Simon Bolivar or George Washington if they were still alive. It still felt sort of strange to be around.

Spence paused in his casting and smiled. "I'm glad to see you two getting a little sun. You spend far too much time working, Sandra. I fear that I keep Thomas fully occupied as well."

Sandy shook her head. "I have to keep working, otherwise, the Dracans will catch up. Sadly, they're not stupid, though they're not as bright as they think they are. At least, their programmers aren't. I've cracked a lot more of their stuff than they have of ours."

Spence nodded. "They depend too heavily on training and not

enough on individuality. Their system produces few outstanding talents."

He inclined his head towards my companion. "For example, they might have sent you to a civil engineering school instead of a programming college, if they'd needed civil engineers that year. They'd have expected you to master the one as easily as the other. On paper the skills are similar. Math, logic, reasoning. If you can design software, you can design highways. Right?"

My companion blinked. "But..."

Spence laughed and false-casted several times before plopping his fly directly in the center of a little pool I knew was full of panfish. "That's the problem with a planned economy. The reality seen by the faceless government officials with quotas to meet never quite matches the truth of things. Potential is wasted, both human and otherwise, because it's not the right potential to forward said official's career. Someone who needs a civil engineer will *make* one, even if they have to throw away a budding genius in another field along the way. The same principle goes for everything from shoe production to spacecraft design. Initiative is trampled, materials mismanaged, and wealth squandered. Yet, it all looks so good on paper."

Suddenly, Spence's line went taut and his long, limber rod bent almost double. "Got one, by god." The fish didn't seem like much when Spence raised it proudly for us to look at, but it seemed important to him.

"Fish," he declared proudly. "This biome successfully produces fish. It's so wonderful. When we first landed, we found nothing but bare rock and slime around the shores. We thought we'd never keep the insects going. It took eleventy-six tries before we managed." He raised his catch again. "And now, fish."

Sandy smiled and nodded. "We were almost ready to release seagulls when the Dracans came." She examined the little goggle-eyed creature closely. "In five years or so. Our very first birds. They'd have been so beautiful."

"They will be beautiful," Spencer observed, nodding approvingly as I first wetted my hand and then gently de-hooked the little rock-bass. I'd learned how to properly handle fresh-caught fish back on Earth. It wasn't a common skill on Churilla. "We'll still release them in five years or so. Promise."

Sandy looked up, startled. "But the Dracans..."

"Will be long gone by then," the big rabbit said as I lowered his catch back into the water and allowed it to dart back into its pool, essentially undamaged. "They'll be gone, or we'll have lost this war and with it everything we ever worked for. We can never keep an organization this large and sophisticated secret that long. We've not a day to waste."

Then he turned to me. "Tell me, Thomas. Are you ready to take a little trip?"

I blinked. The governor and Alicia had left the cave several times each. Sometimes for days at a time. Certain things they insisted they had to do in person, despite the risk.

"I… I mean, why?"

He clapped his arm on my shoulder. "To see someone, of course. Someone very important, who's even less able to move about than we are. He wants to meet both of us. Father Murton is invited as well. How does tomorrow morning sound?"

I blinked again. The travel arrangements were already made. I looked at Sandy and then at Wiston. "Fine," I spluttered.

"Excellent." He broke his fishing gear into several compact pieces and stowed them in an improbably tiny bag. "I'm looking forward to it. We leave at four in the morning."

Chapter Thirty-Nine

We left at precisely four. It felt a little odd, splashing my way so far down the stream and back across the tiny meadow to where a freight train was already slowing to allow us to board. I hadn't been so far from our hideout since I couldn't remember when. I'd last traveled the route as a survival pod. Everything looked different now that I was so much taller. My head now extended far beyond most of the bush tops. I felt as if I could be seen for miles. Not that it mattered so much now. Snipers armed with precision long-range blaster-rifles covered each end of our little ravine at all times.

"Come," Wiston urged me as we dashed for the train. There could be no doubt part of the governor's genome was derived from lapinate stock. I'd never seen anyone move more naturally or effortlessly through thick vegetation. Father Murton and I were hard-pressed to keep pace, especially me with my slow-moving limbs. We were to ride in the third boxcar from the end. Sure enough, its door slid open just as Wiston bounded up alongside.

"Come on," he urged me again. "We have less than a minute."

I nodded, then lowered my head and moved just as fast as I possibly could. Which still wasn't fast. Even Spencer could only do so much with the railroad software before the monitoring systems the Dracans had added began to notice. His jiggery was growing more difficult all of the time, though he remained confident he'd never be shut out of the system altogether.

"They'd have to replace the entire system from the bottom up," he explained to me once. "That's not damned likely to happen. I, more than anyone, know just how expensive and inconvenient that would be."

The door nearly closed on Father Murton when the train lurched into motion with a nasty crunching sound. I'd ridden on passenger trains before, and they hadn't raised nearly so much of a ruckus. My guess was that human freight complained more about such things than foodstuffs, chemicals, and the like.

"Well," Spencer declared cheerily as we all three turned on our handlights. As before, windows were scarce on boxcars, and interior light fixtures rare.

"We're on our way. So make yourselves comfortable. We're riding for a lot of hours."

"Where are we going?" I asked. Up until now, our destination had been a secret even from us.

"Churilla City," Spence answered as he opened his computer. "A little Italian restaurant down in the barrios. Called 'Mama's' of all things."

My tutor's eyes lit up. "I haven't had any fettuccini in months, Governor. How thoughtful of you."

"Hehe," Spence replied, looking up and chuckling. He genuinely liked Father Murton, which flattered the priest and made me feel good inside, too. "I'll see you get some, if it's still on the menu. Not that I expect it will be, what with all the shortages."

His eyes narrowed. "It so happens Mama's is located in one of the oldest parts of Churilla City. Only two blocks from the First Landing site." He smiled again. "Back then, we used to drill tunnels to store stuff. It was quicker and easier than ordinary construction. Mama's basement hooks up to one of those tunnels. The other end of the tunnel connects to the Gambian Embassy. No one ever thinks much about those tunnels anymore. Most have been filled in, but not this one."

Murton blinked. "The Gambians are neutral."

"Yep," Spencer answered, taking off his shirt and making a pillow of it. "They are, on paper, at least. Their sympathies lie heavily with our side. If the United Systems collapsed, what would become of weak frontier worlds like theirs? I rather suspect they remain neutral only because London's asked them to. They're more useful that way."

He yawned, closed his databook, and switched off his handlight. "I've changed my mind. I'm not going to try and do any work after all. Instead, I'll catch a nap."

He stretched luxuriantly, causing little ripples of fur to rise up here and there on his body. "Wake me up in two hours, won't you?" He lay down and almost instantly slept as if he hadn't a care in the universe.

Chapter Forty

Neither my tutor nor myself were self-disciplined enough to fall asleep so easily, though it might have been better if we had been. There were few more boring ways to spend a morning than sealed into a boxcar. For a while, I wandered around the car and checked things out. The car was half-loaded with foodstuffs, including olive oil, pasta noodles, and case after case of tomato paste. Three empty crates, the big expensive returnable kind, sat there. These had brand-new shipping labels on them, dated yesterday. They were easily big enough to hide a man. I suspected they were how we were supposed to get from the railway station to the restaurant.

My best discovery was a small gap in the boxcar's door-seal at just the right height to allow me to see outside. I hadn't ridden in a vehicle in so long the experience was strange and new again. I smiled in delight as the barren hills and scattered buildings rolled past.

We came to a place where a lot of army trucks were parked in a row and gas-masked men under Dracan guard threw what appeared to be bundles of rags into a deep trench. The rags matched the clothes the workmen were wore. I must be looking at was a mass-burial, probably of men and women killed by neutron weapons at the Kammhuber. The wind changed and, judging by my tutor's gagging, the most unbearable of all stinks filled the railcar. Spencer slept through it all just fine, but Father Murton almost vomited. He would have except he realized it would give us away when the time came to unload the car. I'd never seen such a stiff upper lip on anyone before.

We passed more buildings and then row after endless row of greenhouses, many patched from where I'd broken their glass panels with a sonic boom while demonstrating the Skybolt. That seemed *so* long ago.

"It's time," Father Murton interrupted me as the greenhouses were giving way to Churilla City proper. "Would you mind waking our friend? I'm still feeling a little weak."

I nodded and smiled. Father Murton looked a tad green around the gills, all right. I shook Wiston's shoulder.

In an instant his hand was on his old revolver. "Eh?" he demanded, his voice high and querulous like the anciently-old man he truly was. So fast one could almost imagine things had never been any other way, he smiled and stretched.

"Thanks, Thomas." He glanced at his datapad. "We've half an hour to go. Perfect."

"There's a little gap by the door," I said. "You can see out just fine."

"Indeed?" the rabbit asked, his eyebrows rising. He reached for his computer. "The gasket must be bad. I'll make a note of it in the maintenance log."

"But..." I sighed and turned back to my private window. If Spencer didn't want to look around, that was his business. Me, I didn't want to miss a thing.

Churilla City had changed a lot since the Dracans had come. Much remained the same on the surface. All sorts of little things stood out like a misplaced Skybolt. Most of the corner markets were shuttered, and long lines led to the open ones. Sidewalks once crowded with skateboarders, cyclists, and old men sitting in the shade playing chess were nearly barren. Cyclescoot traffic was a fraction of what it had been. Even more noticeable, no one smiled. Churilla City, despite its poverty, had once been perhaps the happiest place I'd ever known.

As I was mulling this over, the tracks swung us left and out over a large river, the same one, I realized I'd once thrown a twenty-credit gold piece into for a boy to dive after. The road bridge ran parallel to the train trestle, perhaps fifty feet away. No daring, swim suited boys my age were anywhere to be seen. It was eerie. Churilla City was the same physical place, but so different in character.

We crossed the river and ran alongside a wasteland. I should've been looking out over the naval airbase, but there was nothing to be seen. Nothing at all, save for a large black crater in the ground that looked big enough to swallow a dreadnought.

"It's all gone." I whispered in awe. "Where the fighters were based, I mean. The hardstands, the hangers, the administrative buildings...All of it, blasted flat to leave a humongous hole. Wow!"

"That's where they scuttled the fleet's molecular battery stockpile," Wiston explained, eyeing the box he was about to climb into with distaste. "So the Dracans wouldn't get them. They didn't want to blow them up, because it would have taken out the whole city and more. Instead they just hooked up a spiderweb of heavy cables and shorted them, the whole pile at once. They say it was some sight. Things got so hot the radiant effect started fires a mile away. The reason there's a hole there now is because the slagheap penetrated so deep down. When the bedrock solidified again, it took up less space."

He shook his head. "I wish we'd gotten hold of some of those batteries. Everything we're using came from local commercial sources. Good, yes, but not nearly so good as milspec. The Dracans are collecting everything they can and monopolizing what little domestic production exists."

Everything ran on molecular batteries. "Maybe you can steal a railcar full of them?"

"Not with the Dracans watching, I can't." He frowned and his nose wriggled. "Well . Yes, to be honest, I could steal us some that way, but it would be waving a red flag in front of a bull. The Dracans would get all excited, and do things I don't want them to do. So, I'll settle for the commercial units, and only steal stuff that they either can't use or don't know ever existed." His grin widened. "For now."

The train's brakes squealed suddenly, and we began to slow down. Spencer glanced down at his datapad again. "Well," he said slowly, pressing his lips together. "I'm not looking forward to it any more than the rest of you are, but it's about that time. Boxes, everyone."

Chapter Forty-One

It probably wouldn't have mattered if we hadn't made it into our boxes in time. Three of the four day-laborers sent to pick up today's delivery for Mama's were members of Spence's personal bodyguard. If I'd been able to see them, I'd likely have recognized them. The fourth was a local Resistance cell leader. She hadn't a clue as to what was in the boxes, only that it was terribly valuable.

So I didn't worry too much when I heard the boxcar's door slide open, and felt a hand-truck's blade slide under my container. It was hot and cramped in the little box, though I was certain I suffered far less than anyone else. The trip was probably worse for Father Murton with his aged and slightly-arthritic joints.

Spencer, I knew, was as lithe and flexible as a real rabbit, and, except for the heat, probably didn't mind the experience at all. It was disturbing all the stuff that Spence and Alicia and I could do that no one else could. It was illegal to gengineer people anymore or to 'borg' them except under very special circumstances. Yet, we modified people were the ones who always were able to function and keep on fighting back when things went bad.

I was thinking about that when my hand-truck pusher swung hard-left in a stomach-wrenching maneuver, and everything went dark. There weren't any holes in my travel-box, but the plastic lid was thin enough to allow the sunlight in. Now I was as much in the dark as I'd had been in the boxcar, and it was equally unpleasant. However, I felt a distinct "thump-thump" as my hand-truck's wheels rolled onto an elevator. It was a slow and noisy elevator, too. Not that I got to find out right away. Box after box was loaded on with us.

At least we received good treatment in the restaurant basement. Someone gave my container two reassuring taps, the prearranged "Don't worry, all is well" signal. Then I was rolled down a seemingly endless corridor, one filled with cool air like the headquarters tunnel where I now lived. At last someone removed my lid, and I rather awkwardly straightened myself. I wasn't cramped. One must have actual muscles in order to be cramped. I'd long-since learned much of the awkwardness of arising after being folded up for a long time is mental. I still had to deal with that part of the equation.

"Well," Spencer greeted me, stepping rapidly across the little room to take my arm. He had to plow through several rather important-looking individuals wearing tuxedos along the way, but he didn't let that slow him down in the slightest. His container had arrived first, probably by pure happenstance.

We were in some kind of basement or other room-shaped excavation, but a very large and nicely furnished one. I saw a long conference-table made of expensive hardwood and surrounded by chairs with cushions on them. I hadn't seen such a chair since I'd visited the Top Banana's ready room and been initiated. More soft chairs were scattered about here and there in little groups. At one end of the table someone had erected a little stage, complete with backdrop curtain and theatrical lights. I wondered what it was for, but before I could ask a third container was wheeled in. "I'll help him," I told Spence.

"Right," he agreed, smiling and nodding.

Then he was off circulating among the dignitaries again, his battered coveralls and oversized revolver every bit as much out-of-place as his tail and ears. Yet it didn't seem to matter. Everyone seemed pleased to see Spence. Everyone. The men slapped him on the back, the women hugged him, even the obvious security-types sought out the chance to shake his hand and wish him well. Alicia excepted, I'd never seen anyone so well-loved in all my life.

As expected, Father Murton was indeed suffering from cramps as the result of his long doubled-up voyage. Our hosts allowed me to help him partway out of the box, but then three medical types zoomed in and somehow managed to take him out of my arms while at the same time remaining respectful and non-threatening.

"Let us help him, Commander," one of them urged. At first I didn't understand because back at headquarters no one ever called me that. I was wearing my lieutenant-commander's uniform because both Spence and Father Murton had insisted. I was also bedecked with my chestful of fake ribbons. So, instead of protesting I simply nodded.

"You'll be fine in a few minutes, Father," I said reassuringly. He was wincing and clutching at his thigh, plus his face was very red. He tried to speak, but, after meeting the attendant's eyes, I cut him off. "These guys will take care of you."

"Damn right we will," the leader of the medical team declared. "Come over here, Father, and sit down. We'll give you a muscle-relaxant. With any luck, it'll still be working for the trip back."

Spence was the only other person I knew in the bustling crowd besides Father Murton, and I felt very lost. Everyone stared at me, but the governor, as usual, had all the leadership-types wrapped up in a little knot around him. Moving carefully so as not to tumble my gyros, I sort of wormed my way in to where he could see me.

"...have weapons, " Spence was explaining. "We have strong ties with the common people. What we require, gentlemen, is support. We'll kill Dracans, believe you me. We'll kill them in numbers that the faint-of-heart peacenik crowd will find appalling, and via means that will give the survivors nightmares for the rest of their lives. We Churillans have no love of the bastards, most of us, and it's becoming more and more unanimous every day. What we need, Harvey, isn't an aid package."

His eyes went cold. "What we need is a fleet and 'hoppers and an army to drive them out. That, I fear, we cannot manage on our own."

There was a little buzz of conversation after that. When it died down Spence noticed me. "Well," he said again. "How's your teacher?"

"H-he'll be fine." I stuttered a little when I was nervous. After five years of speech therapy and a whole new body, I still had trouble sometimes. "I-I-It's just a cramp."

Spence smiled, then reached over and wrapped his arm around my shoulders. "Gentlemen," he said. "You all know who this is, but let me make it official. Meet Lieutenant-Commander Thomas Longo, late of the Top Banana squadron."

Suddenly a forest of hands were extended towards me. I shook them all, trying to keep track of who was who. The Gambian Ambassador was there, his assistant, various military attaches. I didn't know any of them from Adam, though they all were very nice and polite to me.

Then, someone vaguely familiar loomed in front of me. "I'm Charles Wrangell," he explained, his grin splitting his dark, African face. "Formerly charge de affaires at the United Systems embassy, now wanted war-criminal hiding out here. Fortunately, the Gambians have been most accommodating. Helpful, even." His smile faded as his eyes bored deep into mine. "We met at Commander Knight's place, though for you I was just a face in the crowd. We were never formally introduced."

I nodded and smiled. "I do tend to stand out more than most," I agreed, looking down. "Though I sort of remember you."

Wrangell's smile returned. "I assure you, Thomas, I will never, ever forget having met you. It'll remain forever one of the great events of my life."

Then Father Murton came looming up behind me. "Ahem." He

cleared his throat.

“Right,” Spence agreed with a decisive nod. He looked at the Ambassador and raised his eyebrows.

“Yes,” he agreed. “Of course. The time of many of our guests is very valuable indeed.” He raised his voice. “Everyone,” he shouted, “please, take your seats, and let’s get down to business.”

Chapter Forty-Two

It was almost like the dinner at Commander Knight's all over again in some ways. There were names at every seat. Father Murton and I had to look all over the place before we found ours. We weren't to be seated at the main table, it seemed. Rather, we found our name-cards at a little table off to one side, near the stage. I was glad, really. Part of me wanted to sit near Spence so that I could learn about things. He was stationed to the left of the Gambian Ambassador.

That's odd, I thought. Once we were settled, I asked Father Murton about it. We had the table all to ourselves. This was a terrible waste. It was easily big enough for six.

"Shouldn't Spence be seated to the ambassador's right? The seating is all messed up. The way things are, we're the ones to the ambassador's right. I'd have sworn that as chief of state of the host planet, he ought to be in the place of honor. Or, aren't they recognizing his government-in-exile?"

"Oh, they're recognizing it all right," my tutor replied, sipping gratefully at the provided ice-water.

He still rubbed at his thigh sometimes, and looked as though he could really use the drink. Then he sighed and set the glass down.

"Thomas," he began, "I know why we're here today, and I approve heartily. I agreed with Spence to keep it a secret from you. Right up until—"

"Ahem," the ambassador said, cutting off my teacher. Then he tapped his spoon on his water glass, producing a rich, pure tone that cut off all conversation. "Ahem."

Next, the stage-lights went on. I looked at Father Murton again, but he just half-smiled and shrugged.

Once the room was silent, the ambassador stood and began to speak. "Ladies and gentlemen, friends of freedom all. Thank you for honoring both the Free Republic of Gambia and myself personally with your presence."

He smiled. “For obvious reasons, this part of our proceedings isn’t being filmed. There can be no record of Gambian abuse of diplomatic privilege. However, let there be no doubt that the Republic and her people are foursquare behind you. We too believe in freedom.”

I nodded as the others applauded. A small, lightly populated world such as Gambia might indeed be more useful to the United Systems as a neutral party than actively at war.

“That said,” the ambassador continued, turning towards Spencer, “let’s get on with business.”

There were three steps leading up to the little podium. My elderly friend seemed almost to fly up them. Mr. Wrangell ascended more slowly. Once they were in place, a little red light went on and, presumably, the cameras were rolling.

“By the extraordinary powers invested in me by the Parliament of the United Systems I, Charles Wrangell, do hereby recognize the Free Government of the People of Churilla. Further, I also do hereby recognize former governor and now President Spencer Wiston as the legal chief-executive of said government, pending free elections to be held at the cessation of hostilities. We also hereby recognize Mrs. Alicia Wiston as Vice-President.”

He turned to Spencer. “May the day come soon, Mr. President, that Churilla is free once again.”

Spencer bowed deeply. “Thank you, Mr. Wrangell,” he intoned in the deep voice he only used on occasions of state.

He turned to the camera. “I hereby recognize and maintain six of the seven duly-elected United Systems Parliamentarians of the Churillan delegation for the duration of hostilities. The seventh seat, once held by Delegation Leader Duncan Wilde, is open because of Parliamentarian Wilde’s untimely death while vacationing in the Hawaiian Islands. I hereby extend my sympathies to my good friend Duncan’s next of kin. A decision regarding the filling of the Delegation Leader’s seat will be made in due course.”

I gulped. The big naval base on Hawaii had been H-bombed wlth a smuggled weapon. Millions had died. How sad that, even so far from home, a Churillan had been killed by Dracans.

Then Spencer stared at the camera. “Today, Churilla is overrun. We’re a planet under occupation, ground under a hostile boot, and cut off from all aid. To my fellow Churillans, I swear that I shall do everything in my power to throw off the Dracan’s collar of slavery.

“It’s going to be a nasty, ugly fight. More Churillans shall die than Dracans, regrettably. In the end our victory is assured, for no oppressor has ever in all of human history been able to conquer a people whose hearts were steeled to resist. Never. I assure you, shall Churilla be the first.

"We fight from a position of strength, the strength of righteous anger. We have been burned with nuclear fire, yet our anger and defiance glow far hotter than any Dracan fireball. So long as we remain proud and hopeful, our hearts shall remain free. So long as our hearts remain free, the Dracans have conquered nothing. "

Spencer wriggled his nose before continuing. "To our friends and allies in the United Systems, I send this message. Your brothers and sisters are dying every day on Churilla, falling in the name of freedom for us all. We ask that you remain unbowed, as we remain unbowed. We ask that you make sacrifices, as we are making sacrifices.

Above all, we ask that you put aside petty politics, as we have united in the face of this greatest crisis our planet has ever faced." He looked directly at the camera. "I am, obviously, a gengineered being. So is my wife, who could not be here with me today. Yet between us we've been elected to high Churillan office not once but many times.

"We are visibly different, yet in the face of the difficulties of taming a new world my friends and neighbors were willing to put differences aside for the good of all. Once again, I challenge the rest of you to do what Churilla is already doing—genuinely uniting against the Dracan threat."

He smiled and blanked his datapad. "Thank you, in the name of the suffering population of Churilla."

Much applause followed and then a standing ovation. Even though my mannequin-hands didn't move fast enough to make any sound, I did my best. I'd have been weeping if my eyes still did that sort of thing. The line about our anger burning brighter than any Dracan fireball especially touched me.

Only a few weeks back I thought I'd had enough of killing. Now, having just listened to Spence's speech, I'd neutron-bomb a Dracan position in a New York minute with a smile on my face, at that.

Trying to clap with a mannequin-body took a lot of attention I had to watch my hands and concentrate on the motions instead of what was happening on the stage, even though it was less than five feet away. So, I was a little startled when Mr. Wrangell began speaking again. I hadn't even noticed him ascending the podium.

"Thank you, Mr. President. It's a genuine honor to have you here. Now, however, we will move on to our second item of business, the primary reason we have gathered here."

I looked up and blinked. He stared straight at me.

"Courage in time of war is fairly commonplace," Wrangell said, still looking at me. "Men hold their positions until killed. Other men make assault after assault while knowing most of the ones who attacked before them lie dead, covering the ground like leaves. Commonplace courage is noble enough.

Because of commonplace courage veterans are honored and soldiers held in high social esteem. Sometimes, courage goes beyond the commonplace, and men on the battlefield achieve truly extraordinary things."

He smiled at me. "No one, not even a Dracan, could ever claim that the accomplishments of Lieutenant-Commander Thomas Longo on the occasion of the Battle of the Orion Nexus were anything less than extraordinary."

My mouth dangled open. I shut it and turned to Father Murton. "But ... But...But..." I whispered.

"Shush," he ordered, using the same tone he'd employed when I'd been six years old and wanted to talk in church. My mouth opened again, then automatically closed.

"...after volunteering to fly an unbriefed mission with an unproven aerospace fighter..."

"The Skybolt was *not* unproven," I protested. "Father spent years—"

"Hush," Murton ordered, even more firmly than before.

"...shot down no less than five enemy aerospacecraft, making him the first ace of the war. One of these enemy fighters was on the verge of shooting down a squadron-mate, thus, Commander Longo saved his life. This was only the beginning."

"It was a lucky shot," I hissed. "Four of them were just taking off. It wasn't even close to a fair."

"Damnit to hell, " Murton growled, and once again I shut up. When my tutor began using foul language, I knew that I was about to get into really serious trouble, like being grounded.

"....then, as I'm sure everyone present knows, he went on to destroy not only two fully-loaded troopships of the *Grappler*-class, but the brand-new dreadnought *Imperial Throne* as well."

I tried to protest again. I'd had help with the *Throne*, but one look at Murton's hard eyes kept me silent.

"...total casualties may well exceed ten thousand. Even more important, however, is the fact that these unexpected losses are believed to have upset the entire Dracan strategic timetable. By himself, Thomas Longo struck a blow that was felt all the way back to Drakkus and by the Emperor himself."

He smiled at me again. "Thomas Longo, please approach the podium."

My uniform wasn't real Anyone could tell it was a fake if they looked closely enough. It was stained and wrinkled from my having folded myself up in a box for so long. I wasn't really a lieutenant-commander, either. Why on earth no one had told Mr. Wrangell, I couldn't imagine. I froze for a long second, and then Father Murton elbowed me.

"I knew this would happen," he said. "I knew it. That's why we didn't warn you. Now, get up there and do what's got to be done."

I concentrated on how a hero was supposed to help make others strong. I slid my chair back, and everyone applauded again, even harder than they had for Spence.

Soon I stood next to Mr. Wrangell on the little dais. Everyone stood and applauded more.

"God bless you, Thomas," a woman's voice cried out.

"Thank you, in the name of my dead son," another shouted.

Wrangell read something. Though my ears self-tested fine, I couldn't understand a word. Not until he reached the end when he said "...do hereby award you the United Systems Parliamentary Medal of Merit."

He held up a little gold medal on a red and green ribbon decorated with little white stars. I expected him to pin it on me, but instead he held it in the air. "Presenting the award will be Commander Lofton Knight, himself a holder of this highest award for bravery and the former leader of the Top Banana squadron. Assisting Commander Knight will be his son, Lieutenant Theodore Knight, also of the Top Banana squadron. He's the fighter pilot Commander Longo saved."

My mouth fell open again as a door opened in the back of the room. Then two figures moved forward, both dressed in snowy Navy whites.

One of them sat in a wheelchair.

The room went dead silent as Ted pushed the sad remains of his father up the aisle. He was missing both legs above the knee and his left arm at the elbow, plus the lower part of his face was a featureless mound of scar tissue. A round hole there must be a feeding orifice. It couldn't be called a mouth. Someone had rigged a starched napkin to catch the continual flow of drool.

For an instant I had to turn away. Then, I recalled what *I* looked like under the mannequin body. Knight had suffered these wounds fighting for me. If he was strong enough to suffer the wounds, then I could be strong enough to look at them.

"Unh," the elder Knight said as his son wheeled him in front of me. He waved his one good arm. "Unh."

"Hello, Thomas," Ted greeted me, smiling. It wasn't until he stood next to me that I realized he'd been severely wounded too. One of his eyes didn't quite match the other and didn't move when its partner did.

The skin around looked all pink. Only half his face smiled. The rest hung limp.

"My father has asked me to speak for him."

"Unh," the elder Knight agreed.

"He wants me to tell you and everyone else that he's as proud of you as he is of any pilot he's ever had the pleasure of commanding. He also wants you to know the greatest moment of his life was watching the *Imperial Throne* go up in a billion pieces. I'll add that I'm grateful to you for saving my life. If it hadn't been for one of the finest displays of marksmanship I've ever seen, that Dracan would have had me for sure." His single good eye met mine. "Dad's also asked me to inform you that he's pleased with your recent promotion, and approves heartily."

I shifted uneasily and opened my mouth again, but before I could say anything Commander Knight had reached out with his one good arm and pinned the medal to my chest. Was the whole world in on not letting me speak my piece?

Everyone stood and applauded again. Ted finished closing the back of the pin, and his father sat with his arm wrapped around my waist, grunting approvingly.

"B-b-but," I objected. "B-b-but—"

The applause drowned me out. It went on and on and on while cameras rolled.

I gave up. It didn't matter what I had to say anyway.

Chapter Forty-Three

Five long hours later we again sat in a boxcar, waiting out the long, slow ride home. No one talked much. We all seemed to have a lot to think about. I did.

The ceremony hadn't ended with the Medal of Merit. Not by half. Once that had been pinned on me, a veritable avalanche of medals, gifts and awards had come showering me. The District of Japan sent me a rank insignia once worn by someone named Admiral Togo. I wasn't sure who he was, but it had come with a special letter from the Admiralty authorizing me to wear it in place of one of the usual rank-emblems.

The District of Southern Africa presented me with a beautifully hand-crafted and engraved spear-thingie called an assegai, along with an actual, real lion-skin. These remained on Earth because it would've been too difficult to get them to me via diplomatic bag. The holos looked very nice.

The Italians had also given me something that wouldn't fit into a diplomatic bag, a small estate in the Alps. Tons of other stuff, like a white kepi and a big medal from the District of France, a big red star-medal from the District of Russia, and another one very much like it from the District of China followed. It had gone on and on and on, as if the various government entities had competed to see who could out-do the other. They had. The cameras never stopped rolling for a second, so I stood and did what I thought needed to be done, standing as tall as I could and trying to look grateful.

Most of the gifts and medals sort of passed over my head in a blur. I couldn't possibly have remembered them all. Two of them, however, stuck in my memory. One of them was from Spence. He came on stage and gave me an acorn.

"That's a Founder's Acorn," he explained in his penetrating 'public' voice, "from the Founder's Tree, growing not far from my home. It's not much, really. Churilla has little to offer. Our planet is rich only in culture and tradition. By one of these traditions, however, only Founders are buried in the cemetery shaded by the Founder's Tree.

"There's more than one kind of Founder, however. Most are, like my wife and I, individuals who arrived on the first voyage of the *Morning Star*. There's nothing particularly special about us. Most of those would be shocked to see how fondly they're remembered today." He smiled.

"There's another kind of Founder as well. By tradition, a person who has served Churilla in a truly exemplary fashion may also be declared a Founder. The decision is made by consensus of all surviving Founders and is symbolized by an acorn from the Founder's Tree."

Wiston's smile faded. "You are now a Founder of Churilla, Thomas Longo, every bit as much as I am. I very much hope that someday you will choose our planet as your final resting place. In any event, you will never, ever be forgotten here."

Everyone stood and applauded then, and as usual I didn't have the slightest clue as to what to say. So I just stared down at my acorn and smiled my dopey, dumb-looking smile and waited for everyone to stop clapping.

Right after the governor, or president now, rather, left the rostrum, I received the other award that really got to me, this one in a very different way. It was the only one besides the Medal of Merit that I recognized on sight, and it sent chills up and down my spine. Black and crimson, it was instantly identifiable halfway across the room.

"Now, Thomas," Mr. Wrangell said, still smiling for the cameras, "we have an award from your own native Esteppe."

"I…I…" I stuttered, for about the thousandth time. Probably all of my other protests were going to be edited out, but this one I wanted to make stick. I really meant it this time. I had no desire whatsoever to join the Brotherhood.

"The democratically-elected government of the people of Esteppe," Wrangell intoned over my objections, "hereby awards Thomas Longo, their native son, the Ribbon of Blood, making you a Brother of the Order of Blood." He looked directly into the camera. "This medal is awarded only in recognition of supreme acts of courage and achievement by aerospace pilots."

I pressed my lips together in anger, unsure what to do. It'd been the brain-cored 'hopper pilots of Esteppe who'd made the recent war there so difficult for the United Systems to win. The Order had been created to honor the finest of these pilots, and the Brotherhood was the mechanism by which they'd leveraged their prestige and influence within the dictatorship. The survivors still met and plotted, though their fangs had been quite thoroughly pulled. I wanted no part of it. None. What would Father think? Next I'd be painting the nose of my Skybolt red and demanding a noble title.

Just as I was about to turn and walk away Ted Knight came back onstage and stood beside me. "My father, who fought in the Esteppe war, would very much have liked to have decorated you with this award as well," he explained. "However, he's not feeling well and had to go back to his room."

He picked up the evil thing and looked me in the eye. "Bend over, Thomas. I can't quite see what I'm doing."

I false-swallowed, then did as I was told. Technically I outranked Ted, or at least I thought I did. I also knew I was still just a dumb kid, as well. Besides, if Lofton Knight, as busted up as he was, had asked me to accept a medal from Satan himself I'd have knocked down the gates of Hell to collect it. *Why*, I asked myself over and over again on the train ride home, fingering at the red-enamel square that now dangled close up against my throat. Why did the Navy want me to accept a medal with such a dark background?

"I'm not sure, Thomas" Father Murton replied when I asked him. "I saw that you were about to make a scene, and to be honest I wasn't sure how to handle it, especially since I have considerable sympathy for your point of view."

He frowned. "Esteppe is part of the United Systems now. Did you notice how they went out of their way to emphasize that the current government is democratically-elected?"

"Not really," I said.

"Well, it is nowadays. At some point, Esteppe deserves to be readmitted to the family of planets, no matter what its past." His lip curled. "Someday we'll have to do the same for the Dracans, I suppose."

I shook my head. "Not any time soon. We have to win first."

"Of course," Murton agreed. He looked over at Spencer, who was sleeping again. "Our rabbity friend could probably tell you more than I can. I suspect a lot of it has to do with simple pragmatism. First of all the Skybolt is derived from your father's older Esteppan designs. Right?"

"Yeah," I agreed, not liking to admit it.

"When you get right down to it, whose military-industrial complex, even today, is therefore best suited for Skybolt production? Where can officers most easily be found with recent, up-to-date experience on how best to employ Skybolts? Who are the leading experts on Skybolt tactics?"

I grimaced. "The Brotherhood of the Order of Blood."

"Just now, they're probably the most valuable untapped military asset in the galaxy, that's my guess, at least. After all, I'm as many light-years from Esteppe as you are."

He shrugged wearily. "They're not nice people, Thomas. You know it, and I know it. Our leaders know it too or I hope they do. The fact they're not nice doesn't mean they're not vitally important just now. Even more, it's probably vital that the rest of the United Systems worlds accept their help and maybe even leadership, in this one area, at least. That's probably why the award has been resurrected—as a gesture of peace, respect, and healing. Besides..."

"What?" I asked.

Murton looked down at the boxcar floor. "You are an Esteppan, Thomas, like it or not. Esteppe may be thoroughly reconstructed, but that planet will never be so reconstructed that they don't worship their military heroes above all others. You're one of them, from their point of view, and at this point it'd be churlish of you to disown your original home.

"It's important for the United System to have a hero. You've heard me say so a thousand times before, and Alicia and Spence to boot. This goes beyond that, however. You're also the first hero of the newly reformed Esteppe, or so I imagine. That means you have an even larger role to play than I first thought."

Chapter Forty-Four

Conversation sort of died out after that. I had a lot of thinking to do about this and that. I'd decided it was just as well that I was stuck on Churilla for the duration when, quite unexpectedly, the train began to slow. Father Murton didn't seem to notice. It was probably my heightened hearing that tipped me off.

"Mr. Wiston?" I called aloud, but Spence didn't answer.

Father Murton looked up, but the rabbit didn't stir. I reached out with my toe and nudged him.

"Mr. Wiston?"

I'd never met anyone half as fast as Spencer. In an instant he was wide awake and had drawn his gun, ready for anything.

"What?" he demanded.

"We're slowing down," I explained, watching the revolver's muzzle carefully. It wasn't quite pointed at me... "You didn't warn us that we were going to slow down, so..."

"That's because we weren't supposed to" he replied, reholstering his weapon and snapping his datapad open. He flipped rapid-fire through several pages, then his ears drooped.

"Damn," he declared. "It's a checkpoint. They're stopping the trains and inspecting them, about a mile and a half up the track."

"We've got to jump, then," Murton exclaimed.

"We're on a long trestle," Spence replied, looking thoughtful. "A high one, too. With over a mile of it left to run. By the time we're back on dry land, we'll be too close to the soldiers." He frowned.

"It's a devilishly clever place to make inspection stops. I never thought of this little trick."

Just then the boxcar's brakes activated, slowing us further. I closed my eyes and sighed.

"How high up are we?" Murton demanded. "Maybe we can jump anyway?"

"That's not the issue," Spence replied as he began typing again, rapid-fire as ever. "The question you should asking is how deep is the water under us? The answer to that one, I fear, is not nearly deep enough. Just a couple feet, except in a narrow little shipping channel. We're already past it."

Murton stood up, looked around helplessly, and then sat back down. "I see."

Wiston glanced up at him. "Don't give up yet, Ephraim." His eyes returned to the screen. "The game's only just begun. Maybe I can come up with..." Then he smiled. "Yes. Oh, yes. I've always secretly wanted to do this." His fingers went flying again.

I looked at my tutor. He looked back at me, then shrugged. Neither of us knew what was happening, but on the other hand the last thing we wanted to do was interrupt. The train's brakes activated again, longer and harder this time than before. Father Murton tumbled into me and then in turn drove me into Spence.

"Oops," the rabbit-man exclaimed cheerfully. "I didn't do that--honest. Are you two all right?"

We nodded, then I leaned over to where I could see Spence's datapad. His display showed a close-up of two tracks. They ran parallel for a time, then diverged. One ran along the coastline, while the other headed out across the sea. Presumably, this represented our trestle. Our train was represented by a series of yellow dots strung out behind a larger one. I watched the brakes activate again, and our dots became a yellowish orange.

Spence chuckled. "Watch this."

His fingers flew again...and suddenly I realized a second train was coming down the coast. What made me notice it was how suddenly its icons changed from bright red to bright green.

"You see that curve there, Thomas?" he asked, tracing the place where the coastal line joined up with ours. "That's the sharpest curve anywhere on my main line."

"Really?" I said, not sure what a curved track had to do with anything.

"Uh-huh," he declared, nodding happily. "You see that other train? It's only got four cars on it."

I nodded again.

"It'll accelerate quickly, with such a light load." He tapped the screen with his claw again. "Right about there, I reckon. That's where it'll happen. The Dracans will never see it coming. I've disabled the safeties."

I shook my head, confused. "Gov—I mean, Mr. President..."

"I'm never 'Mr. President' to you, Thomas," he declared, looking affronted. "Not off duty, at least. Call me Spence."

I nodded again. “All right, Spence. What’s going to happen? Where?”

“The biggest train wreck in Churillan history, I imagine,” he replied with his sunny smile. “That short freight is going to miss the curve and whammo. It’s really going to be something. With any luck it’ll happen almost on top of the inspection point. Maybe even kill the lot.”

A short silence ensued.

“You mean,” Father Murton said, “that the other train is going to hit this one?”

“Uh-huh,” he answered, nodding. “While we’re still moving fairly quickly, too. It’ll be spectacular. People used to pay lots of money and travel for days to see staged train wrecks. This’ll be my very first, after all these years. Isn’t life full of wonderful surprises?”

“Of course,” my tutor agreed, his eyes narrowing. “Wonderful surprises indeed. I’m quite certain I’ll remember this one for the rest of my life however short a time that may be.” He shook his head. “This train’s a general freight, right?”

“Yep,” Spence agreed.

“And the other one?”

“I never even…” He tapped his keyboard again, then his eyes widened. “Oh my.”

“Oh my?” Murton echoed.

“Oh my,” Spence confirmed, nodding eagerly. “It’s loaded with raw hydrocarbons, for the stinkyworks. Ethanol. Naphtha. Gasoline.” He rubbed his hands together in delight. “What a wonderful wreck this will be. All of us will be right here to experience it firsthand together.”

Chapter Forty-Five

"I suppose," Father Murton said after a very long silence, "it would be asking altogether too much of you if I were to suggest that you consider seeking another way out of this difficult situation. One that doesn't involve a train wreck, I mean, or perhaps, one that doesn't involve tanker cars and gasoline."

"Yes," the rabbit-man replied, snapping his datapad shut and returning it to its usual pocket. "I fear that it would be asking too much, under the circumstances. Especially given that there's only about two minutes left."

"I see," the priest agreed, looking downcast. "In that case, please forget that I ever brought up the subject. "

"Of course," Spencer replied generously, bowing his head in formal acknowledgement. "Well, I suppose that we'd better do what we can to brace ourselves." He shivered in obvious anticipation. "The impact is really going to be something. I'd suggest we box ourselves up again. These reusable shipping containers are much tougher than they look. They're designed to protect fragile goods, as well."

Working together, we hurriedly wedged our boxes up against the left wall of the boxcar, then strapped them down with the heavy cargo ties. Fortunately, the rest of the car was empty. If it had carried a substantial amount of cargo, we wouldn't have had a chance.

"We're going to be hit on the left side," Spence explained, climbing into his. "So, this may look backwards, but I'll bet my house that when we derail, we'll topple over so that the left side is up and the right's down. We won't be able to get out of the door on the bottom."

"Right," I agreed absently. "What about opening the door when the power's off?"

"I'll unlock us once I'm boxed up," he answered. "Then, with any luck the forces of the collision will do the rest." He ducked his head down, then raised it again. "Good luck, everyone."

I'd already spent altogether too long stuffed into a box. Usually, time simply crawled by when there wasn't anything to do or see. This time I felt like I'd hardly gotten myself properly braced when the promised impact arrived. Over the past few months, I'd been around more nuclear explosions than I could easily remember, yet they'd been nothing in comparison. It was as if the entire train had been drop-kicked like a football and then gone spinning across the sky. Then, improbably, it had gone on and on and on, impact after impact, as presumably one car after another was involved.

Boom. Bang. Boom.

Spencer had been so right. This was the experience of a lifetime, far more memorable than being nuked or shot out of the sky. I would have traveled for days and paid good money to see such an event, staged or no. Of course, I'd much rather have not actually been aboard one of the trains. The whole thing climaxed with a huge explosion that simply had to have been at least one of the tanker cars exploding. It sounded as if the sky were splitting—

Ba-Roooooom.

Our car came to rest with the right side down, as predicted, though it was probably a near-run thing. As one impact had followed another, we'd gone careening down the right-of-way, tipping and teetering first this way and then the other whole time.

I opened up my box. What had once been the lid was now a sort of side-mounted hatch.

"Father Murton," I called out, my voice sounding thin and hollow next to the deep bass crashings and bangings still taking place all along the line. Our car's interior was well lit. The illumination was emanating from a sea of flames, judging by its intensity and color. The door was open, then. Good. In the distance, I could hear people screaming in pain. Many of them.

"Spence, are you guys all right?"

Slowly Spence's lid popped open. "I hit my head," the rabbit-man complained. "In fact, I was out for a minute or two and missed the best part."

I shook my head, angry. "Reach over and check on Father Murton."

My body was far tougher than Wiston's, I remembered suddenly and both of us were more resistant to injury than my tutor. Suddenly I was frightened.

"You were knocked silly, Spence. Shake it off, and help Father Murton."

"Right," Spence agreed, his eyes focusing.

Smoke filled the air now, black, thick, smothering smoke. He shook like an animal, taking my advice literally, then stretched out as far as he could and opened Father Murton's lid.

"He's not moving," the rabbit reported.

"Damn," I cursed. I was almost under the door.

Getting out would have been child's play. Electric motors are after all slow, not weak. There was nothing for it but to clamber out and, hand-over-hand, swing from box to box until I got to my tutor's.

"Father," I cried as loud as I could, right into the mouth of his box. "Father." His only reply was a grunt.

I looked up at Wiston, who still didn't seem to be thinking clearly. "We've got to get out, fast. That fire's going to do nothing but spread. There may even be more tankers waiting to go up. You go first, since you've got a gun. Besides, I've got to carry Father Murton." I nodded at the president's box. "If you don't get out, those lashings will have to bear the weight of all three of us at once. They'd probably still hold, but..."

"Right," Wiston agreed, still looking a little dazed.

Then, moving like a trained acrobat, he twisted around, made a smooth long leap, and climbed effortlessly up and out of the sliding door. He didn't make any attempt at stealth, but to give him his due there was rather a lot going on around us just then to distract our enemies. Still, I could only hope that he hadn't been seen. Just as I hoped his head would clear in the fresh air. We needed that head.

If I'd still had real muscles and a normal body, I'd never have gotten Father Murton out. I'd have tried. Things were heating up enough that I knew the fire must be close at hand, and the alternative would've been to watch my tutor burn. If I'd made the attempt using flesh-and-blood muscles, I'd have strained and sweated and popped my joints in the most spectacular of fashions.

Electric motors are more energy-efficient than human muscle tissue, and my molecular batteries were fresh and strong. I simply wrapped my left arm around the priest, locked it into position so that I wouldn't have to worry about dropping him, then clambered out using the other three limbs and the nearly-unlimited leverage they provided. At one point, I had us both suspended by two fingers. Needing to rise a little, I simply ordered the fingers to curl more. The motors, among the smallest in my body, didn't so much as protest. My father had always believed in buying only the very best hardware.

I took a moment to smile. The way my life had been going lately, I'd soon be receiving some sort of gaudy, overdone lifesaving medal for this little stunt. Most likely a gold-plated tanker car from the Santa Fe line back home or something else equally useful. I wasn't exerting myself. I felt no discomfort, nor even any real sense of danger. Just like my one and only combat flight. Normal people didn't understand.

Getting through the door was the hardest part. I gripped the threshold with my free hand, made doubly certain of my grip on Father Murton, and let my feet fall free. Once I dangled, I simply did a one-handed pull up and kept going until the door was at my waist. Spence accepted my burden then, so I was able to sort of fall forward on my face and scramble clear.

"Come on," Spence roared. "We're in the open up here."

Sure enough, we were. Perhaps I was a little dopey from the impact, too. Or, more likely, I'd been too focused on the task at hand to notice much of the world around me. Not that it would've mattered. Spence's train wreck had altered the local landscape beyond easy recognition.

Fire and flame and accordioned-railcars and spilled cargo heaped all around us. I couldn't make sense of anything at all. At least the equally-stunned Dracans couldn't make any sense of anything, either. A single wide-eyed soldier came wandering out of the darkness beyond a large fire, rifle in hand.

"Spence," I cried, pointing. The soldier turned and stared at us instead of raising his weapon. It was his last mistake. The rabbit's oversized slug took him square in the center of the chest, the revolver's thunder a pale and pathetic thing against the deeper, far more profound detonations we'd experienced earlier.

Spence lowered Murton to the ground and dashed up alongside the Dracan. The soldier was still alive when slower-moving me arrived a few seconds later. His mouth worked struggling to say something. Whatever it was, he never managed to speak.

Spence snatched the man's rifle out of his unresisting hands. In two quick motions, he dismounted the bayonet and plunged it deep into the Dracan's throat. "We don't have much time."

He took two more seconds to slash the Dracan's cheeks and stab out his eyes. Mutilating dead Dracans whenever possible was official Resistance policy. Watching it happen bothered me until I remembered that innocent hostages were being shot in retaliation, and probably would be again for this night's work. What came around, I reckoned naturally went around. War was like that, I was beginning to understand. It simply had to be, or people like the Dracans would win every time. Sheer savagery offered an unbeatable advantage unless countered with more of the same.

"Stay close," Spence continued, tossing the bloody bayonet down onto the now-unmoving corpse. "There's still two tankers ready to blow, and we don't want to be in the same county with them when it happens."

Chapter Forty-Six

Spence's datapad was networked through the rail system's computers. Because of this, the big wreck had effectively disconnected him. Too many cables or whatever had been cut. Since he didn't dare try to log onto a public frequency, we were totally dependent on his memory as we staggered through the darkness. I was carrying Father Murton over my shoulders and unable to move quickly even if I hadn't been so burdened. Fortunately, the president's memory was a remarkably good one.

To his credit, Spence never once asked me to hurry. He was unflappable, except when knocked silly.

"There's an access road that parallels the coastwise line," he explained as we walked away from the scene of the wreck, our path lit by upheavals and explosions that, even at this distance, appeared to be ripping apart the heavens. "We'll have to commandeer some sort of vehicle, and that's all there is to it. Anything else would be even riskier."

I nodded. We needed to get Father Murton to a doctor, and fast. My tutor didn't appear to have been badly hurt, but he remained unconscious so long, it couldn't be a good sign. His left shoulder had been dislocated, but Spence had fixed it with a nasty-looking twist-and-shove. Otherwise, neither of us could see anything wrong with him.

Sometimes he'd sort of half-regain consciousness, and twist and groan, but then he'd black out again. It had already happened two or three times, and I didn't like it one bit. We were still thirty miles or so from the cave, a good day's walk even in daylight. If we had to sneak around it might take us a week, and he couldn't wait that long.

"In an hour or so," Spence assured me, "this place will be absolutely crawling with salvage teams. Firemen, railroad engineers, accident investigators...Hell, I'm probably still on the 'to call' list for an incident this big myself. Not that I'm expecting my phone to ring.

"The Dracans will be here soon as well. They've got men they can't contact and will be expecting sabotage. Half of Churilla will be coming, I'll bet. Right down the same access road we need to use."

I pressed my lips together for a second before replying. "If the Dracans are coming, why are we headed towards them?"

He shrugged. "There's a key precondition to our plan of commandeering a vehicle, son. Said precondition is there must first be a vehicle available to commandeer. For all we talk about there not being a lot of land area on Churilla, this is still an empty planet. You won't find many vehicles per square mile, especially out here in the boonies where there still isn't any soil.

"So, we simply *must* go to where there are vehicles, Dracans or no Dracans. The good news, at least, is they won't be expecting us."

A little while later I found myself lying in the middle of the road, playing dead. Spence was covering me from the ditch. He'd found a nice rock pile to hide behind. Twice he'd whistled me back to cover because the oncoming vehicles had been trucks. He'd been right to do so, as they'd each contained a squad of Dracan soldiers oohing and aahing at the light show just beyond the horizon. I could tell by the sound the third vehicle to approach was a cyclescoot. Perfect.

I kept as still as I could. I didn't even breathe. My uniform and medals were wadded up in a ball in the ditch. Because my rubber like skin couldn't itch or chafe I never wore any underwear. From a distance and in the flickering firelight, I probably made a passable imitation of a naked corpse.

"Aw, geez," the cyclescoot's driver said as he came skidding to a stop. "We've got victims already this far from the incident site. Toxic fumes?"

"I haven't got anything on my sniffer," a second voice answered, sounding puzzled. "It self-checks just fine. If only the damn Dracans—"

"Freeze," Wiston's voice rang out, loud and clear and authoritative. "Don't move a muscle." He sounded impressive. Even I didn't move for a moment and I was *supposed* to. Just a little late, I sprang to my feet and tried to look threatening. That didn't work well.

Spence more than made up for my lack of threatening skills. He emerged from cover and waved the big revolver.

"Get off that bike," he ordered, voice still booming. "Move."

The cyclescoot's riders surprised at being stopped stared.

"Governor Wiston," the driver said, "are you here to help with the investigation, sir? I mean…"

"Shut up," he ordered, his voice taking on less-menacing tone "I don't want to have to hurt anyone. Especially not one of my own employees just trying to do his job."

"Don't shoot, sir," the second agreed, raising his hands. "I got an 'excellent' rating on my performance review last quarter. I like working for you."

Spence shook his head and rolled his eyes. "Get off the bike," he ordered. "We need to borrow it."

"Of course, sir," the driver replied, nodding with vigor. "You don't need the gun. It's your cyclescoot, not mine. We just put in a fresh battery, too."

"Good," Spence agreed, lowering the revolver a little. "Very good."

It didn't take nearly as long to get Father Murton situated as it otherwise might have. The two railroad employees assisted us.

"What are your names again?" Wiston barked as he settled in behind the handlebars.

it was a tight fit for the three of us, with him driving, Father Murton in the middle, and me on the back holding him upright. We'd manage.

"Paul Hartmann, sir," the former driver replied.

"Mitchell Lester," answered the one with the excellent performance review. "Free Churilla."

Wiston chuckled, reaching under the vehicle's dashboard. He ripped something free and examined it critically. Then he pulled out two gas masks with his other hand.

"I'd make myself scarce, if I were you two. Walk to the wreck and get busy. A few hours from now, you can claim you parked here when your sniffer-warning went off and walked the rest of the way, making checks every few feet. That's standard procedure, when gas is suspected. The scoot was stolen while you were gone. You don't know how or by whom." He handed Mitchell the part he'd removed, then the masks. "This is the vehicle locater. You're an excellent on-the-job performer, Mitchell. Get creative. Figure out something interesting to do with it. Like, maybe toss it in a Dracan Army truck."

"Gotcha, sir," Lester replied, eyes glittering. "We'll take care of you every way we can. It's an honor."

"I'll take care of you as well," Spence replied, extending his hand and shaking each of theirs. "Expect a bonus in next week's pay envelopes. A big one." He started up the scoot. "See you later and thanks."

Chapter Forty-Seven

The rest of the trip was a lot easier than it should have been for several good reasons. One was we didn't have all that far to go anyway. Our train journey had been nearly over before it was so rudely interrupted. Second, the spectacular flames and explosions drew everyone's attention. Even Spence and I kept turning our heads to look. Third and most important, the disaster-response units crawled around like ants from a disturbed hill, totally disorganized. The chaos probably didn't last long. We only needed those first few precious minutes.

Spence had been prescient enough to turn my uniform inside-out while I lay naked in the road. When I put it back on it looked enough like work overalls to pass on a dark, flame-lit night, especially while zipping by at forty or so miles per hour. Spence's helmet didn't fit well. It rattled around on his head so badly, in fact, he had to constantly adjust it or the faceplate would turn sideways. Between the helmet and his own coveralls, the only things about him looking at all unusual were his big bare feet and puffy cottontail.

Father Murton's unconscious body effectively concealed the tail and his feet blended in with the cyclescoot's floorboards. Besides, who ever looks at a cyclist's feet as he zooms past, especially one riding behind a dazzling headlamp and a night otherwise lit by brilliant explosions? We had one close call when a squad of Dracans jumped down from a truck to create a checkpoint. They hadn't gotten set up yet and most faced the wrong way. Instead of pulling off the road and cutting cross-country through the rocks, which almost certainly would have resulted in them chasing us, Spence instead simply blew his horn and rode right through their midst.

"Gassed rail worker," he cried out as we wound and twisted our way right through the startled enemy soldiers. "Coming through. Emergency! Watch out for the toxic gas leak."

Once through, having offered the unprepared Dracans at most a second or two to see what we were and make up their minds as to what to do about us, we continued on our way. We passed an oncoming

Dracan truck a couple miles later and the driver pulled over so we could pass without slowing. The soldiers in this truck wore gas masks. They looked terribly uncomfortable.

After that, everything was relatively simple. Spence took us past our turnoff, not even slowing and making certain that several more vehicles saw us before pulling off the highway. Then he turned off the headlight and crawled through the rocks for a time. Eventually we found a sort of natural lean-to and rolled the cyclescoot into it. No one ever went out among the rocks. Unless we'd left tracks, which I doubted, given the hard, unyielding barren surface, the cyclescoot was nearly as unlikely ever to be found again as it would've been in a similar hidey-hole on the surface of the Moon. I was unhappy at the thought as we dismounted.

I'd never ridden a cyclescoot before because Father considered them too dangerous. Even with all the Dracans about the ride had been a lot of fun. It seemed such a pleasant, inoffensive, little vehicle. What a terrible waste if it would never be ridden again.

Did war ruin everything it touched?

We made it to the canyon well before dawn, but Spence decided it was too dangerous to approach in the dark. We'd likely be shot by our own sentries. Father Murton was groaning and near-waking more often now, which I took to be good news. So I took my time turning my uniform right-side-out again, while Spencer freed up his ears. They were what would show up best in a sniperscope so we agreed he should keep them sticking straight up and wiggle them a lot. I was to stay close to him.

"Halt," a voice rang out as we waded down the stream.

I closed my eyes and relaxed a little for the first time in many hours. Our snipers were under orders to shoot first and not bother asking any questions if they had the slightest doubt our hidey-hole was in danger of discovery.

"Freeze."

We froze. Not three minutes later, we were back home.

"Oh, Spence," Alicia wailed, the tears flowing freely as she hugged and squeezed her husband over and over again. "I thought you were dead."

Then Sandy hugged me, blubbering just as freely as Alicia. My support team smiled and slapped each other on the back. Apparently, pretty much everyone had given up on us.

Didn't they have any faith at all? I mean, it hadn't been all that hard to escape. Spencer had been resourceful like he always was. Why was it a surprise we survived? The whole thing hadn't even been all that exciting except for the train-wreck. Adventures I realized were highly overrated.

The holovids were more exciting and entertaining than the real thing.

Chapter Forty-Eight

I found holovids more interesting than the nuts and bolts of an actual, real-life resistance movement. No sooner had the breakfast dishes been cleared and I'd visited Father Murton, who was recovering well from a severe concussion, than we were back to meetings, meetings, meetings. At least by now I understood what they were all about a lot better, having been involved from the beginning.

"...no reaction to the wreck yet at all," our Chief of Security said, "which strikes me as odd. You say you're certain they know it was sabotage?"

Spence nodded. "Yes. I was pressed for time and left traces. Besides, any idiot can figure out the safety interlocks were bypassed, and that it took a high-level password to do it. Wrecks like that don't happen on computer-controlled rail networks. At least not since the last bug was cleaned out of the software."

"They are rounding up hostages," Alicia said, sipping at her coffee. Spence hated the stuff, but his wife drank enough for the both of them. "Over a hundred, so far."

Spence and I lowered our heads. We'd both grinned like little kids while describing the wreck itself, right up until the point when we remembered lots of innocent people would be beheaded on live holovid because of it. Spence had sworn he would watch and then avenge every single execution, but I couldn't. No one press me. They all understood I'd already seen more than enough death and dying.

"Well," said a new voice. "Maybe we should take this as a turning point, then. It's a good one psychologically. Unplanned, but the best opportunities usually are."

Spence looked at Bob Knudsen sent by the United Systems to advise us. He described himself as an "officer" of the United Systems government, which Alicia explained was a nice way of saying "spy."

Bob was an unusually short man with dark skin and a Michigan accent. Officer Knudsen was out-of-place on Churilla, and I didn't think he'd last long if he ever tried to blend in with Churillans. I guessed he was a different kind of spy than the sort I was familiar with.

"You did a wonderful job laying the resistance groundwork," he said, "better than we'd imagined possible back home."

He rubbed his chin with stubby fingers before saying more. "Feelings will run high against the Dracans after so many beheadings. They performed a handful before and gave halfway plausible explanations that they slaughtered only "class enemies" like lawyers and stockbrokers. Now, I expect they'll lose any last lingering traces of credibility. Even if you don't like lawyers or stockbrokers, you can only stomach so much."

Spence and Alicia nodded while they unconsciously took each other's hands. They'd always been touchy-feely, but since the train-wreck, the two had been in almost constant physical contact.

"They'll probably fly Fowler in again," Spencer agreed. "To tour the barrios and try to calm them down."

"Almost certainly," Knudsen agreed, his eyes still distant. Then he inhaled sharply. "Spencer, Alicia, I have some highly classified information to share with you and no one but you. Can you clear the room? It may just be that outside events are about to force our hand."

Chapter Forty-Nine

Whatever it was that Knudsen told Spence and Alicia stirred up our little world something awful. Suddenly Spence called twice as many meetings, most of them now held in the extra-secure new conference room at the far end of the tunnel. My Skybolt support staff had dug it in their spare time when they weren't caring for me. They were pleased and proud it was put to good use so quickly. They had already begun another.

The best thing about the new flurry of conferences, from my point of view at least, was that I didn't have to attend any of them. The rabbits weren't seeing stinkyworks owners anymore, or bankers, farmers, or anyone else they needed to impress and reassure. They didn't need me and my fake uniform and unearned medals to impress potential supporters. That suited me just fine.

It was cool to sit with Father Murton and help him recover just as he had twice done for me. We had all day to sit and talk, except when he tired and wanted to nap. Mostly, we talked about the war.

"Things are bad all over," he agreed with me after I read an article about yet another lost space battle to him.

My tutor still had difficulty focusing his eyes. The doctor was a little worried, but said he figured everything would be all right in a couple days.

"We lost five cruisers, they said?"

I nodded. "That's over a thousand men. All dead. Almost no one in a big ship survives a lost space battle."

Murton shook his head and lay back. "Even worse, the Henderson Nexus is almost as important as our Orion Nexus. Losing them both means a good number of United Systems worlds are cut off. The escape of the Orion fleet from here is the nearest thing we've seen to a victory. You have to do a lot more than retreat successfully to win a war."

"They're only two jumps from Earth now," I agreed, shaking my head. Interstellar journeys closely resembled a large-scale game of hopscotch, with ships leaping from the Nikita points in one system after another until they arrived at their destination. Sometimes they had to Jump hundreds of light-years past that and then double back because the Nikita points didn't line up right. A political map of the galaxy made no sense at all unless superimposed atop a chart displaying which Points connected to which. Until the basic framework was explained, everything was an incoherent mess.

"Just two Jumps," I repeated.

"The Dracans will sterilize her if they think they have to in order to win," Murton replied, looking glum. "There's not a doubt of it in my mind. Old Earth, dead and gone. She's still home to almost half the human race. It's hard to imagine."

I nodded. There wasn't anything more that either of us could do except talk. It wasn't like I had a Skybolt to fly.

For three days Spence and Alicia hardly left the secure conference room. Father Murton was able to get out of bed and go back to being my tutor. The tunnel buzzed with voices and activity at all hours of the day and night.

Even Sandy was doing extra hacking work she couldn't talk about. That was fine and dandy with me. We discussed other things when we went wading up and down the creek.

Then, eventually, it happened. It was inevitable all along, but, I'd kept up hope right to the bitter end I'd be left out. At long last, Spence and Alicia summoned me to the secure briefing room. I was now to participate in whatever they planned.

"Hi," I said from the airlock-like entrance foyer.

A female guard tried to scan me for bugs and the like and then gave it up as a bad job. I was made mostly of metal and electronics gear. Having no viable alternative, she surrendered and waved me by.

"Hello," the two rabbits greeted me, smiling and looking as fresh as if they'd actually been getting more than a couple of hours of sleep a night. Their personal aides were the most pitied individuals in the tunnel. They could easily be recognized because they were the ones with dark circles under their eyes who kept passing out at the dinner table with their faces in their food.

"How are you, Thomas?" Alicia dimpled. "How's Father Murton?"

"He's fine. Doctor Evans says he'll make a full recovery. He had a subdural hematoma."

Spence'e eyebrows wrinkled. "Ouch!" Then he smiled again. "And how's calculus coming?"

I frowned. The fact was while I wanted to be an engineer like my father and brother, my talent for higher math was proving limited at best.

"Not so well," I said. "The good news, though, is that I started the course early because I was worried that I might have trouble. So even if I fail this time, I can still catch up."

Spence nodded. "People say I'm very bright, but, I'll tell you a little secret. I'm not very good at math either. Because I built the original railroads, I belong to all the planetary engineering societies. I never got a degree in the subject or in any other subject for that matter."

He reached around and squeezed Alicia up close to him. "Neither did my wife. Frontier worlds tend to be informal about such things. Personal abilities and skills are what matter when you've got a new planet to develop, not diplomas. It seems to me we get away from that basic understanding of what does and does not matter, the more stratified and inefficient our society grows."

Tilting his head to one side, Spence considered me. "There are many careers open to you, Thomas. If you really and truly want to be an engineer, that's all well and good, but for a young man in your position, who knows? The universe, as they used to say, is your oyster. Don't limit your choices before you must."

I shrugged, not knowing what to say. I'd never really thought about doing anything with my life except working in one of the family businesses.

Then, Spence got down to brass tacks. "I understand," he said "you're subject to an ongoing problem with your gyros?"

I nodded. "If I move too suddenly, they tumble and have to reset themselves. For about three or four minutes, I'm pretty much helpless."

Alicia's eyes narrowed. "I've never seen it happen. Neither has Spence. It must not be a common occurrence. "

"It mostly happened when I, well…played. Rough-housed. Stuff like that." I'd have been blushing, if I could. "I don't do that sort of thing very much anymore. I've grown up a lot since then."

"A pity," Spence observed, though I didn't understand what he meant. "How quickly do you think that you could climb a flight of steps? Like, say, the fire stairs in a big office building?"

"It depends. I mean, I've never timed myself. I'm slower than an ordinary person because I have to watch my feet. Most of the time, I take the elevator because I'm so slow."

"Right," Spence agreed, tapping his oversized incisors with a pencil. "That's unfortunate, but it can't be helped." Then he put the pencil down and looked his wife in the eyes.

"Yes," she agreed to the unspoken question. "We must. It's unavoidable."

He nodded, then turned back to me. "Thomas, you've seen and heard a lot. We trust you completely, but now we're planning an real operation of great difficulty. The information is being compartmentalized as tightly as possible. You are to say nothing to anyone, not even Father Murton, without our permission. Furthermore, I can't promise to answer any questions you may have. I'd much rather you didn't ask any questions at all. Do we understand each other?"

I blinked. "Uh-huh."

"Good," he answered, smiling again. "Now, I need your best possible guess. How fast can you climb stairs? Half as fast as an ordinary person? Two thirds?"

I raised my hand to my chin and considered. "Half," I said. "Half a normal human's walking speed, more or less, but I don't get tired and need to rest. If there's a whole lot of flights to climb, that might matter."

Spence nodded and smiled while Alicia took notes. "Excellent," he replied. "We feared it would be worse."

His brows furrowed again. "Do you think that you can fly a 'hopper?"

I blinked. "Of course I can. I flew the Skybolt."

"No, Thomas," Alicia explained. "That's not what Spence means. We need to know if you can fly an ordinary, human-pilot-configured 'hopper."

My mouth opened, then closed again. "I'm not sure. I mean...The basic operating principles are the same, but I've never had to physically move the control levers or anything like that. My hands are awkward and slow." I hated to disappoint him. "I've never thought about it. It just sort of never came up. My license is only good for the Skybolt, if that matters. It's a special deal—they had to pass new laws, just for me."

"Humph," Spence snorted, giving Alicia another quick little squeeze. "If the Dracans issue you a citation, we'll reimburse the amount of the fine." His face grew serious again. "So, we can't and shouldn't count on you being able to fly a normal skyhopper?"

I considered it some more, then shook my head. "No, it's something I might be able to pull off or might not. You couldn't count on it."

Spence's ears drooped. He hadn't wanted to hear that, but he took it well. "All right then, Thomas, thank you for your honesty." Alicia scribbled more notes. "It's far better you tell the truth up front instead of making promises you might not be able to keep."

"It's good to see you, Thomas," Alicia echoed, smiling brightly and dimpling again. "I miss our little visits. Maybe someday I can draw for you again. For now, though..."

I nodded and clumsily turned to leave. Over the past few weeks I'd already used up far more of the Wiston's time than anyone should. I was a lucky person just to have met them at all, much less to have actually helped them with their revolt.

"Good luck." I was relieved my inability to fly kept me from participating in yet another adventure. "I hope you can find another 'hopper pilot."

"We shall," Spence assured me just before the soundproof door swung shut. "We most certainly shall."

Chapter Fifty

Presumably they did find another pilot because the frenetic new tempo of events in the tunnel continued day and night. At first, nothing much changed for me. I sweated over my calculus, while Father Murton, who seemingly had even less of an aptitude for math than I did, tried his best to stay a lesson ahead so he could help me along.

He'd become my tutor when I was still a baby and had taught my general studies classes. Everyone knew and understood he wasn't qualified to train me in higher math. Eventually, Father would've hired a special tutor for me. He'd sent several to meet me before I left on my Skybolt demonstration tour. Despite everyone's best intentions and efforts, my grades remained poor and progress slow. Both Father Murton and I found it frustrating.

It became more frustrating when I thought I was beginning to understand the equations a little and a Churillan guerilla I didn't know began taking Father Murton and me aside for run-throughs of our role in the big event to come. First we had to learn how to get out of the cargo compartment of a moving van as quickly as possible. Lots of other people had to get out with us. So we rehearsed it over and over again to make certain I wouldn't be in the way any more than could possibly be helped.

Most of the others at these rehearsals were young muscular men who carried unloaded slug guns and backpacks laden with simulated explosives. When I realized this, I wanted to ask questions, but I remembered Spence had told me about my not needing to know so I kept my mouth shut.

According to the rehearsals, the guerillas were supposed to run off somewhere, presumably to break things and hurt Dracans, while Father Murton and I calmly walked into some kind of building and climbed fourteen flights of stairs together. Then, we were supposed to stand and wait patiently in the vestibule until someone opened a locked door for us. That was all anyone told us. More instructions would be issued when the time came. It was probably a breach of security for me to even think about the plan. However, I couldn't help but put two and two together.

It looked to me as if Spence and Alicia wanted to steal one of the little VIP 'hoppers that even under the Dracans were still shuttling Churilla's richest and most influential citizens from rooftop to rooftop in downtown Churilla City. Why else would they have asked me about piloting if a skyhopper wasn't involved? Besides, where else except in the city did one have to climb so many steps to get to a 'hopper's landing zone? It still didn't make any sense.

For the life of me, I couldn't figure out why I was involved in the affair if I couldn't serve as a pilot. Even worse, when Father Murton was called away to talk to Spence and Alicia about his part in the plan, he was gone for three hours, where the rabbits had spent perhaps that many minutes talking to me.

When he returned, he didn't say a word about what had happened. He seemed unusually quiet and thoughtful. I wanted to ask him about his interview more than anything else in the world, but I knew better. I kept my curiosity to myself.

After all the preparations, it wasn't surprising when one afternoon, while my tutor and I were fretting unsuccessfully over Mean Value Theorems and what to do with them, Spence himself came knocking on my door.

"It's on, gentlemen," he said. "Be ready tonight at midnight." He looked each of us long and hard in the eyes. "Godspeed and the best of luck to the both of you."

He shook my hand. "It's been an honor to know you, Founder."

"Best of luck at what?" I couldn't help, but observe after he was gone. "At crawling out of the bed of a truck and then climbing a couple hundred stairs without tripping over my own feet?" I shook my head. "I wish I knew what this was all about."

"Security can be tough," my tutor agreed, looking away so that he wouldn't have to meet my eyes. I could tell he knew far more about what was going on than I did, but wouldn't tell.

He shook his head and allowed his gaze to wander about our little shared room. "Get some rest, Thomas. Forget about calculus for now. Take a nap and I'll deal with everything else that needs doing." He looked around the cubicle again. "Not that there's much to do. Who knows? Maybe I'll be able to get a little shuteye myself."

Chapter Fifty-One

Riding in an empty or near-empty boxcar was a lot better than riding in the back of a crowded moving van. Something had gone wrong at the last minute with the large truck we'd planned to use, so a shorter one had been substituted. It was so crowded there wasn't enough room for everyone to sit down at once. We had to rotate the privilege except for me, of course. I never got tired so I stood up all of the way and let one of the older men have my turns.

Things were so unpleasant that it's hard to say which was the worst part. If you place enough frightened men in a moving, fully-enclosed and poorly-ventilated van on a hot day, certain things become inevitable. Many will become motion-sick and then vomit. Others will find the pressure in their bladders intolerable. We couldn't stop and open the doors to accommodate either group, so the air soon grew thick and full of stink. That didn't bother me, but Father Murton and the rest had to suffer and be careful where they stepped or sat.

Our ride seemed to take forever. All through training, the Churillan guerillas, while treating me with the greatest of respect, had remained cold and distant. This was so far from what I'd experienced of Churillan culture that I figured they must've been ordered not to socialize with me. It was probably because of more security stuff. I'd returned the cold silence while also at the same time trying my best to show respect. It worked well enough. We were all on the same side. We got along. Besides, I didn't reckon the guerillas had any more idea of why I was along with them than I did.

At last the monotonous sensations of highway travel gave way to the shorter, sharper turns and accelerations of city streets. We were getting close.

"Are you still sure?" I asked Father Murton, who now stood next to me gripping his borrowed carpet-bag. It'd originally belonged to the Wistons. "Don't I need to know anything more?"

"Not yet," my tutor reassured me with a gentle smile. "Our mission might be compromised even at the last second. Those of us who know the entire plan have sworn to commit suicide if that happens. No matter what, the Dracans can't be allowed to know our real goal or why we're attacking here and now. The stakes are too important."

He took a deep breath and then released it. "None of us wanted to ask you to make a promise like that, Thomas. We just couldn't. Not with your youth."

I false-gulped, impressed. Father Murton a devout Catholic. What could persuade him to vow suicide? No wonder the Wistons had met so long with him.

The guerilla leader gave the order for us to prepare. I waited. The others scrambled to stand and strap on their packs. He gave the order none too soon.

The truck skidded to an abrupt halt. We'd been warned that this would happen, and all of us were as ready for it as run-throughs with no actual truck could make us. Only a man or two here and there tumbled because the vomit and urine made the floor slick. We hadn't planned on that.

Then suddenly the truck emptied except for Father Murton and me. I'd been walking towards the open cargo doors all along, but even so the last guerilla was out before I reached the end of the cargo bay.

"Damnit," I complained, looking down at the ground.

We were parked over a mud hole. No one had ever said anything about a mud hole. If I slipped in it, my gyros would tumble for sure. If that happened, Father Murton might have to, might have to…

"Hold on, son," the priest cried out, leaping off of the back of the truck like a man half his age.

He'd been around me long enough to understand my problem with a single glance. For a wild, timeless moment his head rotated back and forth with machine-gun speed as he sought a solution. There seemed to be none.

We were parked over a mud puddle, and it might ruin everything. A mud puddle. Could anything be sillier? I heard a ripping sound I knew came from one of the guerillas slug guns. The report of a blaster followed.

Then my tutor had an idea. He threw himself, carpet bag and all, facedown into the mud right where I needed to step down. "Come *on*, Thomas," he urged. "Move."

"I…but…" Then there was an explosion so close it made the truck rock a little. The driver blew his horn, impatient to begin his getaway.

Beeeeep.

There wasn't anything to do. Father Murton was right. I took a single step halfway down the back of the truck, to where a little connector-bar attached to the chassis. The new truck was identical to the old one in this detail. Trying not to land any harder than I could help, I stepped down first onto Father Murton and then dry land. My companion leaped to his feet.

Blaster-bolts filled the air all around us, and I could also identify the snap-crack of slugs zipping past us. We stood right in the middle of a firefight.

Father Murton slapped the truck's side twice in the pre-arranged signal, and the vehicle roared away, leaving us more exposed than ever. My partner tugged my arm. Unresisting, I followed him towards a large building.

The *Octavia House* a big sign over the entrance read. Even as I watched, a wayward submachine gun burst from a guerilla's primitive slug-gun shattered the capital "O" into a million pieces. My tutor walked bent over half-double, as if into a heavy wind, but I had to remain fully erect, regardless of the gunfire. If I didn't employ proper posture, I couldn't walk at all.

I felt I was in a slower mode than usual. It must've been worse for my tutor. If I got hit anywhere except directly in the brain or spine, I'd just malfunction. It wouldn't even hurt, but, he'd die.

A large explosion burst behind me and a second followed. I spun my head around much further than a normal person could and boggled. All of this time there'd been two Dracan armored vehicles behind us to cover the hotel entrance. Before, the truck had blocked my view. Both burned, now broken, though at least a dozen dead Churillans lay clustered around one of them. The blaster fire wasn't nearly so thick now. Most of it must have come from there.

Not that it was entirely gone. As I turned around to look where I was going, a Dracan in full battle gear dashed out onto a third-story balcony, where a blonde woman in a bikini stood gaping at all the sudden violence. He shoved her aside and raised his rifle.

A shot from behind by someone with a hand blaster killed him. The shooter wore hotel livery. *If only Spence were here*, I thought inanely as I walked through the chaos, arm held firmly by my tutor. I felt maybe six years old. He'd be loving every second of this. It's almost as exciting as a train-wreck.

The hotel staff had taken full possession of the lobby, and expected us. A housemaid carrying a wicked-looking submachine gun and a bloody carving knife smiled and curtseyed at us as we passed through the large revolving door. An equally heavily-armed valet opened the fire stair door for us and gestured us through with a flourish.

Now I faced the endless stairs. Shots and explosions echoed and rang out around us. I tried to hurry and half-stumbled on the third riser. Father Murton caught me or it might have been over right then.

"Come now, Thomas," he said, using exactly the same tone of voice he'd employed when I was still just little and doing something extra-stupid. "Take one step at a time. It's just like solving a calculus problem."

I opened my mouth to complain that so far as I could see climbing stairs in the middle of a firefight wasn't even remotely like solving a calculus problem. Then I recalled how bad I was at doing calculus, and admitted to myself that I was hardly an expert on the subject. So, instead of arguing the matter I shut my mouth and climbed.

It would've been a long ascent at the best of times. Under the circumstances, it felt endless. When we were about seven floors up the fire door two levels beneath us flew open and a high-ranking Dracan officer in full dress uniform burst through, bleeding badly from his left shoulder. Father Murton reached under his cassock for something, but before he could grasp it the door burst open again, so hard that it knocked the Dracan half off of his feet. Before he could regain his balance a valet surged through and pressed the barrel of his submachine gun against the Dracan's belly. They both screamed in rage, then there was a ripping sound and lots of blood. I turned away. By the time I looked again, all there was to see on the landing was the Dracan's bloody corpse.

How many Dracans were there in this hotel, anyway? Was it a headquarters?

Good lord, the Dracans had beheaded almost two hundred hostages over Spence's train wreck. One by one they'd been marched to the bloody headsman's block, some weeping and pleading, others singing patriotic songs. How many would die over this? It didn't even bear thinking about.

I continued to climb, pulled along by Father Murton's remorseless arm.

"Freedom's never free, Thomas," he explained, as if reading my mind. "All throughout history there have been barbarians at hand who seek to take it away. Remember always, Thomas, the ultimate foundations of every church, university, hospital, and library in the galaxy were laid upon the bones of the barbarians we slaughtered in defending our right to build them."

That was true enough, I decided. There was genuine civilization, and there was barbarism parading around behind a mask and calling itself civilized. I didn't have any doubt which side represented which. Nor did I have any trouble choosing between them, once conflict became inevitable. Nor did most Churillans. Knowing that they fought for what they believed and for what I believed helped with the pain.

At least it did a little. We weren't interrupted again until we were on the tenth floor landing. There, the door opened virtually in our faces and an elegantly dressed girl about my age came surging through. Under very different circumstances, she might've been described as beautiful.

"Aaaaah," she screamed, looking us each in the eyes in turn, but apparently not finding what she sought. "Aaaah."

Then she passed us and ran down the stairs as fast as her heels and tight dress allowed. It all happened so quickly that she was almost out of sight before I realized that her left arm was missing below the elbow.

The firefight and explosions had been audible all the time we climbed, but the noise increased at the fourteenth floor landing, where we were to wait. We did that once we reached it. We waited and waited.

Father Murton didn't look happy. He pressed his lips into a fine line, and his free hand made a fist and then relaxed, over and over again.

"Come on," he muttered. "For God's sake, come on."

I frowned and pressed my bare hand against the metal door. It quivered and shook with the intensity of the battle occurring on the other side.

"We may have to go back. I mean, if the plan's—"

At that point the door flew open and a wild-eyed valet dressed in the ruins of a tuxedo stood before us. "Come in," he shouted. "I don't know how long we can hold this hallway."

Neither of us needed to be asked twice. Our arms intertwined out of habit, and we stepped down the hall.

"Hurry," the valet urged. "You've got to—"

Just then I heard a new barrage of blaster-bolts. Our escort took one right in the throat, blowing his head half-off. Father Murton shoved me down and forward, then landed on his belly himself.

"Take cover, Thomas," he urged. "Take—"

The rest of his sentence was drowned out by the roar of at least two Resistance submachine guns ripping away just inches over my head. My gyros tumbled when I fell. It was inevitable. Suddenly down was up and left was right. I couldn't tell the difference except that I was sort of stuck to the carpeted side of things. This hallway was no place for me to remain while I reset myself.

I took Father Murton's advice and dragged myself along as best I could until I reached a door. A closet. Perfect. It was halfway open already. Crawling in wasn't much of a problem even with the pseudo-dry-heaves caused by malfunctioning gyros. Lying as still as I could for a time, I listened to the battle, but couldn't make much sense of it.

Ladies' shoes filled the closet floor. I lay in a huge disordered pile of the things that spun, spun, spun endlessly around me. At last my x-axis gyro reset, and I could tell down from up. That helped a lot. Given a wall to lean on, I could even stand.

I extended my hand to steady myself. I touched a nylon-stocking-clad leg.

"Oh," a female voice exclaimed, inhaling sharply.

The leg trembled under my touch. The woman acted terrified.

"It's all right," I reassured her. "I don't mean you any harm."

I gathered my feet under me and stood. The electric motors in my hips and knees whined.

"Thomas? Thomas Longo?" I blinked. The woman's voice sounded familiar, but I couldn't quite place it.

A grenade went off somewhere nearby and knocked me off my unsteady feet. I ended with my arms around the woman, leaning on her for support. "I…I'm so sorry," I stuttered. "I mean—"

"Thomas Longo?" she demanded again. This time there was a hysterical edge in her voice. "Oh my god, of all the ridiculous…"

I was all wrapped in the closet's coats and dresses and frilly whatevers by then. By the purest of luck one of my hands brushed up against the light switch, and I turned it on.

"Help," the woman screaming, struggling to get past me, but there was no room. "HELP! Guards!"

All I could see for a moment was pink silk. Then it fell away and I stared into the panic-filled face of ex-Parliamentarian, now Assistant Governor, Sara Fowler.

"HELP," she yelled again, trying to knee me in the groin.

She should've known better. Perhaps it was sheer reflex.

"Someone help." She tried to twist her way past me once more. "Help."

Reflex works both ways. When she kicked me, I grabbed her left upper arm and squeezed. Remorseless little electric motors spun, and I clamped onto her like a vise.

"Oww," she screamed, thrashing and kicking harder than ever. "You're hurting me. GUARDS!"

I was, in the middle of a huge firefight in a Dracan headquarters building. Things weren't going according to plan. Father Murton might be dead already. The guerillas were either all dead or soon would be and I was on the verge of dying myself or ending in a POW camp where Dracan captors forced privates to kill their own officers for amusement.

Why should Parliamentarian Fowler live, when I might well die? I said to myself. The Wistons and everyone else I respected might die.

She had sold out to the Dracans. Sara was under a death sentence. What did it matter if I was her executioner instead of the assigned guerilla who was most likely already a casualty in the misfired attempt?

I squeezed a little tighter and Fowler screamed again. Then something sort of crunched, and she stopped struggling. That moment was all that I needed. Once she quit moving, I secured my other electric-muscled hand around her throat.

It takes a long time to strangle a healthy woman to death I learned in that closet. It seemed to take an eternity. If I'd gripped her a little differently I could've broken her neck and perhaps made a cleaner end of things. She was half-gone before I thought of that and by then it didn't seem right to start all over again.

Perhaps the shooting in the hall made the minutes seem longer than they were. Perhaps it was the way she first pleaded with me or the way she kicked and fought against me, her blows landing with as much effect as those of a butterfly and growing ever weaker as the darkness enclosed her.

Her eyes glazed over and she died. To me, took an eternity, but in the end she died regardless of who won the battle for her penthouse.

I wiped the filth of her voided bladder and bowels off of my pants with one of her fanciest dresses. I'd received a ton of awards and recognitions, but only two of them really mattered a damn to me. One was having been accepted into the Top Bananas. Sharing their brotherhood and wearing their insignia was one of the greatest honors of my life. The other, even greater in its way, was having been named a Founder of Churilla by Spence and Alicia. A Founder, like a Top Banana, carried responsibilities and duties as well as benefits. This I understood and accepted.

One of these duties was ensuring Churilla was never troubled again by the likes of Sara Fowler.

Chapter Fifty-Two

Sara hadn't been dead long when the firing slackened off. I waited a good long moment to be sure before opening the closet door. I and stuck my head out.

"Father Murton?" I called.

"Thomas?" he answered. His voice sounded thin and weak. He still lay in the corridor, pointing a small hand-blaster towards where most of the Dracans had been. The calf of his left leg was bleeding. "I—" He didn't get to finish whatever he was trying to say.

Suddenly the entire sky was ripping itself apart. A deep rumble shook the building to its very foundations. One of the big picture windows cracked and the sound began to fade.

"That was a fleet taking off."

I stepped towards the ruined pane and looked outside. Sure enough, a dozen balls of light rose rapidly in the sky.

"Right," my tutor agreed. He checked his watch. "The Dracan standby squadron. Almost dead on schedule. Too bad we're not."

"There's a little slop built in," a new voice commented from behind us. It was Ted Knight, of the Top Bananas.

Now I knew where Spencer had found his alternate pilot. He was carrying a heavy military-type blaster, and the barrel was still glowing. "We've got to get moving. Like, right now." He looked at me and grinned. Half of his face might not work anymore, but the rest still smiled as well as ever.

"Hi ya, kid, will you copilot for me? I'm gonna need all the help I can get." He pointed his thumb over his shoulder. "Our 'hopper is back that way, warm and ready."

"Sure," I agreed, assisting my injured tutor to his feet and helping him limp as fast as possible in the direction Ted pointed. "Whatever I can do, I will."

Dead Dracans and hotel workers lay everywhere, many more Dracans than workers. The surprise had been near-total. One of the Dracans in the kitchenette had his head split wide open with the pointed end of a clothes-iron. I could see it still wedged there. Someone had snuck up behind him Maybe he'd been the first to die.

Hardly any hotel workers remained alive. A valet and a maid were the only ones I saw. They guarded the 'hopper as Father Murton and I arrived. They left when Ted waved them away.

"They're as entitled to get away as much as G god knows the odds are stacked against them. "

The 'hopper was just what I'd imagined. It was a little eight-seater meant for VIP's. A full one too I saw as I helped Father Murton through the little cockpit and into the main cabin. Commander Lofton Knight and his son Tommy, who I'd once played *Rocket Sledder* with and who now looked thin and worn were already seated and belted up. Four other kids there I didn't know sat there with Alicia Wiston, elegantly dressed and looking for all the world as if she were on her way to a formal dinner.

"Hello, Thomas," she greeted me, showing her dimples. "We're headed for Earth. Care to share the ride?"

"I…I…" I stuttered as Father Murton released my shoulder and painfully lowered himself into a seat. "Uh…"

"Hurry up, Thomas," Ted called from up front. "We're minus on minutes."

"Right," I agreed, turning around and climbing into the co-pilot's seat. It was only a step or two away from the cabin on such a small 'hopper.

That proved to be a good thing because even before my butt hit the cushion Ted was lifting us skyward with everything he had.

Chapter Fifty-Three

Our little intra-city 'hopper wasn't by any stretch a military aerospacecraft, but it was still good for enough thrust to leave Ted slumped in his recliner, struggling to breathe. This was partly because he wasn't wearing a G-suit, like he did when piloting a Polecat. More importantly, however, it was because, down so close to the planet's surface, even our little taxi could manage an acceleration of several times Earth gravity.

"How can we be going to Earth?" I asked, speaking effortlessly despite the G-forces. That was one of many advantages of being equipped with a speaker instead of a mouth. "We can't translate a Nikita Point in a taxi."

"Uh," Ted answered, trying to control his breathing. With effort, he got everything in sync so that he could reply intelligibly, a couple syllables at a time. "Our fleet…is here…on a raid. They'll pick…us up."

My eyes widened. A raid? Here? So far behind enemy lines? Then again, the Dracan fleet had launched…

A little red light began blinking on the control panel, and the thrust began to lessen. *Engine overheat* the light's label read. I shook my head in disgust. Just those paltry few G's? For that short a time? It was incredible. We'd never get out of this alive. Maybe I'd never really appreciated what a Skybolt could do after all. This was pathetic.

"Erk," Ted exclaimed, reading the same display I was. "Well, we're doing our best. We can't go any faster, no matter what. While everything's nice and light,"—Ted reached under the control panel and pulled out a little box—"your flight crew wired this up for me," he explained. "We owe them a beer, if and when."

He plugged in the standardized leads, then flipped a switch. I was looking into a military-type pipper.

"Yes," Ted said, as the red and blue dots and vector-arrows appeared to float over our control panel. "I was so worried because we had no way to test it."

I frowned and leaned forward. Our ship, labeled *Churilla City Taxi*

Service Seven appeared in red. Just above and ahead of it, the Dracan defense squadron also lit up in red. I counted five fast light cruisers and seven destroyers. This squadron was far weaker than the United Systems fleet that had once called Churilla home. Just beyond them were five of the most beautiful blue blips I'd ever seen, two light carriers and four destroyers. One the carriers was named *Saintes*. The second was *The Glorious First of June*. I'd never heard of either vessel, even though I followed fleet stuff more closely than most boys my age. I hadn't heard of any of the destroyers—*Red Cloud, Roman Nose, Chief Joseph,* and *Tecumseh.* Since when had the United Systems started naming destroyers after great AmerIndian warriors? These ships must all be new.

That made perfect sense, once the display settled down enough to show us the vector arrows. They were moving along at a god-awful clip, just like the Dracan light carriers when they raided Churilla on Army-Navy game night, to open up the war. We'd figured out how to jump at high vectors too. At least we'd figured out how to do it with brand-new ships.

"We've got to match vectors with the squadron," Ted explained. "Otherwise we'll run right past each other."

We were already heading in something close to the right direction, which meant that he'd gotten a head's up beforehand and launched accordingly. Carefully, he played with the miniature joystick mounted on the arm of his seat until the alignment was perfect. "They're braking just as hard as they can, and we're accelerating just as hard as we can. The Dracans are doing the same thing. They want a close engagement with those cruisers on their side."

He frowned and studied a readout. "It's going to be close. Mighty, mighty close. All three of us are running like hell towards the same point in space and time. It's when I've got problems like this one to untangle that I wish we could mount real computers aboard a skyhopper. Someday your father needs to figure out a new antigrav that doesn't scramble up the circuits so badly."

I nodded. If he ever invented such a thing, then I could have non-mechanical gyros, too. Ones that didn't tumble. Then I wouldn't have to hide in closets and then—and then…

I didn't want to think about Sara Fowler at that moment. I never wanted to think about her again.

Instead of dwelling on the look in her eyes as they'd died, I asked a question. "We're squawking Red Force," I pointed out. "Won't we get attacked by mistake?"

"Not likely," Ted replied, smiling his easy smile.

He pointed at another control, a non-standard one mounted all the way over on the left. “This is a Dracan distress call. We’ve been screaming bloody murder before we took off. Presumably, their admiral thinks Fowler or some other VIP is on board and seeking shelter from the sudden storm.

“Look at how there’s a space growing between those two Dracan destroyers. Their force-leader is inviting us into that nice, safe spot. If it comes down to a traditional fleet action, the Dracans hold all the high cards. Probably, we’d survive just fine there.”

He looked at me and shook his head. “They lost a lot of their leadership back at the hotel. Much of the rest is incommunicado, trapped in their rooms or leading mop-up parties. There were other assassinations up and down the entire archipelago. Their second-string is running things just now. Maybe even their third. Most of their fighters were sabotaged on the ground.”

He pointed at the screen, which so far was nearly empty of small aerospacecraft. Only three tiny red blips rose to combat the carrier forces. Easy meat for two entire carrier-groups, even if only light ones. It was a brave gesture on the part of the Dracan pilots, but certainly a futile one.

“So, we’re better off squawking red than blue. Especially since the Blue forces actually know who we are, and consider it their primary mission to get us out.”

“Ah,” I nodded my understanding.

The fix was in. For the first time, I began to understand how it was that we might actually survive a taxi-ride in a sky full of high-performance warbirds.

“Churilla Taxi Seven,” our radio said just then with a distinctly Dracan accent. “Churilla Taxi Seven. Do you read?”

Ted and I looked at each other, then sat silently. Let them think that our set was broken.

“Churilla Taxi Seven,” the Dracan repeated. “You are entering a combat zone. Turn around at once. Urgent, Urgent, Urgent.”

Ted remained silent, but pointed towards where the two Dracan destroyers were making room for us in the formation. So long as that was happening, we could believe shooting us down was the last thing on their minds. The little red *Engine overheat* light went out. Knight’s finger flashed out, and once again our anti-gravs fired for all they had, struggling to help us match velocities with our friends.

Chapter Fifty-Four

The warning beacon had just lit up again for a third time when *June* and *Saintes* launched their combat groups. First came the Polecats, all twenty-four of them braking hard and vectoring off for attack runs on the planet proper. The carriers were still pretty far out, and the antigravs on the Polecats were all mushy and slow-acting from being so far away from any good masses to work against. They weren't able to hold a proper formation. The thruster-fighters launched next. They were the latest-model Gladiuses, according to the pipper, with long sleek noses and twin blaster-cannon.

Twin blaster-cannon or no, I realized before five minutes had passed that my Skybolt and I would've been capable of shooting down every single United Systems fighter in the sky unassisted. The only thing that might save one or two would be if I ran out of ammunition. The Polecats were too distant from the planet to maneuver properly. Granted, they were headed in the right direction and would grow more deadly soon. For now they were wholly dependent on the thruster-fighters for escort, and no one anywhere had yet made a thruster-fighter that worked worth a damn.

I remembered the four I'd personally taken out in as many seconds and shook my head. The basic concept was wrong. Thruster-fighters couldn't obtain a high-enough power-to-weight ratio to be effective in a battle-zone. The only reason people kept trying was because once in a while they got lucky in combat sims and torpedoed a major ship before getting scragged. They were useful for defending against other equally-incapable thruster-fighters. The Gladiuses were pretty things, but they were sitting ducks before the close-range secondary and tertiary mountings that dotted the sides of major warships

"It's the Adam and Eve squadron," Ted said, pointing at the pipper. "The Polecats, I mean. That's what the little apple symbol beside their vector arrows represents. Not a bad outfit, really, but not a particularly good one, either. Just average."

I nodded. I'd never flown against them and had no opinion to offer.

"The Gladiuses are the Faith, Hope, and Charity squadron. Reservists, out of Canberra. Surprisingly good for part-timers. Considering the junk they're flying, I mean."

I nodded again, then pointed to the three Dracans. They were turning towards the blue fighter-pips. Not much distance remained between the two opposing fighter forces.

"How long do you give them before they're dead? Once the shooting starts, I mean."

"Thirty seconds," Ted opined. "From first shot to last dead Dracan. How many defensive kills?"

"The Dracans will get one Polecat," I predicted with reluctance, "if the Adams and Eves are as average as you say. These three Dracans are real go-getters or they'd still be on the ground."

He sighed. "Probably. Things must be really bad for the Adams and Eves to be used on a big raid like this. Normally a mediocre group like that would be given a nice, quiet rear area to watch."

Sure enough, things went down pretty much as Ted and I predicted. The little lines of fire lanced out, crossed, and in about thirty seconds the only red fighter-sized pip left in the sky was damaged and retiring rapidly towards the safety of Churilla. The odds were heavily against it ever arriving there. Two blue pips were also missing.

I'd underestimated the Dracans abilities by exactly one hundred percent. About that same time the Faith, Hope, and Charity reservists in their thruster fighters swung around and grimly began their long, slow accelerations towards the Dracan fleet itself. We were accelerating hard on the Dracan's heels as well, though with our piddly little civilian antigrav we appeared to be lose more ground than we gained.

No one was shooting at us, and the Dracans were still holding a slot open in their formation. That was all the good news there was.

Slowly but surely, it became evident we weren't going to make it. Our motor was overheating too much.

"Mr. Knight," I began.

The pilot smiled and cut me off. "Ted," he corrected me. "For god's sake, Thomas. My name is 'Ted'. I'm not that much older than you and you outrank me to boot, sir."

My lips curled in disgust. "I'll make you a deal, Ted. I'll use your first name from here on out, if you never, ever 'sir' me again. It gives me the heebie-jeebies. Deal?"

"Done," he agreed. "I kinda figured you'd feel that way about the rank-thing. It's part of what makes you so likable. The Navy hasn't had time to ruin you yet."

I tilted my head to one side. "How come you aren't ruined?" I demanded.

His grin widened. “They keep trying,” he replied. “Oh, but how they try and try again to ruin Dad and me both. Somehow, it never quite takes.”

I shook my head. “Ted, we don’t have time to joke. We’re falling behind.”

His smile faded. “I know, kid. I know. This taxi is a real piece of shit.” He sighed and looked away. “With the people we have in back…My kid brother, among them.”

I nodded. “What can we do?”

“Nothing, pretty much,” he replied. “Unless you have any bright ideas.”

“Fresh out,” I admitted, looking down.

“Well, then…” Ted's good eye went cold for a moment, then the irrepressible lopsided grin was back. “I suppose we’ll have to just keep right on going like we are and hope something comes up.”

His face brightened for a moment. “If not, we can always ram the Dracan flagship. Wouldn’t that surprise the shit out of them? It’s hardly the kind of behavior one expects from a taxi full of friendly VIP’s.”

Chapter Fifty-Five

It didn't take long for the United Systems task force commander, whoever he was, to figure out his primary mission was in jeopardy. The Polecat raid was going fine so far as we could tell. There had been two nuclear flashes over the area of ocean where the Dracan fleet floated when not spacing. Presumably the facilities there were now toast, as were any unspaceworthy warships they'd left behind.

A gaggle of Polecats could cause quite a bit of mischief when properly configured, and life must be interesting indeed for the Dracan occupation authorities. By normal raiding standards, that success would have been enough to call the whole thing a success. If it left the Vice-President of the Free Churillan Provisional Government adrift in hostile space and gasping out the last of her air supply, well...

It wouldn't do much for the commander's career. It was inevitable the Gladiuses deployed into a line-abreast for fleet attack, three of the four United Systems destroyers began braking harder than they already were, thus closing the range with the Dracans and us as well.

Our radio sprang back to life. "City Taxi Number Seven," the same Dracan voice warned us. "You are about to enter a combat zone. I repeat, you are about to enter a combat zone. Abort, abort, abort."

We were thrusting again, and Ted was pasted into his couch. Our taxi was substantially further away from Churilla now than it'd been only a few minutes before. The acceleration produced by our antigrav was reduced accordingly, but it was still enough to prevent a normal human from functioning. Ted managed to roll his eyes, however, even if he could manage little else.

"Fight...soon," he grunted.

"Yeah," I agreed, watching the pipper nervously. The Gladiuses were closing in, and one by one their little lights were going out. Just like Lieutenant Eaglish's light, I remembered. It must've been a death ride, trying to attack modern warships with a squadron of Gladiuses. "I think so too."

Just then the whole line of Dracan cruisers opened up with their big main guns, sending fireball after fireball towards the smaller United Systems warships. Even before the first rounds arrived, however, the destroyers made tiny random changes in their courses and accelerations. The pipper went wild. The vector arrows twisted this way and that from second to second. The same thing happened to the Dracan fire control systems I hoped.

"Co-ordinated...torpedo...attack," Ted gasped. Sure enough, everything came together in my mind and I saw it too. The destroyers were moving up in front of the Dracans, while the remaining Gladiuses, almost wiped out, were lined up now so that their own torpedoes would cross at a right angle to those of the big ships. It was perfect.

"Fire," Ted grunted. He called it to the second.

Tiny blue pips swarmed the sky and we were slewing to port. It took me a moment to recall we were headed for the torpedo trap too. At times, war seemed far too much like a big video game.

Then the there were red torpedoes in the sky as well, even more than there were blue ones, though they were all going the wrong way to worry us. The United Systems destroyers swung almost as one towards the line of advancing torps, an evasive tactic denied the Dracans because of the fact that they were getting hit from two directions at once. Instead, they twisted and turned and maneuvered independently, just as they had when threatened by my lone Skybolt so long ago.

Was this their standard response? If so, it seemed a bad one. Their formation was ruined and with it a substantial part of their combat capability. Ships turned here, there, and everywhere. Their volume of outgoing fire halved as they masked or threatened to mask each other. Still the torpedoes came.

I shook my head in awe. There were *so* many of them. If they could have been equipped with "smart" warheads, not a single ship would have survived. If computers had been able to function so near a modern power plant, they wouldn't have needed me to fly the Skybolt. I wouldn't have been within parsecs of the war in the first place.

Wasn't that a nice thought?

The torpedoes weren't the first weapons to draw blood. Rather, *Chief Joseph* took a direct hit from a large-caliber Dracan gun and went up in a single flash. As distant as we were it was painful to look at. Seconds later a dozen or more red-colored torps flashed through the place where the proud destroyer had once been, but there was nothing left for them to hit.

The same was not true of the multitude of other nuclear-tipped projectiles hurtling about blindly. Two hit Dracan cruisers. One of them died in much the same way the *Joseph* had while the other reeled out of the line of battle and crept away, staggering and sparking and, in places. It glowed from the severity of the blow. Another Dracan cruiser took a lesser hit, and remained in the fight.

At first it appeared the Dracan destroyers had worked their way free of the danger zone, but almost the very last blue speck hit their squadron leader. Another Dracan destroyer collided with it while still trying to dodge the torps. At the impact, both exploded much as *Joseph* had. Finally, a single torp slammed into *Red Cloud* and she too swung out of the battle, glowing and sparking and badly or perhaps even mortally wounded.

"Damn," Ted whispered, his single working eye wide in awe.

Our drive had cut out again. I'd been so riveted on the fleet action that hadn't noticed. Some kind of pilot I was.

"We inflicted better than two for one, but it's still not enough," Ted said. "Now, the torps are gone."

I nodded and frowned. Torpedoes were the only real ship-killing weapons carried by destroyers or carrier-fighters. The destroyer's guns weren't big enough, except for soft targets. They'd already fired their entire complements of torps, and who could blame them for holding nothing back? They'd probably never see such a perfect setup again. There were almost no Gladiuses left to re-arm.

On the other hand, we were much closer to the nearest surviving United Systems destroyer, *Roman Nose*, than we had been. Her vector was now reduced to something approaching our own, as well. If we could just mate hatches with her...

The *Nose's* captain figured this out as quickly as we did. In an instant he charged the Dracan fleet, closing on the severely-damaged cruiser with the single-minded ferocity of a sailing-master of old determined to carry the day by boarding. The Dracans, formation already broken, closed in like locusts. Once again they masked and disrupted each other's fire, so that *Nose* was able to pour salvo after salvo into her crippled foe while the Dracans were limited to single, careful potshots. One of these finally hit home, and Ted inhaled in the expectation of another huge detonation, but nothing happened. Apparently, *Nose* was a lucky ship.

Just as our taxi clearly was not. For, just then, we took a stray round square in the middle of our passenger compartment.

Boom.

The thing sounded like a grenade going off in the confined space, and then the air went roaring out.

"Shit," Ted yelled, startled by the suddenness of it all. This wasn't at all according to plan. "Get in the back," he ordered me, disabling the drive and reaching for his emergency suit. "Get them—"

He never finished the sentence. The control panel itself exploded. There were secondaries elsewhere in the ship as well. The original hit had overloaded something. This was a taxi, after all, not a warship. The control systems weren't hardened.

The windscreen blew out, and shrapnel whistled through my body. Red lights flashed in my brain. My left leg was now inoperative and my waste systems were toast. That was all right. Now we were in free-fall, I didn't need both legs. My shit could boil off into the vacuum for the time being. It didn't seem likely that I'd be experiencing any shortage of vacuum any time soon.

I wasn't explicitly designed to function outside the atmosphere, but I was still a lot better adapted to it than the typical human. Father had build in a small reserve of oxygen into my brain box that'd keep me alive for a few extra minutes in case anything ever went wrong while I was in the act of being moved from body to body. As a result, despite the fact the fact that I was now breathing vacuum, I was still doing fine.

For the moment, at least.

With the windscreen blown out and the main cabin holed, there was no way we were ever going to hold pressure. So, with agonizing electric-motor slowness, I hand-over-handed my way back to our passengers. There I found Alicia unstrapped and floating in the main aisle like the saltiest spaceman in the fleet, sealing a survival balloon over two of the kids we were carrying to Earth. Both of them were bleeding from their noses and ears, but they looked to me like they'd make it. Even as I watched their balloon pressurized, and the boys doubled over in agony at the sudden change.

Meanwhile Father Murton was similarly bagging up Tommy Knight and his crippled father. The elder Knight was bleeding from one of his leg stumps, as well. It looked serious, but Tommy already had his belt loose to make a tourniquet, and it wasn't like the commander could lose the leg again. So I turned my attention to stuffing the last two kids I didn't know into their own container and zipping it shut.

By the time I finished Father Murton and Alicia were trying to help each other into yet another bag. But my tutor, bless him, was clearly losing consciousness. He was fighting to get out, not in, and Alicia looked seriously vexed. So I gently grabbed the opening in one hand and shoved his forehead down and in with the other. That did the trick. Once he was clear the zipper shut itself just fine. The balloon pressurized itself... and I realized that I was trapped in a cabin so full of survival balloons I couldn't make my way back to the cockpit without straining and maybe popping one of them.

I shimmied my way out of the hull through one the holes. They were much larger than I'd imagined. Then I hand-over-handed again along the outside of the 'hopper and re-entered through the ruined windscreen.

Ted had problems of his own. The left hand of his emergency suit had taken a shrapnel-hit in between the thumb and fingers of his mitten. It leaked badly, so badly that I couldn't imagine he was generating much pressure. Even worse, it was one of the few nearly-impossible places to try and lay a patch.

I looked him in the eye, and he shook his head in a definite no. So I reached around into the main cabin, fished around a little, and yanked out a survival bubble for him as well. Once he was safely inside and pressurized, then I could climb into one too. And after that, I supposed, we'd just have to float and wait and see what came next. Our ship was so shot up that it was a wonder any of us lived at all. There wasn't anything for us to do except drift and hope. We couldn't even ram the Dracan flagship anymore.

Ted was Navy trained, just like Father Murton, but he wasn't so oxygen-starved as my tutor had been. The lieutenant slipped into his balloon so quickly that I never did anything to help. He activated the seal from the inside. It popped, and before he too doubled over, grabbing at his ears.

Now, it was my turn. I reached around behind the bulkhead for another balloon. It was harder to grab one this time, for some reason. I reached and reached and reached... and came up with an empty dispenser. The balloons were gone. Every last one. The copilot's emergency suit would never fit me. My head was too large, my torso too long.

I looked over at Ted, who stared at the empty dispenser with his mouth gaping open. Survival balloons didn't carry enough air to fill them more than once. If I tried to enter his or any other, all I'd accomplish would be to kill them and not do myself any good at all.

"Jesus," Ted's lips said, though of course my ears didn't work in the absence of air. "Oh, sweet Jesus."

Yeah, I thought to myself. Sweet Jesus indeed. What the hell am I going to do now?

Chapter Fifty-Six

I looked around the cabin, experiencing an increasing sensation of panic. So far everything was fine. I wasn't seeing black spots or otherwise experiencing any of the signs of hypoxia. How long could it last? Not more than another two or three minutes, I figured. Father was famous for his meticulous over-engineering, and heaven knew he'd taken his obsession to new heights with his son's life at stake. There were limits, and I was pushing them too far.

Yet, what could I do? There was nothing in the cockpit that could help me. The whole 'hopper was dead and blown to hell. Even our pipper was out. I couldn't tell who was winning anymore and would die without knowing if anyone else would be saved.

I was going to choke on nothing just as surely as Sara Fowler had, and my eyes were going to… going to… going to…

My mouth opened in a feral scream, and I bared my steel-cored teeth in raw primate rage. Damnit. I was dead, as dead as if my dosimeter had turned coal black, like Mendes's had. He'd died swearing to kill Dracans. I vowed to do the same.

Not that I had any evident means to do that. Lacking any other ideas, I turned towards the shattered windscreen. Ted was shouting again, the still-working parts of his face all twisted and contorted. Evidently he'd seen my scream and had figured out what it meant. Ted didn't matter anymore, except I hoped he make it. Sealed up in a little ball like that, he was as helpless as a kitten. So I smiled and waved my last good-bye, then crawled outside.

We'd come a long way while I was sealing people into balloons. Now we floated right through the midst of the Dracan fleet. I could read the names on the ships. *Conqueror*, a nearby destroyer was called. Her captain must've been annoyed at us. We drifted along between his ship and *Roman Nose* so he couldn't fire at the United Systems destroyer for fear of hitting us. I could easily picture him up on his bridge, stamping and kicking and spitting curses at the idiot VIP's in the taxi who'd ignored all the warnings.

Meanwhile, *Nose* had a plethora of targets to choose from, and blasted away with great enthusiasm at everything that moved. Except us, of course. Not that we were moving much, come to think of it.

Just then a big searchlight stabbed out from the *Conqueror* and focused on me. We were passing through her shadow. I scrambled behind some crumpled-up metal as best I could, but apparently they saw me because the light didn't go away. Instead, it flashed three times, clearly in acknowledgement.

I frowned. If this was what I thought it was...

Sure enough, a moment later a big hatch on the Dracan destroyer swung open, and a launch burst out under high acceleration. Apparently, we were being rescued under fire. How heroic. We were being rescued by the Dracans.

Frantic, I looked around for something, anything, to fight with. There was a pipe sticking out of the ruptured hull. I gripped and twisted, and it ripped away easily. It had a nice heft. I wasn't much at swinging, but perhaps I could find a place to stick it in the launch's hull and lever it open .

Not that I stood much of a chance of ever finding such a place. My field of vision, I noticed, was shrinking. It was, however, the effort that counted. Dying game, I was beginning to understand, counted for quite a lot.

Then, out of nowhere, a huge ball of energy zipped past so close to my skin that I was sure the plastic was charred. It hit the Dracan launch dead-on, instantly vaporizing the brave souls in it who were rushing to our aid. It was *Nose* that'd fired. She was paying attention after all.

I turned around, and my jaw dropped at how close by she loomed. Her lean, menacing bulk took up half the sky. Good lord, but she was a frightening sight. Her lines reflected nothing but business, and that business was death.

Then she fired again, a full broadside, the big rounds missing both ends of the taxi by mere inches. Reflexively, I cringed and hugged the broken hull as tightly as I could while bright lights filled the sky and silent explosions ripped apart my universe. The taxi shuddered. We'd picked up a few fragments from the *Nose's* broadside, but that didn't stop her. She fired, fired, and fired again.

Eventually the *Conqueror* was forced to reply, and suddenly things were twice as bad. The gunners in both ships were trying to miss us, or one had to at least assume so. How long could they manage?

Then the Dracans got lucky. There was a huge explosion aboard *Nose*, and all her turrets forward of midships ceased functioning. Even her rear turrets were firing more slowly now, more deliberately. Even worse, another Dracan destroyer stood just beyond her, pouring in more broadsides from the other side. At least I thought she was a destroyer. It was getting hard to see.

How odd it was, I thought, *to run out of oxygen without a real body*. There was no stomach-wrenching vomiting, and I wasn't flailing about at all. Even better, I had no bowels to void. When the Dracans collected my corpse they wouldn't have to hold their noses. That was nice.

Nose tried to break off the fight then, broken and defeated, but it was impossible. She was as much locked in death's grip as I was. I shook my head and looked away, not wanting the last thing I ever saw to be the final end of those who'd given their all to save me.

Then the last United Systems destroyer, the one that had remained with the carriers to cover them, came charging in like an implacable, avenging god. Her main guns spat fire, and suddenly the Dracan destroyer pouring fire into the helpless *Roman Nose* exploded so violently I actually felt and heard what seemed very much like a shock wave, vacuum or no.

Now the whole Dracan fleet fired at *Tecumseh*, or those of it who could bring their guns to bear. Like *Nose* before her, she seemed to lead a charmed life. Suddenly she turned broadside to her enemies, screaming sideways through space, and one after another a dozen missiles streaked out. Torpedoes. By god, she still had her torpedoes. That was why she'd been held in reserve.

The Dracans took full notice of the torps. They couldn't to ignore them. Suddenly they twisted and turned again. The lightly-damaged cruiser swung too slowly and took another hit, knocking her out of the fight. For the moment, only scattered shots came our way. I nodded in approval, wanting to cheer.

Nose turned away and ran with her engines apparently undamaged. Good for *Tecumseh*. At least she'd extricated her brave squadron-mate, even if it was too late for us. It was hard to see now, with everything so dim, but who could ask for a better end?

I kept waiting, waiting, and waiting for *Tecumseh* to turn away and cover her retiring sister, but she didn't. Instead she loomed larger and larger. It was the lack of oxygen, I decided. That was what made her look bigger. After all, she wasn't going to ram us, was she? Then something moved in her big dark mass. It was a cargo hatch opening, like a gaping mouth.

The mouth was coming straight at me.

By then it wasn't just my eyes that weren't working right. I wasn't thinking very well either. So instead of doing something intelligent, I tried to scream, then blindly scrabbled my way through the shattered windscreen once more, to hide like a child from the big bad monster-thing chased me. At the last moment the Dracan destroyer began firing again, but the fireballs did no harm.

Or, at least they did no harm compared to what happened when our taxi slammed first onto the edge of the open "mouth", then flipped over, and was swallowed. It was like the train wreck all over again, except that my mind was all weak and fuzzy and I did nothing but silently scream like a mute baby.

"Sheer bloody-minded aggressiveness," Commander Knight's voice was whispering in my ear for some reason. "Sheer bloody-minded aggressiveness. Unnh. Unnh. Unnh."

Even a warship's structure wasn't designed for this sort of thing. We fell through several decks before the crashing finally stopped. Then it started all over again, as *Tecumseh* obeyed the laws of physics and went on to ram the Dracan destroyer that had Stayed so close beyond us.

Everything shook and rattled and exploded. A folding I-beam sheared off my useless left leg, then my right was crushed between two vague somethings I felt like I ought to be able to identify, but couldn't.

There still wasn't any air. How could there be, with *Tecumseh* so full of holes? None at all, I reminded myself as I stared into the blackness and thought my muddled thoughts. No air. No air. No air...

Dying of hypoxia wasn't so bad, except it took much too long. For a little while there, I'd blacked out. Now, my brain was working again if not very well. A cool breeze blew on my face. I blinked, but all I could see was a senseless kaleidoscope of light—yellow with bright blue flashes.

"Lay back," a voice yelled. It was twisted and distorted and somehow very thin.

I blinked again...and found myself looking down the maw of a huge pipe. It was blowing air on me like a hurricane. Just beyond were two vacuum-suited Navy ratings working with cutting torches. On me, I realized suddenly. They were cutting me.

"Easy," the helmeted man with the air pipe ordered. He was blowing the thing right on the air-intake above my sternum, I realized. Not quite directly on my face.

I turned my head, looking this way and that. The ship lurched suddenly. Apparently the battle was still in progress.

"You're in hard vacuum," the man yelled at me. Now I knew why he sounded funny. Not only was the air thin, but what little there was of it must've been filled with odd pressure-layers and ridges from all the turbulence.

"Hold still. We've almost got you cut out."

I shook my head. "What about the others?" I asked.

The airman shook his head. "What?" he demanded. The ship shuddered again, this time not so badly.

"The others? What about the others?"

He shook his head again. Then something broke loose, and I floated free of the wreckage. For just a moment the air-hose drifted away and I felt my eyes go wide in panic. I didn't want to die again, not so soon. I was stuffed into a survival balloon, and the seal was activated. I discovered my ears didn't hurt like everyone else's always did when I was repressurized.

"Are you all right?" the medic demanded, and I was able to give a weak thumbs-up. Then he smiled so wide I thought his helmet was going to split open. He and the rest of his crew began giving each other high-fives.

It seemed to take forever for them to airlock me into a pressurized part of the ship. I doubted there was much pressurized ship left to airlock. The port they used was spattered with blood residue.

"How are the others?" I demanded again, as soon as I was able. "Did they make it?"

The medic frowned, and for a moment I felt an icy chill in the heart I no longer had. "Yes," he said. "A couple of them sucked almost as much vacuum as you did. One, the triple-amputee, is in surgery. The rabbit-lady has a dozen broken bones, though you'd never know it to talk to her. It's as if she's not injured at all. They all took a lot of rads, though the hull protected them somewhat. They'll be on anti-radiation drugs for months, if not years. Especially the kids." He looked at my middle, where I now terminated in a mass of once-molten metal and frayed wires. "I don't have proper facilities to treat you, Commander. Nor even to diagnose you, really."

I nodded. "It's okay. The really important lights are all still green. I'm just going to leak stinky stuff, is all. I won't need a servicing for another four days and it can be a minor one. I'll be able to talk you through it. We have many wounded to treat, sir."

"Right," I agreed. "I'll be here when you get back, I promise. In fact, I may never go anywhere ever again." I sighed and lowered my head onto the nice, soft pillow. "Certainly not by taxi."

Chapter Fifty-Seven

Splashdown on Earth as bad as I'd feared. A storm roiled the North Atlantic, and, for a time it looked as if we might not land at all or divert to Ceylon. In the end, the wind and waves cooperated, if only barely. The *Spratley Islands*, our luxury liner, splashed down on schedule.

Half of Earth's VIP's awaited us in the rain at Kings Cross Skyhopper Station. It wouldn't have pleased them for someone to tell them they should have gathered in Bangalore instead. It had been more pleasant when the bulk of Earth's space traffic was routed through Hawaii. The Islands were the planet's natural spaceport, but it would be years before the facilities there could be used again.

The deck swayed and lurched as we transferred into the big black government 'hopper sent to ferry us ashore. The rest of the passengers had assembled before we arrived, and they cheered and applauded as the eight of us, six riding in wheelchairs, bumped and limped our way through the icy winds and sleet.

"Wave back, Thomas," Father Murton instructed me. He already was. So I waved as well. As I did, the cheering increased in volume, and I felt myself trying to blush.

Waiting for us aboard the 'hopper was a Navy lieutenant. He smiled and was the very image of polished diplomatic efficiency. "Welcome home," he repeated over and over, in-between arranging for wheelchairs to be tied down. "Welcome, welcome."

"Welcome home" was the traditional greeting given to all spacefarers when landing on Earth—it was considered appropriate even for the starborn. It had felt odd to me when I'd been so greeted upon my first arrival from Esteppe. Now, it felt odder still.

Then the lieutenant fussed again, making sure that everyone had a drink that steamed, intoxicated, or fizzed before seating himself and seeing to his own straps. When we took off, it was with the gentlest of acceleration. Air traffic controllers hated low acceleration. I guessed our aches and pains were more important than the controller's protests. I wondered how long traffic would be backed up before the flow returned to normal.

I gazed down at my drink, a cherry-cola, my favorite flavor. I wondered who'd told them that? Not that many other people liked cherry-cola. They must have bought it especially for me. What a waste, given that I couldn't taste it even if I drank it. Would people be wasting cherry cola on me at every social event I attended for the rest of my life?

"Well," Father Murton said from his seat next to me. He understood, at least. "It's the thought that counts, Thomas."

"Of course," I answered dutifully, picking the cup up again and sipping at the straw. My holding-bag was far from full, so I could pretend to enjoy the stuff.

"Good," he answered, smiling.

He just wanted to help. He always wanted to help. That was why I loved him as much as I did Father, but sometimes...

I turned and looked over my shoulder, where Alicia Wiston and Tommy Knight sat on each side of the protocol lieutenant. Alicia was drinking a cup of coffee. The ride was so smooth she balanced the saucer effortlessly atop one of her leg-casts.

She caught my eye and smiled, dimples and all. "Enjoying the ride, Founder?"

I smiled back. For some reason I couldn't understand at all, I'd broken down in front of her during the long trip back home on the *Spratley*. Without warning, I'd begun weeping my heart out and couldn't stop. She'd held me for hours despite her own injuries, and made everyone else leave.

I told her how I'd strangled Sara Fowler. That made me cry worse than ever. I was so embarrassed. She stroked my hair after that for what seemed like forever, saying nothing at all. It was exactly the right thing.

Eventually I felt better, and she told me to ask for her anytime I needed her, day or night. She'd drop everything for me, she promised. No one else knew about Sara, not even Father Murton. Someday, I'd have to tell him. Not yet, though. Not yet.

Before I knew it, we landed at King's Cross. I'd gotten a window seat, and, curious, I pulled the curtain aside. Oh, my, I glimpsed thousands of people out there, maybe even tens of thousands, waving Union Jacks and Rising Suns and Star-Spangled Banners and who knew what all else. Above them all, tall and proud on the single flagpole we'd landed beside, flew a huge United Systems ensign.

Every last member of the crowd waved a copy of the comic-book version of my adventures Alicia had drawn back in the cave on Churilla. I closed the curtain again before I got too scared. Then Father Murton laid his hand on my shoulder.

"It'll only last a moment," he reassured me. "Everyone knows you've been hurt, though I fear most of them will never understand what really pains you."

I shook my head, not really sure myself. Then the 'hopper's crew released my wheelchair, and I was on my way to face the masses.

They cheered and cheered and then settled down while the Prime Minister spoke of pain, necessary sacrifice, and the inevitable triumph of good over evil. He was an excellent speaker when he put his mind to it. I found the part about being able to promise only "pain, tears, and suffering" especially poignant. When he ended, he turned to face us.

"Madame Vice President," he greeted Alicia, and then the rest of us. "Honored heroes. Welcome refugees welcome home. Welcome to a world that honors your sacrifices and does not forget that others suffer still under the Dracan heel of tyranny. Welcome." He shook each of us by the hand, one by one, to the most thunderous applause I'd ever heard in my life. I was the last in line.

"Welcome home, Thomas Longo." he said to me as he took my hand. "You'll be pleased to know that there are some people here who've been very worried about you."

A little door opened, and out walked Father, looking as always a little rumpled and out of place. When he saw me, his eyes widened, and suddenly I was in his arms, being hugged so tight that it was just as well I didn't have to breathe any more.

"Mein Gott, mein Gott," he said, over and over. "I never imagined, Thomas. I'd never have asked…I mean, if I'd known—"

"It's all right, Father," I interrupted him, my own eyes aching to shed the tears they no longer had. "It wasn't anyone's fault. It just happened that way, that's all."

Then Sven rolled out Dean, who beamed ear to ear in his silly, not-quite-there way. "Look," he declared to the whole world, "my brother has a power-chair now too. We can race."

"We can indeed," I answered, reaching out for my siblings and hugging them as everyone else in the world cheered and waved flags. The Prime Minister looked very pleased indeed, but it didn't matter. I was home again, physically at least. If the rest of me wasn't quite back yet, well, miracles happened every day. Didn't they?

Then Father Murton joined in our family hug. Father, all blubbery-faced, welcomed him. Then Alicia horned in as well, as did everyone else. Tommy even wheeled his busted-up father over. The Knights were crying now, too.

"Wel-come Home," the crowd chanted now. "Wel-come Home," in a dozen accents and dialects. "Wel-come Home. Hurray."

Then in my heart I knew we free peoples couldn't be conquered by the Dracans, not if they had a thousand battleships and million sailors to man them. Not ever. For no one could defeat such strength. Spence was right. The Dracans could never win the battle that mattered most.

The one in our hearts.

Glossary

Aerospacecraft— Flying vehicles meant to operate within and not far from the atmosphere. Examples include aerospace taxis, aerospace passenger shuttles, and aerospace fighters.

Angels—A shorthand term used by pilots to denote altitude—"Angels ten" is ten thousand feet.

Antigrav—A type of engine used to power aerospacecraft. They create severe space-time disturbances, so unless they're heavily shielded, computers won't function anywhere near them. Antigravs are only effective near a planet-sized mass—in deeper space they're helpless.

Autarch, The— A deposed and deceased ruler of the planet Esteppe who began as a benevolent transhumanist, but later went mad and turned into a tyrant.

Churilla—A planet mostly covered in water very near the highly-strategic Orion Nexus.

Cyborg—Short for cybernetic organism, or something part living creature and part machine. Creating one is illegal except under the strictest of governmental supervision. Thomas Longo has become a cyborg.

Cyclescoot—a two-wheeled mode of transportation quite popular on the frontier worlds.

Dracan Empire—A group of planets unified under a despotic Emperor. Highly aggressive. They broke away from the United Systems during a mini Dark Age in interstellar travel.

Drakkus—Capitol world of the Dracan Empire.

Esteppe— Home world of both the Autarch and the Longo family. Also the leading planet in cyborg technology. Currently experiencing a major ice age. In a past war it took the entire might of the United Systems to defeat this one world largely due to its skill at cyborging.

Founder of Churilla—The highest honor Churilla can bestow. There are two ways to become a Founder. One is to have been aboard the first colonizing ship to land there. The second is to be selected by a consensus of all other Founders. The award is symbolized by an acorn from the Founder's Tree.

Fubar— Common military slang. Stands for "Fouled Up Beyond All Recognition," or something very close to that.

Furball—Military slang for a fighter-versus-fighter air battle involving a large number of participants.

Gengineered/gengeneering—Slang term for "genetically engineered". In the past the United Systems dallied with the practice of gengineering sentient beings, but eventually it was banned. Then-current laws required animal DNA be the primary component. A handful of these beings still survive, including Spence and Alicia Wiston.

Kammhuber Pass— Military key to the planet Churilla, in ground-fighting terms. It's impossible to control the surface of the planet without holding the Pass and its railroads.

Molecular battery— Nearly universally-used power storage device, sized for everything from cyclescoots to dreadnoughts.

Nikita Point—One end of a space warp, named after their discoverer. The Points are the only means by which interstellar travel is feasible—traversing them is near-instantaneous and they only hook up to each other in certain ways. Some have special peculiarities, such as only being active during certain periods of time. Others are asymmetrical, meaning that reversing back through takes you to a new place entirely, rather than where you started.

Order of Blood—An Esteppan military order of semi-nobility. Its membership is limited to successful aerospace fighter pilots who've been brain-cored.

Orion Nexus— One of the key strategic and mercantile hubs of the galaxy. It consists of five Nikita Points all located conveniently close together. The nearby planet Churilla was colonized specifically to support a fleet that could defend the Nexus.

Parliamentarian—The United Systems endorses a Parliamentary form of government at both the planetary and interstellar level. Therefore there are two levels of Parliamentarian. The lower is elected to serve at a world's capital, while the higher is sent to Earth to represent all or part of the world in the United Systems Parliament.

Polecat—A type of manned aerospace fighter fielded by the United Systems, the latest and best of its kind.

Skimmer—A high-speed boat, often raced for pleasure by the young and affluent.

Skybolt—A superfighter designed by Willy Longo, Thomas's father. It's a logical development of the Stormcrow, which was once flown by the dreaded Esteppan Order of Blood pilots. Due to the time-space distortion and hard radiation created by its engines as well as the huge accelerations it's capable of creating, only a disembodied and heavily-shielded brain can fly one. All Skybolt pilots, therefore, must be cyborgs.

Skyhopper, or 'hopper—A slang term for any aerospacecraft powered by an antigrav. Polecats and Skybolts are both skyhoppers, as are any number of taxis, shuttles, etc.

Superfighter—A new breed of aerospace fighter far more capable than anything that came before. Superfighters are characterized by extraordinarily powerful antigravs and a level of performance that no human body could ever withstand. They can be piloted only by brain-cores. In a recent war, thirty-six of the first superfighters ever built stymied the entire United Systems Navy for months and caused thousands of casualties. They're game-changers, capable of altering the basic nature of warfare.

Thruster fighter—A form of space-fighter capable of operating in deep space. Employing thruster-based motors like larger spacecraft, they're easy meat for any antigravity-engined 'hopper type fighter if a planet is nearby.

United Systems—The largest single coalition of planets. A parliamentary democracy, the United Systems once represented all of humanity. However, during a sort of mini Dark Age interstellar travel nearly ceased. During this era large blocks of planets such as the Dracan Empire broke away.

www.ingramcontent.com/pod-product-compliance
Lightning Source LLC
Chambersburg PA
CBHW020316260626
47156CB00004B/1247

* 9 7 8 1 6 1 2 3 5 1 8 0 3 *